MIDDLE FINGER RIGOR MORTIS

ANDREW ADAMS

MADAXEMEDIA.COM

Book Cover by Drew Huff

Print ISBN: 978-1-966497-19-6

E-Book ISBN: 978-1-966497-21-9

PRAISE FOR MIDDLE FINGER RIGOR MORTIS

"A deep, riveting dive into the world of survivors, retribution, and murder, *Middle Finger Rigor Mortis* is a bloody, unique take on the slasher genre. This is required reading."

—**Pedro Iniguez, Bram-Stoker-Award(c)-winner and author of *Fever Dreams of a Parasite***

"*Middle Finger Rigor Mortis* dissects the heart of the slasher genre from a final girl's point of view in an intense, page-turning, tour de force exploring the depths of survivor psychology while also delivering a gory good time. A must-read for any fans of revenge horror."

—**Emma E. Murray, author of *Shoot Me in the Face on a Beautiful Day***

"*Middle Finger Rigor Mortis* is a fierce tale of a final girl forever stamped into the bloody footprints of massacre after massacre. But she's got edge, wit, and an unshakable f*ck-them-all attitude that might make her the perfect murder consultant. Unflinching and undoubtedly wicked. This is not to be missed."

—**Haley Newlin, author of *The Film You Are About to See***

MIDDLE FINGER RIGOR MORTIS

1

SENSATIONALISM

"We have a very special guest speaker here with us today! You may have seen her on the news before, or heard her incredibly unique story from friends, but please put your hands together and give a warm welcome to our very own local legend—Marilyn Soroka!"

Rapturous applause follows the somewhat obnoxious announcement as Marilyn feels her heart knock in her chest with an off-kilter rhythm. This always happens before she speaks in front of a crowd, which she's been asked to do far too often lately. Deep breath. Smile. Be what they want.

Marilyn waves as she turns the stage corner and faces a sea of rabid fans like some sort of celebrity. This isn't something she ever wanted, and certainly didn't expect, yet she tries her hardest to play the part of a reluctant role model well for the crowd.

"Hello, every—" She begins to greet them as the speakers send screeching feedback through the streets. Marilyn clears her throat uncomfortably and begins again. "Hello, everyone. Thank you for having me here today."

Deafening applause erupts once more from everyone in attendance, though no group among them is more enthusiastic than the young women. Linda Delaney, the mayor, brandishes a pearly politician's grin and eggs the crowd on further for at least thirty seconds until the television crew signals for quiet.

"Marilyn, I believe I speak for everyone here when I say this—thank *you*!"

She grins weakly with a plastic smile, feeling overwhelmed by her own accomplishments, or lack thereof. She didn't necessarily do anything special to be considered a hero in her own eyes, much less a *local legend*. The whole thing feels foreign and forced.

"In case any of you at home are unaware, Ms. Soroka was the lone survivor of the recent Miles Heights Massacre but hold your applause until you hear the rest! Tell us, Marilyn—how many such massacres have you survived before?"

"This was the eighth."

"Eight massacres! Do you hear that, folks?! Marilyn has successfully fought off an attack on her life *eight times*!" Linda shouts as the television crew gives the okay to the crowd for more explosive applause sprinkled with oohs and ahs and adoration. "Yes, you heard that right ... Marilyn has staved off the *same* serial killer ... *eight different times*. You've obviously become an icon for the hopeful people in our city, but the entire nation is beginning to wake up to how magnificent you are. Frankly, I find it inspiring. What's the thought process like during those harrowing moments? What goes through the mind of a true survivor?"

"Defiance."

"Excuse me? Did you say defiance?"

"Yes," Marilyn responds with a face of stone. She scans the crowd again. "The first time it happened, our first encounter, he killed all my friends in the house. We were having a graduation party to celebrate some of our friend group finally getting out of college, although I was the only one who actually walked away in the end. By the time the killer got to me, I gave him two middle fingers, sat down on the couch, and told him I wasn't going to give him the satisfaction of my fear. He would have to kill me while I was relaxed and watching a movie. I simply didn't allow him to be in control of me in any way."

"Show us the fingers!" someone shouts from the middle of the crowd as more cheers take over, their echoes carrying through the tall buildings.

"Would you mind?" the mayor asks off mic as she leans in. "The cameras would love it for the folks at home."

Marilyn hesitates briefly, then she nods and stands with both middle fingers pointed tall and straight toward the television audience. The skyscrapers still seem to shake from the thunderous clapping, and the vibrations carry upward into the stratosphere. The image of Marilyn's pose has become iconic throughout the state as it has been decimated by tragedy. The stuff of legends.

"We love you, Marilyn!" another woman belts out. Her voice carries over the crowd noise.

"When you say *he*, are you referring to the Bardstown Butcher?" the mayor asks.

"I don't acknowledge his name. He doesn't deserve one. All he craves is attention and control."

"Okay, so go on from there. He kills all your college friends and finally stops when you sit down on the couch. Was he wearing a mask?"

"Yes, he wore the familiar mask that you all know and fear. I just flipped him my middle fingers like I said then relaxed, believing it would be my last few seconds alive, and I wanted to enjoy them as much as possible. Death felt inevitable and immediate, so instead of running away ... I embraced it. I took control. But then he left." Marilyn recounts the happenings casually as if reading something as plain as a recipe.

"That was it? He just got up and left your house?"

"It wasn't my house, but yes."

"Amazing, truly amazing. You also said that you were a college student at that time, and now I'm curious—what was your major?" the mayor asks, leaning forward in her seat, clearly eating up her own moment of publicity.

"I was a psychology student but never pursued a career in the field after that first incident. It seemed as though I had already dug into the darkest depths of the human psyche and lost interest."

"Extraordinary. So, that was the first time, but what about the following seven? What happened then?"

"He followed me again, killed everyone around me, and waited once more for me to be afraid of him. Why would I be *more* afraid the second time?" she scoffs. "Yeah, he killed my friends, but I had already suffered through that same feeling before. I shoved both of these fingers in the air and dared him to try it again."

"How many friends and associates would you estimate to have lost to the Bardstown Butcher?"

"Sixty-three."

The crew members flip a sign that signals for gasps.

"Wow! That many? Are you certain?" the mayor asks in disbelief.

"Without a doubt. Sixty-three."

"Oh my. That must have been incredibly traumatic for you. I'm amazed that you're still standing! Is there anyone in that group of people that you would like to commemorate by name today?"

Marilyn's thoughts race through best friends and boyfriends, classmates, coworkers, neighbors, and family members. "All of them."

"You want to name all sixty-three of them?"

"I'm not going to say their names individually—they were all special to me. Listen, all this information is public record, and you can research every single massacre if you wish. The killer followed me over the course of several years from parties to jobs to gyms and even ruined a wedding once. It's always the same thing—he kills everyone in sight to scare me, and then I refuse to acknowledge the events in his presence. I don't want to acknowledge them now."

"Sorry to interrupt, Marilyn, but I'm sure people would love to know just *how* you do that? It's one thing to put on a brave face as a defense mechanism, but how do you prevent yourself from feeling afraid in such a helpless moment?" The mayor scoots forward, her burgeoning eyes soaking up the spectacle.

"There is no how—you simply have to reject it. I absolutely and vehemently deny this man the right to make me fear him. I refuse, rebuff, oppose, and contradict him in every manner possible, and, in fact, wish him a violent death. But I will never be afraid. It's always the same process, predictable as can be, like we're in a staring contest waiting to see who blinks first. At some point in time, those near me will be murdered, and that's an inevitability. He's probably in the audience right now, unmasked and watching me. Taking notes."

The crowd begins to stir and leap from their chairs to leer at those around them. Families glare at each other judgingly and clutch their children closely, exclaiming in fear and shuffling about nervously.

"Folks, I'm sure there's nothing to worry about! Our security team is top notch, and they would never let a murderer on site!" Mayor Delaney shouts, trying to soothe them.

"How would you know? Nobody has ever seen the Butcher!" someone screams back.

"He could be any one of us!" a woman exclaims in a panic.

"See? This is what he wants," Marilyn says. "All of you out there running around in circles, you're as good as dead already! This is the sensationalism he craves, driving an entire state to act solely out of fear. If he *is* here now, then he's surely eating your emotions up for fun."

They all stop fretting abruptly and stare at one another wide eyed, each of them slowly realizing that they may be the next victim. And there's nothing they can do about it.

"You see how differently people act when the threat directly involves them?" Marilyn continues, her condemning voice booming from the speakers. "Suddenly, the fun is all gone once you realize these have been *real* people dying. This isn't a scary movie. And you might be next."

"Then what are we supposed to do, Marilyn? Tell us," the mayor bellows.

"Stop talking about him. He's nothing without that which you give him for free."

2

IDEALISM

"**N**ow you're watching *yourself* on TV? Wasn't actually being out there punishment enough?" Tara, Marilyn's friend and current roommate, grabs the remote and shuts off the interview replay.

"I'm not watching it to see me." Marilyn takes a sip of coffee and trails off, feeling her blank eyes still staring at the black screen. "I have a question, Tara—don't you ever get scared about being my friend?"

Tara scoffs. "Why would I? A very wise woman on the television just a moment ago said that fear is what causes the killer to come after us."

"I'm serious."

"So am I. You're the only person to survive an attack from the Butch—I mean the killer, and you did it *eight times*. If you aren't scared, then why should I be?"

"Oh, I don't know, maybe due to the fact that the people I hang around have a literal zero percent survival rate. If you do a quick inverse calculation, that's one hundred percent mortality."

"What can I say? We're in this together. I don't want to abandon you out of fear, especially if that apparently only makes things worse." Tara clears her throat and leans forward, her elbows on her knees. "I'm curious, and don't answer if you don't want to, but what does it feel like to know he's still out there? That he could be literally anywhere?"

Marilyn stifles a sigh. "It feels like end times. I know there will be a conclusion at some point that won't be good for one of us, though the urge to fight back and kill him first has begun to build inside. I don't care so much about my own fate, but I also can't deal with losing too many more loved ones."

"I don't really know how you've dealt with it this many times already, if I'm being honest. The rest of us would've folded."

"Disconnection. Removing my personal feelings from the situation because otherwise it would drive me insane. I will say that every time he attacks, it strips me of a bit more humanity—then to go out in front of those cameras and talk about it endlessly with nosy, obsessed fanatics ... Disgusting."

"Well, I think what you're doing is a good thing. You're raising awareness and exposing the monster living among us. Think about all the lives you've saved—do you ever consider that? How many people *didn't* die because of you? Your story has helped thousands of people. Maybe more," Tara says, the light of encouragement in her eyes somewhat infectious.

"I wish I could sincerely agree, but thank you. I'm giving networks major revenue and increasing awareness, that much is true, yet the more afraid they are the more power he has. Ignorance is bliss in this case."

"You're a hero, Marilyn. A beacon of resilience and survival in an increasingly dark world. People don't only idolize you; they want to *be* you. They wish they had even a tenth of your courage."

"That's just it, Tara. I didn't do anything to deserve this attention. Who would've known defiance would be such a desirable trait?" Marilyn shrugs.

"Exactly! You're a symbol of hope that no matter how frightening these times are, we can always laugh our problems off and flip them the bird. It transcends the killer—images of you with your middle fingers raised have become synonymous with strength. You're like Rosie the Riveter, except we would have to call you Marilyn the Middle Finger Giver," Tara laughs. "You also aren't just some rebellious teenager trying to cause trouble for their parents ... You defied *death*, Marilyn, and it seems to have no answer for you. I'm sure you're well aware that normally doesn't happen."

"I guess so. I wish it felt better." She takes another sip of coffee and gazes out the window with a thousand-yard stare, simultaneously spacing and fighting through racing thoughts as a firm knot develops in her throat.

"Anyway, you did a great job out there today. You'll be a worldwide celebrity in no time."

"I don't want that, Tara. Actually, that's the furthest thing from what I want, and I hope it never happens. I might even have to start sabotaging myself to be sure."

Tara giggles nervously. "I'm sure it's all so overwhelming, but you wouldn't want to ruin any opportunities for yourself, would you?"

Marilyn maintains her gaze and ignores the goading. She grits her teeth as the thoughts continue to roll unopposed, and her only comfort lies inside the darkness of the coffee cup.

Tara still stares with a face resembling concern. "Hey, maybe you just need some good food to cheer you up? I was planning on going out anyway. Do you want anything?"

"No, thank you. I'll be fine here with my coffee for now," Marilyn replies, detached and looking into the ripples inside her mug again.

"Suit yourself. I'll be back soon."

The door latches, and the key turns within to lock it. Marilyn couldn't care less whether or not it was locked and has nothing to hide from at this point, but Tara insists on keeping her safe. She turns the television back on to catch the tail end of the broadcast replay out of curiosity.

"*Is there anything else you would like to share with everyone out there?*" The mayor grinned proudly as if she herself had just contributed a good deed to the community by hosting the event.

"*Yes. You need to let go and live your lives. Fear isn't real until you allow it to grow within, at which point it will spread rapidly and never leave.*" A brief pause, music, credits.

Marilyn rewinds the broadcast and stares at the great mass of people in attendance, all of them loving every moment as if watching a rock concert in a football stadium. The obsession coursing through the crowd is contagious at the very least, though that's the last thing they all need—including Marilyn. She is *the survivor*, of course, though that has led to her own identity becoming synonymous with the killer's. The ... *Butcher* ... and Marilyn Soroka will be mentioned as a tandem for generations to come. Is this her fate? Her only contribution?

The message she left the crowd now echoes within her own mind yet was the sentiment for their benefit or hers? Their compulsions that anchor them to the legend of a very real threat in town render them blind to the truth and slaves to desire. Idiots. If only they knew the reality about what they're so enthusiastically hollering over—death, loss, pain, and endless despair, though through their eyes this situation is nothing more than a scripted reality show to enjoy.

Marilyn decides to retire to her bedroom in order to sift through her thoughts from the long day. She relaxes with the light off for a bit too long, and instead, falls into a deep sleep devoid of indecent thoughts where even the dead can't be reached.

3

———

MOCKERY

The key clicks in their front door lock, and it swings open on loud and creaking hinges, causing Marilyn to sit straight up in bed. She had forgotten about Tara going into town, although this isn't entirely out of character for her roommate. She's as much a free spirit as Marilyn is an encumbered homebody. The time is after midnight now, but a glass of water sounds nice before returning to bed for good.

Marilyn exits her bedroom and sees Tara standing still in the kitchen and facing the refrigerator, looking down at her phone without acknowledgement. The screen flickers on the ceiling above as if playing a video. "You were gone for quite a while. Did you get everything you wanted?"

Tara ignores the question and continues to stare at her illuminated phone in the darkness, still as stone and quiet as a corpse. Someone wails their car horn on the still-busy city street below, a common occurrence throughout all hours of the day.

"Jesus, Tara, did you go out drinking again? I just need some water before going back to bed, and then you can do whatever you like out here." Marilyn tiptoes by in the dark to avoid running into anything sharp or hard. She glances and scoffs at her aloof roommate while reaching for the fridge, and notices Tara's long, curly locks draped over the phone, streaming the publicity event with the

10

mayor from earlier in the afternoon. "Why are you watching that trash again? Never mind, it's too late to worry about it now. Goodnight."

Tara grasps Marilyn's shoulder abruptly and digs her fingers in as Marilyn walks by and flips the phone around to force her to consume the news broadcast.

"I don't want to watch that anymore!" Marilyn lashes out, instinctually backhanding the phone onto the ground facedown to shroud them in darkness again. "I'm sorry, Tara, it's just … It's been a long day. It's been a string of long days, actually." Marilyn squats down to grab the device as she hears footsteps creaking on their upstairs apartment floor.

Tara turns and flips the overhead light on and bounces her lively curls as she trounces toward the couch and sits on it, gently patting the adjacent cushion. Her eyes are black and sunken with a single trail of drying blood running from each corner, and her mouth hangs loosely and disheveled above a zipped windbreaker. She pats again with less patience this time and waves Marilyn over.

"Oh. It's you." Marilyn exhales, cold and stoic on the outside as her heart knocks within. The killer cocks his masked head to one side, and she can only imagine him absolutely beaming behind Tara's facial skin. She's only ever seen the well-known black mask concealing his identity, though never heard a word spoken. "Back to waste your time again? Or are you just a glutton for punishment?"

The Butcher crosses one leg over the other and taps his knee rhythmically, going from pinky to pointer several times while continuing to stare through the vacant eyeholes of the ridiculous and sloppy Tara mask. He rises and walks by Marilyn as she stands firm.

"Are you going to try and find her brush now, too? It's in her bedroom, the first door on the right, though that'll never be your hair no matter how long you primp yourself in a mirror to feel pretty." The Butcher ignores her taunts and bangs around several cabinet doors clumsily in the kitchen. "I would have a hard time facing me, too, especially when you're wearing my roommate's face. Bad job on the skinning, also—such a shame, she *was* very pretty. Look, I really don't have the patience for you tonight, so please, finish the charade already because I would rather just go back to sleep. This is asinine."

The killer returns to the couch with two crystal glasses and a bottle of bourbon, clanking all three down decisively on the coffee table between them. Marilyn stares into her best friend's facial features hanging loosely off the skull of a deranged man. Her arch-nemesis. He pulls the cork unnecessarily loudly and sloshes a hefty pour of whiskey into each glass and sighs with the air blowing out of sunken, black eyeholes that don't quite fit.

Marilyn thinks of a great many witty and sassy things to say in response, but she takes the glass instead. Sharing a drink with this demon seems to be the only way forward now, no matter how masochistic it may be in the moment. If she's being honest with herself, the constant public obsession and attention has created a complex that one might call the first inkling of fear. A sense of dread has formed revolving around the Marilyn Soroka traveling shitshow and what her life has become. How many more times must she tell the same goddamn stories? How many more adoring fans will pack the streets to idolize her for ... what? What kind of legacy is this? She quickly downs the drink and pours herself another, clinking it against the Butcher's which is still resting on the table.

"This is how far we've fallen, then? Well, I guess you already killed all my other friends, so now I have nobody else to drink with. The company could be worse—we could both be alone tonight." She takes a slow sip with her pinky finger pointed facetiously outward.

The Butcher finally grabs his whiskey and takes a long drink, making a mess of it down Tara's chin and his own behind. He places the empty crystal glass on the table as Marilyn leans forward and fills it for him once more, immediately noticing Tara's lip gloss imprinted on the rim.

"So, what can I do for you tonight? Did you miss my presence and want to come back around for another hearty dosage of *fuck you*, or did you just need a place to stay? I obviously have a room open as of tonight. What is this, our ninth meeting now? Can't wait to add to my growing legacy, even though I did very little to earn it," Marilyn sneers as she tops off her drink. "They act like it was hard work to do what I did, but look at you. Who wouldn't want to scream *fuck you* whenever you walk in a room? I've been biting my tongue not to shout it every second since you've been here, but the liquor is loosening my lips rather quickly, so take one more. *Fuck you and your stupid hidden face.*" Marilyn outstretches her right middle finger hard while raising the glass with her left. She begins to giggle, which quickly rolls into a cackle. "That's right! Ah, it feels so good to finally speak freely without a fucking camera shoved down my throat from every angle. If only I could tell them all the same! Fuckity fuck fuck everything about you! If it wasn't for you, I wouldn't have to sit through those ridiculous fucking interviews and answer their stupid fucking questions! I wish I could curse you for every person you've taken from me, but there isn't enough time in the day, nor booze in the world, to keep me here that long. So fuck you, anyway."

The Butcher takes another pour and shoots it down. "You ruined my life," he bemoans finally, the words muffled behind the mask with a soft, yet grizzled voice from shooting whiskey.

"Excuse me?" Marilyn sneers, holding back either the heat of mockery or whiskey-burn in her throat.

"You ruined my whole life!" the killer screams, ripping Tara's face off to reveal a broken and sobbing woman beneath. Smears of dried blood coat her skin like some sort of tribal paint.

Marilyn feels her lower jaw pull tight as if a weight hangs from it. She stares into the face of a woman that could, in some alternate universe, be a relative of hers. Maybe even some twisted version of herself had she gone further wayward from a younger age. Her heart skips a beat, as if the news cameras and stage lights all just turned to focus on her from an uncomfortably close distance, and her throat feels dry enough to force an involuntary gulp. But she only grits her teeth externally. She can't quite place her finger on it, but the revelation that the killer, this person that has utterly ruined the entirety of Marilyn's adult life, is actually a woman has her feeling a bit shaken. Hits a bit too close to home.

"*I* ruined *your* life?!"

"Yes, *you*! My life was great until I found you! And you talk incessantly about the people you've lost, but you took *everything* from me! My confidence, my willpower, my reason to live! Nobody in the entire state is afraid of me anymore, and do you know why? Because of you! I'm a laughingstock and a disgrace, but I'm sure it will all get *so* much better when you trounce your pretty little ass onto the next news broadcast and tell them all the vaunted Bardstown Butcher has performance anxiety! Right?! Answer me, bitch!"

"That must be horrible for you," Marilyn deadpans with a sip as her thoughts run amuck with questions and emotions.

"I fucking hate you for making me feel this way. I wish nothing more than to deliver you endless pain ... but I'm unable to do so. My confidence is destroyed."

Marilyn feels a boiling sensation begin to rise within her chest while trying to take a drink, and she spits whiskey all over the Butcher's face as she wheezes through a belly laugh. The absurdity of life's idiosyncrasies proves to be too much for her as she falls into a fit of hilarity. "Fuck you ... and fuck ... your ... confidence!" she squeaks between gasps for air.

"Stop it! Stop your laughing!" the Butcher screams. She jumps up to throw the crystal glass at Marilyn, but it whizzes by her head and smashes on the wall behind instead.

"Oh look! Missed again!" Marilyn allows the breath to escape her as she mocks the defeated killer, who sinks back into the seat across from her. "Listen, if you came here for sympathy, then I don't know what else to tell you," she continues, wiping her eyes at last, followed by a deep breath. "You'll get nothing but middle fingers and mockery from me forever. I'll be screaming *fuck you* from the afterlife then beyond for everything that you are, everything you've done to *me*. I hate you with every fiber of my being, and now that I can see your stupid face, I somehow hate you even more."

The Butcher pulls a small revolver from her coat and points it at Marilyn with a quivering hand. She wavers for a second before pulling the trigger several times to dry fire, the hammer uncocked, then she roars in anger. She pulls the hammer back and turns the gun around on herself to fire through her own forehead. The exit wound releases a spattering of blood and solid matter on the plaid sofa and the wall behind her. Her head falls backward, lifeless, followed by continued drops descending to the floor behind the couch.

Marilyn wipes her eyes sleepily and gets up and grabs the bottle of bourbon, then she shuffles to turn off the lights before returning to her comfortable chair. Her ears still ring from the shot fired, and the pungent scent of gun smoke lingers in the air. The persistent noise from the many tenants and the city street below will assure that nobody else in the building paid attention to the sound of gunfire.

She plops back down and yawns deeply, taking swigs from the bottle as she chuckles intermittently. Marilyn falls into a peaceful slumber that she hasn't experienced in years, sleeping through a media event scheduled for the next afternoon.

4

———

RETRIBUTION

Marilyn finally stirs in the cozy chair with her head slumped over on her shoulder and her neck stiff. Her eyes flutter as she wipes them through blurry vision that reveals the lifeless Bardstown Butcher stuck in the same position, the abstract mess resembling a Jackson Pollock painting still behind her. The evil woman sits pale and gray with the corroding bullet hole in her forehead as expected. Some events feel like nothing more than dreams until they're confirmed as reality. Too strange to be non-fiction, yet too abstract to be considered normal.

She grabs her phone and scrolls through the twenty-seven missed calls and countless text messages headlined by '*WHERE ARE YOU?!?*' at the top. It's half past four in the afternoon. Fuck it.

The Butcher's dark eyes dangle open beside the bullet hole and look like prosthetics from some old horror movie, already affected by the kiss of death in the nearly sixteen hours since she shot herself. The mess of blood and white bits of skull within the spatter pattern have dried in a gelatinous mixture that also seems to be something more fitting in a haunted house attraction than Marilyn's living room. But no. It isn't corn syrup stuck to the walls and furniture nor red food dye that releases such a pungent stench. And this will surely ruin any chances of getting the safety deposit back.

The woman's face is still heavily pained, as she was at the time of death, though it's even more unsettling to see the serial killer in this sort of vulnerable light cast upon her than it was for Marilyn to lose all her friends. As another lifeless victim. Beneath the mask and wildly prolific killing streak, underneath the revenge obsession and the rabid bloodlust and ability to kill innocents at will, the Bardstown Butcher was still human, on the outside at least. The thought of which makes Marilyn feel ill.

This ghastly woman had a real name once, maybe even something pretty like Brianna or Heather. She might've had a family of some sort, too, a couple loving parents and perhaps a few siblings with which to play. She had an identity as a simple citizen that at some point turned from average to infamous with the first kill of many. Maybe she was an unfortunate victim of abuse, or psychopathy, or some other sort of mental illness. Maybe she had a miserable childhood, like the type they talk about in true crime shows, where those loving parents became monsters behind closed doors and unknowingly created the beast she became. Or maybe she really was just born this way. But fuck her all the same.

Marilyn yawns and lifts her cell phone apathetically and dismisses her dozens of missed calls and even more unread text messages before she dials 911 with the Butcher's glazed eyes watching her all the while from whatever wicked realm awaits on the other side.

"911, what's your emergency?"

"This is Marilyn Soroka. The Bardstown Butcher broke into my apartment. She killed herself here."

"She?"

"She. And she killed herself."

Marilyn tosses her phone like a frisbee onto the couch beside the Butcher while the operator continues asking questions, her miniscule voice still audible from this distance. She floats into the kitchen for coffee while wiping the extended sleep from her eyes. The responders know where she lives—the whole city does. It's never been a secret nor would she care to make it one.

The last shred of privacy she would ever know went up in flames long ago, on a chilly early summer night where her white blouse was left painted with the crimson blood spatter of her college friends. Their pandemonic screams stuck inside the house and seemed to reverberate long past the time when the last kill occurred, and Marilyn sat catatonic on the dearly departed Dalilah's sofa without moving until morning—much like how the Butcher spent last night. Then she was discovered on the road babbling outside the house and that was it for her. Marilyn was thrust into the public eye for nothing more than accidentally deterring the killer with reverse psychology, a last-ditch effort to try the wildest thing she could think of to live.

That attitude of uncompromising nihilism in the face of death felt like a Hail Mary play at the time when Marilyn was only just a young college student celebrating the accomplishments of her classmates. She also *believed* in the sentiment at the time. The old saying is true—there really is nothing to fear but fear itself, and that moment when Eric Holden, the vaunted local high school quarterback, was stabbed through the back of his neck with the knife's tip protruding just beneath his Adam's apple, was the last time Marilyn Soroka would ever be afraid of anything. Stressed? Yes. Lonely? Absolutely. Existentially destitute? All the time. But never afraid, not again. The Butcher didn't deserve the satisfaction at that time, and she damn sure doesn't deserve it now in death.

Marilyn stares daggers at her stiffening arch-nemesis that might as well be her spouse for all that binds them. Their stories are sure to be tied together forever more. Not even death will break that bond. The Bardstown Butcher and Marilyn Soroka—the former more famous for failing to kill the second than actually murdering dozens while the latter's only contribution was absolutely refusing to die.

Marilyn lunges forward in a flash and punches the Butcher in the jaw with her tiny fist that has never hit anyone before. A molar skitters across the apartment floor as the killer's neck cranks to the left and stays there. No bruises. Marilyn sidesteps with her hand ablaze and throbbing and releases all her pent-up primal energy as she knocks her on the left cheek to straighten the head back to roughly the same position where it started. She pants from both the adrenaline rush of a rare showing of emotion and the pulsating pain throbbing across all eight of her knuckles.

Sirens arrive outside, though they're several floors down and situated on a noisy city street. Marilyn walks calmly to the sink to wash the remnants of filth from her aching and suddenly swollen hands. A sense of serenity overtakes her as she anticipates the immense gratification that is to come. The resolution of a nightmare.

Three hard knocks shake the front door and echo into the apartment. "Ms. Soroka? It's the police here to answer your call!"

"It's open!" she shouts back as she dries her hands on a dish towel.

A mixture of first responders pours into the apartment wearing various uniforms and badges that Marilyn pays no attention to. She yawns and reaches for the cold coffee mug that she forgot about the day before and heats it in the microwave.

"Ms. Soroka? Do you remember me?" an officer asks. He's middle-aged and clean-cut like the rest of them with wings of silver traversing the corners of his flat top.

"Of course. Simmons, right?"

"Officer Simmons, yes." He smiles at her and fidgets as if he wants to reach out his hand for a shake but doesn't. "I was on scene for three of the massacres. Maplewood, Evergreen, and Sycamore."

"I have a hard time remembering the details of each individual incident, but I do remember you." The microwave beeps, and she opens it and takes a sip of coffee, knowing damn well she can recall every detail about each massacre down to the names of every single person in attendance and what they were wearing. "Do you want some coffee? Bourbon?"

"No, thank you. Marilyn ..." Officer Simmons clears his throat and steps forward and pauses before speaking under his breath. "Did you do this? Because it would definitely be understandable if you did. We wouldn't mind covering the crime scene to protect you, but I just need to know the truth before we begin."

"No, Simmons. I didn't. Like I said on the phone, the Butcher killed herself. I'm sure your ballistics team will back that up when they discover the blowback inside the gun barrel."

"Okay." He turns and looks at the blue corpse and the congealed mess dried on the wall behind the killer. "Then I have another question for you. Can I ask why you waited so long to call us?"

She shrugs. "I fell asleep. I've been very busy recently and exhaustion finally caught up to me. Am I in some sort of trouble?"

"Not at all. We're all on your side here, but *I* don't want to get in trouble, either. Just trying to get the story straight so I can make my report. The boss doesn't much care for inconsistencies."

"Right." Marilyn watches a paramedic wearing rubber gloves check the Butcher's vitals, and she laughs. "I wonder if they can save her?"

"Standard procedure. So, would you care to give me the details of the incident? Also standard procedure."

"Sure. I have nothing to hide. My roommate Tara left to get herself dinner, and the Butcher came back here several hours later wearing her face like a latex mask. She poured us drinks, proclaimed her hatred for me for ruining her life, and then she shot herself."

Officer Simmons scribbles in a notebook and nods. "That's everything?"

"Yes."

"And you're certain that's the Butcher?"

Marilyn scoffs. "Well, she was definitely someone that has intimate knowledge of our time together, and she also killed Tara."

"Could be a copycat?" He shrugs. "Sorry, I was only shocked to see that the Bardstown Butcher was a woman. I'm sure you know it just isn't very common, especially these days."

"I know." Marilyn pauses, remembering the experience of first seeing the

Butcher's face like looking into a funhouse mirror. "I was shocked, too. But it's her. I could feel it."

"Okay. Well, like you said, this should clearly be determined as a cut-and-dry suicide if that's the case. And I'll change the official time of death to something a little closer to when you actually called." Simmons nods and writes more before clicking the end of the pen to close it.

"That's fine. I have nothing to worry about either way."

"Of course, not. We're all big fans of yours, Marilyn. What you've accomplished has been nothing short of heroic."

"Thank you. I wish it felt a bit more gratifying. But thanks anyway."

"Absolutely. Aside from surviving the attacks, you've now done something else that our entire police department, with all of our resources, couldn't do. You brought down the legendary Bardstown Butcher."

Marilyn shudders inside to think of herself as some sort of hero. That horrendous woman walked into this apartment and killed herself due to homicidal impotence. She even had the key from Tara. "I'm glad she's gone, but I'm no war hero. The Butcher beat herself because she couldn't beat me. That's all this is."

"You're still a hero in society's eyes no matter the details. I hope that means something to you."

"I suppose it does. Her death will definitely save a lot of lives."

"And relieve a lot of anxiety in the city," Simmons says. "Anything else before we wrap up the scene? It'll be a few hours yet until we can leave."

Marilyn looks into the blackness of her coffee cup and sees nothing reflecting back, not even her own impression. "Can I see her one more time before you cover her up?"

"Of course, whatever you need."

She nods and places the mug on the counter then walks with an assured gait toward the Butcher. The other officers and first responders look at Simmons for guidance, but he only nods, and they back away to allow her space.

Marilyn stares into the woman's black eyes beside her corroded gunshot wound. Her skin continues to turn a shade of slate blue with time, and she remains stuck in the same position as when she was confessing her innermost conflicts.

"Bitch," Marilyn whispers, never before wanting to curse someone with more vitriol, yet she can't find the right words to properly convey the boiling emotions. "I hope you find the same amount of torture in death that you afflicted upon others in life. I hope you find it a dozen times over. I've never been one for prayer, but I pray that you're subjected to eternal anguish. Remember this face that will spit on your grave for as long as I live. Suffer my memory forever."

5

CONSUMMATION

"We gather here today, not to honor the life of a wicked being, but to celebrate the death of one. We as a city must come together to recognize the memory of those we've lost and keep them in our hearts forever." Mayor Delaney pauses at the podium and clears her throat. Thousands of citizens line the cemetery grounds as far as the eye can see with faces of both jubilance and sorrow. "But most important of all, we must use this opportunity to come together and rebuild our communities! A sadistic reign of terror finally came to an end yesterday—an epoch of immense pain and suffering that won't be fully understood for years to come. The Bardstown Butcher is finally gone for good! But with her death comes a whole lot more wounds to re-open in our quest of recovery."

"*Her?*" several people ask in return.

"Yes, her. I know it's incredibly rare, but the Butcher was a woman, and *she* is finally dead! Happy Death Day to all!"

The crowd erupts into uproarious applause and cheers that echo from the makeshift podium to the far reaches of the cemetery grounds. Marilyn watches from afar beneath a black veil and sunglasses as families jump up and down with expressions of relief and joy. So many parents who might've been next to mourn their slayed children, so many teenagers who could've been the Butcher's next drunken party victims, and they all scream in delight to know that the streets are now that much safer for them to meander. Until the next one comes around.

The funerary gospel continues, yet the attendees are dressed in celebratory white clothing instead of the traditional black suits and dresses. There's nothing to grieve over, not today, except for the tragic death of Tara. She will be forgotten in the annals of history as a necessary sacrifice to lure the Butcher into her self-made trap. But Marilyn will always remember her as the sixty-fourth and final victim. And her crooked skin mask will be the image stuck in her head whenever she thinks of Tara.

"Ms. Soroka. Pleasure seeing you here today," a man says from behind, although quietly enough to not draw attention from any nearby fans. "Didn't realize you were in mourning."

"I'm not. I'm in hiding."

"Hiding? Why? The Butcher's dead, and nobody here will hurt you now. They love you."

Marilyn turns to glare at him with her piercing eyes burning holes through the black glasses, and then she turns back. "I'm hiding from people like you."

"Like me? What did I do?"

"You're near me. That's enough. The whole place would swarm me if they knew that I was here, and you're not helping with anything."

"And how do you think I recognized you? Might there be others?" he asks with a tone of playfulness, like a child trying to push their mother's buttons.

The mayor continues to speak to a quieted crowd, and her demeanor has calmed down considerably following the early outburst of energy. A politician's rhetoric.

"Not if you keep your mouth shut. All of these people will go home feeling a false sense of undying security because she's gone. But there will be others. That's how it always goes. It's only a matter of time." Marilyn continues to stare straight ahead through her dark disguise with a growing concern that she may be exposed. "There will always be more monsters to replace the ones we finally kill."

"Then why are you here?"

"Isn't it obvious? And why are you here? Just to annoy me?"

"I'm here for the same reason you are. Looking for something more gratifying than a simple funeral," he answers, his tone smug.

"I'm here to celebrate that bitch's suicide all over again. I almost feel giddy about it."

"I doubt you feel much of anything at all, which is why you're still alive. Congratulations, by the way."

Marilyn stifles a sarcastic snort. "What are you, my psychiatrist?"

"I'm *a* psychiatrist, and a big fan of yours, too. Dr. Hudson." He places a hand on her shoulder and gently taps. "Nice to finally meet you."

Her shoulders drop as if the weight of his palm forces them both downward. She can't go anywhere without being recognized, without being *seen*, but she'll never be anything more than the middle-finger girl to all of them. The defiant survivor. Damaged goods. "What do you want? I didn't have your antics in my plans today. I was supposed to show up quietly and pay my disrespects then leave."

"I just wanted to—do you mind if I stand next to you? I feel silly."

"Yes."

"Okay." Dr. Hudson walks around her so they stand face to face, and he grins.

"I mean yes, I do mind."

"Don't worry, Marilyn, there's nobody around us for fifty yards in any direction. They can't hear us, nor do they know who you are." He's a handsome man for his age, objectively speaking, with salt and pepper sprinkling throughout his classic combed-over haircut and five o'clock shadow.

"Regardless. You didn't say what you wanted, which is perfect because I have nothing to give you." She blinks hard and sarcastically behind the sunglasses and veil, and she hopes the unwelcoming attitude is felt all the same as if she were fully exposed.

"Oh, I beg to differ, but you're right. I didn't tell you why I'm here, and I must apologize for my manners, or lack thereof. My name is Dr. Dan Hudson, as I said before, and I'm a psychiatrist who specializes in treating those affected by serial killers. I'm sure you could guess that I've been quite busy these past few years," he chuckles.

"You've got the wrong person. Didn't you see the news? I survived my serial killer. Outlived her, even."

"Very humorous, as always. I'm not here to treat you, Marilyn. I'm here to *help* you. Part of that specialty is studying how they think and predicting their actions to save as many lives as possible."

Marilyn turns her head slightly to avoid his gaze, and she stares at the Death Day celebration in the distance. "Yeah, well. The Butcher is already dead, so I'm safe now. Thanks anyway."

"It's not the Butcher I'm worried about. Obviously. Do you really think that all of the other killers out there will see your media charades and *not* take them as a personal challenge? Do you think they won't take offense to it?"

"I never asked for any of this. I never wanted the attention."

"Of course not, yet it found you anyway. Only a certified narcissist would crave the sort of publicity you've found yourself mired in, but you're still in danger all the same. You're the *unkillable woman* in their eyes, and they will want to conquer you. We don't yet know who these people are, but sure as the sun rising each morning, they *will* come out of the woodwork eventually." Dr. Dan pauses and stares in equal parts inquisition and stoicism. "You need me, Marilyn. I fear that you'll be ambushed in that apartment of yours sooner than later and especially so if you refuse to lock the doors. Come stay with me. We can work together, and I can keep you safe."

"I don't know you."

"But you might die otherwise."

"I don't care." She removes her sunglasses at last and flips back the veil and tosses them both to the ground. "What if I'm ready to die? What if the thought of being chased by rabid killers like wild game for the rest of my life isn't appealing anymore? And the biggest irony is that my lack of will to live is what attracts them to me in the first place—both the killers and the fanatics."

"What if I give you a reason to live?"

"And how are you going to do that? My entire adult life has been simply surviving an accident. Despite my many pleas otherwise, the universe absolutely refuses to kill me, but it also refuses to let me live."

Dr. Hudson scoffs. "So come with me and help others. Use your real-life experiences to supplement my expertise. We could save countless lives together, Marilyn. Here, take this." He steps forward with a lavish business card stuck between his two outstretched fingers and Marilyn takes it. The black letters are ornate and raised high above the thick cardstock like braille text. The card is fancier than it should be and suggests success in the field. "Give me a call when you decide you want to join the living. It's quite nice over here on this side, having something to fight for." He smiles and winks and removes a pair of sunglasses of his own from his jacket pocket then puts them on as he leaves.

She runs her fingers over the bone-white business card with raised black lettering, and she stuffs it in her pocket apathetically as the mayor finishes her lengthy speech.

The cemetery has finally cleared out after nearly an hour of aimless bystanders chatting with one another nonchalantly as if they weren't already standing in the middle of a graveyard full of the dead. She shuffles quickly toward the portable stage and podium still left standing, now with the sunglasses and veil covering her face again.

A cardboard box waits for disposal at the back of the stage where Marilyn saw the groundskeepers tuck it behind a stack of boxes earlier that morning, long before the mayor and townsfolk arrived to holler and cheer for matters foreign to them. They don't know true loss, not most of them, but they damn sure did celebrate it in full.

She flips the flaps of the box open to reveal a thick plastic bag secured at the top by a twist-tie, and she unwraps it to expose the Butcher's ashes that the groundskeepers will probably only trash later. Marilyn pulls a small glass vial typically used for blood samples from her pocket and scoops it through the dust like a cup in a punchbowl until it's just about full, and she closes and clutches it tightly.

She looks over both shoulders before kicking the box off the stage. It hits the ground below and projects a plume of ash upwards, just narrowly missing Marilyn's face as she pulls back to avoid it. The dust settles, and she looks down again to see the moisture of the very green grass seeping into the gray soot of the Butcher's remains. Marilyn spits into it and cracks a slight grin as she flips a middle finger, then she spits again.

She unfolds her white knuckles clutching the vial and stares at it with immense pride like a serial killer celebrating a trophy of their own. "I win, bitch."

6

REFLECTION

Marilyn turns her unlocked doorknob and enters the apartment that has only recently been made her own. Tara's belongings still remain in every corner like antique relics of a time period long since passed, even though she's only been dead for less than forty-eight hours now. Pink fuzzy slippers sit innocently beside Tara's favorite chair, her empty coffee mug resting on the end table with a few more sips left inside it, sure to start growing mold soon. Framed pictures of her family line the walls and offer a reminder of all the post-mortem work Marilyn needs to do and all the messes she still needs to clean up. Calling Tara's family would be a good start, but then again, they'll probably find out on their own soon enough anyway.

The glass vial rests warmly against her abdomen as if burning a hole in her jacket pocket simply for still being there. Marilyn removes it and inspects it in her open palm like some ancient artifact that she excavated from a dig site, but no. This was *earned*. Sixty-four confirmed innocent lives were sacrificed to bring down just one wicked soul, to encapsulate all the great many horrors the Butcher afflicted in one small glass container like a spiritual prison. Marilyn shakes the vial and envisions the Butcher suffering one more humiliating defeat with the same distressed expression as the moment just before she shot herself, hopefully in even more pain. And then Marilyn smiles.

Cars screech and honk on the crowded street below, and the sounds of the cityscape echo in her now hollow apartment. Tara's body hasn't been recovered yet and likely never will. All the other victims were left where they were slain to send a message to Marilyn or so many mental health specialists have told her over the years, as if the sentiment was meant to be some sort of pacification of fear she had stopped feeling. The Butcher, at that time still assumed to be a man, likely grew an obsession with her apathetic nature and ruminated on how to finally kill her, how to finally make her *afraid*. One always wants what one can't have, even when that one in question is a serial killer. The human element is undefeated.

Marilyn pulls out the slightly ostentatious business card from her other jacket pocket and reads it over in her head. *Dr. Daniel Hudson, Psychiatrist.* Marilyn immediately shudders at the thought of dealing with another *smug fucking shrink*. Sitting through countless hours of court-ordered psychobabble bullshit and the idiosyncratic deconstruction of her experiences could turn even the sanest person into a serial killer themselves. The Butcher's visits were almost a welcome relief compared to being forced to talk about her *feelings*, or at least the faking of such.

There was a time, early on during the first couple massacres, where police understandably didn't always believe Marilyn's survival stories. They arrived on the scene to find her as the sole survivor in a house or building filled with bloodstained walls and floors and corpses galore. There was no evidence to implicate her as a formal suspect, although she was only released on the condition of working with a psychiatrist for one hundred hours of rehabilitation in total to determine if she was mentally fit to rejoin society after all she'd seen. Then the second massacre happened less than a year later, and another hundred hours were tacked on for good measure. Then the third massacre happened, and on and on went the torture.

Marilyn groans and makes the phone call nonetheless with regret already flushing her face. She paces the apartment, past Tara's slippers and family photos, and sighs when she hears the other side finally pick up.

"Marilyn ... I knew you'd call sooner than later."

"So, what can I do for you today? Are you experiencing any symptoms? Any thoughts of harming yourself or others?" Dr. Hudson clicks his expensive-looking ballpoint pen and stares at her with his eyebrows raised, the cuffs of his cardigan clinging annoyingly to his wrists.

"Jesus Christ, I knew this was a bad idea. Nevermind." She scoots her leather-covered chair backward and starts to rise when he laughs. The cackling echoes off the high ceilings and ornate vases circumscribing the room.

"Marilyn—just a joke. Please sit back down."

"You mean a horrible joke."

"Yes, well, most of the people I talk to are mentally ill," he snickers. "But in all seriousness, I'm glad you called. I can't imagine there's another person in the world with more people wanting to kill them for sport. Especially with that unlocked front door of yours."

"Keeping tabs on me, are you?"

"Someone has to."

"The whole fucking town is," she scoffs.

"No. They're *watching* you, like a spectacle, like an entertainer, like a reality show character. They want to see your next move, what sort of sensational, quotable nuggets you might drop next in the face of death. They *enjoy* you, Marilyn. But they don't *care* about you."

"Hm. And you do?"

"I do, but I digress—I care about your wellbeing more than most, yet I must admit to having my own selfish agenda, as well." Dr. Hudson stands and grabs a manila folder from the filing cabinet behind him and tosses it onto his walnut desk. He then grabs a carafe of water and fills the two crystal glasses before each of them. "Open it."

"What is it?"

"Just have a look."

Marilyn sighs in a tone that closely resembles a groan, and she flips the top cover of the folder open. "Jesus."

"Exactly. Remember when I told you that I specialize in those affected by serial killers? Well, that's one of my patients' files."

"So much for doctor-patient confidentiality."

Dr. Hudson stares at her and eventually releases a hearty laugh. "Well, I suppose you got me there. It's really more of a gray-area subject anyway. Besides, this particular person has given me consent to share her story with you, and by coming here today, you're legally one of my clients now, too."

"I was only being a smartass, you know."

"I know. You tend to do that."

Marilyn clears her throat and looks back down at the high-definition photographs of a bludgeoned and dismembered corpse staring into the camera lens with one eye protruding from its socket and resting on the dirt beneath. More pictures from different angles reveal the victim's throat to be bruised and slashed and battered in what was an assuredly unimaginably agonizing death. "This can't possibly be your patient."

"No, that was her daughter, Danielle, and my patient is deeply affected by it. So affected, in fact, that she's thought often about some sort of retaliation to settle the score. Something permanent."

"Mm, can't say I blame her." Marilyn continues flipping through the photos nonchalantly when her face turns. "Wait."

"I didn't want to shock you with everything all at once. She wishes to take revenge on her daughter's killer, preferably in a brutal fashion, and we need your help in doing so."

"*Mine*? Why the hell do you need *my* help?"

"You're the only person I've ever heard of who's evaded a serial killer multiple times when very few have done so even once." Dr. Hudson smiles and takes an unnecessarily long sip of water from his glass. "Shelly deserves her vengeance in full, and I intend to help her achieve that closure. She needs this—for her recovery."

"I fought off *one* killer several times, and I inadvertently unlocked the Butcher's secret insecurities. On accident."

"All the same. My research indicates that nearly all serial killers share a great deal of similar characteristics in their psyches. Chaos theory, I believe it's called, when certain patterns are discernible within such lawless darkness. Killers are actually incredibly predictable ... if only one knows how to decipher said theory."

"I'm not sure if you remember this, but the Butcher came to *me*, and all I ever did was wear her down with obstinance until she killed herself. That's all. I'm a nobody. I did nothing," Marilyn says as she stares at him with conviction, the same sort of stubborn resolve she showed the Butcher.

"Then why are you still alive?"

"I don't know."

"Why are you here?" Hudson asks with an eyebrow raised and hands connected at the fingertips. "Why are *you* still talking to me, still alive now, still breathing when dozens of others died? Could've easily been you in their place."

"Probably should've been."

"But it wasn't. And why not?"

She sighs. "I don't know."

"Because you have a purpose to fulfill. A duty."

"Didn't realize I was coming to a sermon." Marilyn grumbles and rubs her burning eyes. "Look, I don't mean to offend you, but I don't believe in any sort of god for a reason, because it's impossible to follow the same old prescribed bullshit of karma and destiny and purpose and whatever the fuck else after you've seen what I've seen. I've heard it all before. If there really was some grand old plan, then I don't think I deserved to lose everything and everyone

I ever loved while being forced to live this miserable fucking existence alone in perpetuity." She raises her crystal glass and downs the water in two gulps with memories of doing the same in the face of the Butcher.

Dr. Hudson laughs. "You see? That's why people love you, Marilyn! You represent the courage they don't have, and you inspire them to fight despite the fact that they can never *be* you! Do you get it now? *That* is your purpose."

"What if I don't want it?"

"Since when did anyone ever *want* the hand that's dealt to them? But you learn to play it nonetheless, and you'll play it well if you want to live."

Marilyn rolls the glass by its base across the table as she bites her bottom lip. "I still reject it. I don't care about helping anyone, I don't care about being an inspiration, and I damn sure don't even care about living. Don't *you* get it? The Butcher couldn't kill me because I legitimately didn't want to live anymore after what she'd done. It wouldn't have worked if it was an act."

"Yes, I get it more than most. And yet ... I fear you don't understand that sort of attitude only draws them to you more." Dr. Hudson sips his water slowly and savors it as if it were the finest of single malts. "I hate to be the bearer of bad news, but that seems to be the way of life, my dear. We're conditioned to hate that which is good for us and dream about the opposite outcome instead."

"And what about you, *Dr. Dan*? Are you saying you didn't want to be a therapist, but you *have* to because of some sort of destiny?"

"Psychiatrist. And no. I *enjoy* powdering my nose in Vegas and pulling a jackpot on the slots while a cocktail waitress keeps my drinks flowing two at a time until I can't walk back to my room. But my work is fulfilling. It gives my life meaning, and I take great comfort in it."

She snorts. "I didn't take you for the type. Do you have any of that right now? Because I could use a real drink."

"Maybe. Or maybe I was lying the whole time, but the point remains the same. We have to find purpose in our daily routines or else the rest becomes a bottomless pit of misery. Drowning in your own sorrow, existential nihilism, that sort of thing. Balance is the only answer."

Marilyn swallows hard, having been drowning for the past seven years in what has become the open grave of her own existence. Death has plagued her since she was barely an adult, waiting only for the next opportunity to strike whenever she tries to meet new people and move on from the spiritually taxing trauma. Murder, stasis, rebuild, repeat. And the only time she ever felt truly alive was when staring directly into death itself. Something primal maybe, like the feeling of conquering inevitability, or at least facing it head-on as an impossible hurdle to cross. Then the rest of life began to feel horribly mundane by comparison. Unbearably so. "Balance in what way?"

"Every way. Pleasure and pain. Misery and joy. Work and leisure. You can't be Marilyn the Savior at all times. You need rest, peace, *purpose*. You need people behind you and beside you. These aren't wants, but necessities, and I know for a fact that more adversaries will be on the lookout for you soon. Eventually, one of them will grow the nerve to kill you once and for all, even if it means sacrificing themselves in the process. It's only a matter of time now, because your life makes the definition of chaos seem rather vanilla by comparison."

"Feels normal to me at this point."

"Of course, it does. You've adapted well. I can't figure out *how* for the life of me, but you did." Dr. Hudson leans forward and empties the carafe into their glasses, and he slides over a folded piece of paper. "Here's my home address and phone number. Everything we need to cover about the plan is much too sensitive to talk about here. Just think about it, okay?"

7

———

REBIRTH

Marilyn takes the final drag of a cigarette and flicks the glowing butt still lit onto the street. She was once a heavy smoker but mostly quit the habit out of a growing disgust as opposed to any quantifiable health benefits from doing so. Like Dr. Dan said, her immediate life expectancy is nearly zero, not that anyone else will fare much better in the long term. Death is the only certainty—some take it as comfort while others fret.

She stares at the exterior of his house, the lavish estate that a psychiatrist's salary can afford, with an intermingling of regret and wonder. It's a countryside mini-mansion situated on at least an acre of land and surrounded by tall hedges along the property walls.

Why is she here? What seemed like such a horrendous idea an hour ago somehow now seems even worse, like walking headlong into everything she despises all in one. *Mental health experts* ... there aren't enough therapists in the world to fix the type of fucked up she's fallen into. Who else could be so rotten that the bastion of hell itself wouldn't touch her? *Positivity ... mindfulness ... spirituality*. What a crock of shit, all of it.

Marilyn eventually called Dr. Hudson when the well of emptiness seemed to hit the rock bottom of nihilism. It's difficult to care too much about living any longer after making a life out of laughing in the face of annihilation. He set up a meeting between the two of them and the patient in question, Shelly something or the other, and said they would all share a nice dinner together. Nothing else, he promised.

She sighs with an exhalation that resembles the last billow of cigarette smoke in the night sky but is actually only her own breath in the suddenly frigid weather. Just dinner. Dr. Dan opens his ornate wooden door and waves her toward the house in a quirky-patterned sweater that could only be worn by a psychiatrist. She scoffs.

"Come on in, Marilyn. You're right on time."

She clenches her jaw and walks up the long driveway reluctantly, careful not to stomp on his perfectly manicured grass which looks ridiculously pristine for wintertime. Everything inside her feels wrong for being here, wrong for getting involved in something that has nothing to do with her, wrong for sticking her neck out for someone else when her survival instinct as a lone wolf has never led her astray, wrong for abandoning her laissez-faire attitude toward the world's unfortunate happenings in favor of *help*. "Hello."

"Come in. Shelly is already here, and she simply can't wait to meet you."

Marilyn swallows hard past the burgeoning lump in her throat and walks onward as if she wasn't already sweating bullets internally. "Charmed."

Dr. Hudson disappears in a closing tunnel of darkness constricting Marilyn's vision. Her legs continue to carry her onward through muscle memory alone. The sheer terror of the mass murders as her loved ones shrieked and their blood pooled on the floor and their anguished cries and the following silence that left her alone staring in the black eyes of the Butcher stone-faced and stoic doesn't hold a goddamn candle to a single session with a mental health professional. Not a *goddamn* candle. Killers only want to kill her, but the *shrinks* want to *see* her, and for some reason the former seems preferable to peeling back the mask in a private room and feeling *seen*. Maybe Dr. Dan will pull out a knife or a gun and threaten to murder her and make her feel more at home.

He motions her inside again with a smile instead where a woman smiles, too, as she appears to wave. The figure approaches in a cosmic blur of bending light, an angular visage like a faded Polaroid, getting very close before whispering something unclear. She hugs Marilyn.

"What?" Marilyn asks at last.

"I said you have *no* idea how much this means to me. Thank you." She releases the embrace and steps back with her eyes full of tears, and she wrings her hands in front of her chest. "My name is Shelly Carlisle. My daughter was taken from me one year ago."

"I'm sorry to hear that, Shelly. My name is Marilyn Soroka."

"I know. Everyone knows." Shelly laughs as she wipes her eyes with her index finger, though the bold black bags beneath them surely developed long before tonight. She seems to be a woman of about forty, though the past year must've wrung her inside out based on her twitchy nature and overall residue of shell shock and visible trauma. "But I can't believe I'm standing here in front of you now. Suddenly, I feel ... I feel like there might be some hope."

"You see, Marilyn?" Dr. Hudson approaches and places a hand on each of their shoulders. "You have a *purpose* yet to fulfill. And it seems to be seeking you out."

"Mm. Well, it's nice to meet you, Shelly. I wish it were under better circumstances, but here we are." Marilyn clears her throat and realizes that she would never have been asked to the house if she didn't also lose several dozen loved ones herself, though never a daughter. Bonded by blood. "I'm happy to help however I can."

"Thank you. You have *no* idea how much this means to me." Shelly repeats as she lunges forward with another teary-eyed embrace then immediately recoils in embarrassment. "Sorry."

"It's okay, Shelly. Really."

"Shall we sit and get started?" the doctor asks. "I'm not much of a cook, so I've called in for delivery, but I can promise you that it's the best in the city."

Marilyn and Shelly take their seats at the table across from one another while

Dr. Hudson selects three bottles of wine from a cooler in the corner. He places one in front of each of them, and the third before his own chair with a wine glass set beside them next.

"Is this prescribed medication, Doc?" Marilyn asks facetiously.

"We're way past using formalities, the three of us. Please, call me Dan. You're in my home as honored guests and, once again, we're past the point of small talk now. Enjoy yourselves as you see fit." Dan uncorks his own wine bottle with a pop and passes the opener to Marilyn as he pours a glass and noses it carefully. She pops hers and drinks directly from the bottle, causing Shelly to giggle with her hand over her mouth.

"Marilyn, we're up against a man by the name of Wayne Taylor," he continues and then pauses to acknowledge Shelly's shudder. "He's murdered three that we know of, although the number of confirmed victims is nearly never correct. Shelly was recommended to me as a patient once her daughter was taken from her, and we've been in pursuit of him ever since."

"I don't mean to come off as callous, but how do the two of you know about him when the police don't? Why isn't he doing life by now?"

"Lots of reasons. Many serial killers fall through the cracks when they aren't as highly publicized as the Bardstown Butcher. In fact, most of them won't be caught anytime soon, leaving a whole score of broken people drowning in guilt and mourning. Like Shelly. Between police departments being poorly funded, understaffed, and overworked, many killers walk among us freely, killing the homeless, prostitutes, drug addicts, and others who are commonly not missed as much as others. But every now and then, they attack a bright young mind like Danielle, a college student with excellent grades and what was once a promising life ahead of her. I may be a professional who swore an oath to serve all patients in need, but I say Danielle's death was infinitely more damaging than some strung-out junkie getting killed on the street with no family to notify post-mortem. No offense to them, of course."

"But how can that be? How could the police not go after Wayne if you already know his identity?"

"Because there was no evidence," Shelly says. She pours herself a heaping glass of wine at last and takes a long sip. "Wayne would frequent the coffee shop where Danielle worked between classes, and he would bother the young women there. She told me about him one night when she got home. She said he would often sit in his car and seemed to wait for her to get off work. She took a picture of him and the car."

"Forgive me for playing devil's advocate, Shelly, but shouldn't that count as evidence of some sort? Shouldn't Wayne be a suspect?"

"Of course, and he was, at first. But the police said that it could've been a coincidence that he was waiting outside the coffee shop for whatever reason, and it was within his rights to do so. Everything else fizzled out from there."

Marilyn swallows several more gulps of wine. "So, how do you know for sure that it really was him?"

"Because we began to follow him after Danielle's death," Dan interjects. "Illegally. And we saw him transporting another body, but it was too late to gather any legitimate physical evidence to present to the police. I was conflicted about going that route anyway, given why we were following him." Dan clears his throat. "Wayne has killed at least two people that we know of, likely several more, and he displays all the classic signs of intending to kill again soon."

"Okay. Sounds like you have everything you need without me."

"If only that were true. Shelly and I lack the experience and expertise to engage a serial killer face-to-face, who would frankly be several steps ahead of us. And, for lack of better word, neither of us have the balls to lead something like this. We're outmatched."

Marilyn smirks. "Or scared?"

"Can't it be both? I'm an expert in serial killer psychology, which includes *why* they do what they do, but I have no experience in pursuing nor dealing with them once we inevitably end up making contact."

"I'm not scared of anything anymore," Shelly says. Her eyes have gone dull, and she holds the wine glass under her nose without drinking it. "Wayne could kill me and torture me all he likes, but the only thing that keeps me up at night is the dread of dying before I can deliver him the pain he deserves. I made a certain sort of peace in losing my daughter within those first few months after it happened, when I had to fight day and night not to kill myself to numb the pain, when I thought the world had no use for me anymore. But Dan convinced me to rise up and *fight*. That's the only thing that drives me now."

"And I'm immensely proud of how far you've come, Shelly. That's where you come in, Marilyn." He nods at her. "We know where Wayne lives, but we'll need your help once we're inside his home with him, behind enemy lines. That's where your expertise will carry us to the finish line. I believe your reputation will have the opposite effect if we take the offensive instead of allowing them to come to you—if we strike first, he'll likely feel powerless just knowing that you're there."

"And that's all I need to do?" Marilyn asks, still unsure of her commitment to the cause.

"That's it. Advise us, guide us through the process, and we'll do the rest. Shelly has been to hell and back in preparation of getting her revenge. She's ready."

Shelly nods.

"And what about *you*, Dan? Are you prepared to die? What if shit hits the fan in his house?"

"I'm okay with the idea of it, but I wholeheartedly believe in you to deliver, Marilyn. Especially if we catch him off guard. And I believe in the prep work we've already completed." He twists in his chair and reaches for a manila folder identical to Shelly's file and hands it to Marilyn. "Have a look. We've figured out his routine, when he leaves the trailer and for how long, how to distinguish between when he's calm or anxious, and much more. But we must move quickly—his current routine is likely bound to a potential victim, and it could change quickly if we don't act before he kills her. He'll begin to get more agitated as time goes on, which could either play to our advantage or cause us to meet him at his most aggressive."

Marilyn flips through several photos of Wayne, the almost stereotypical serial killer with a greasy mullet, pale skin, and empty eyes. He wears denim overalls in the pictures with nothing beneath them. "How are you so sure that the next victim will be a woman?"

"That's been his MO so far. Young women, all of them college students."

Further pictures show more of Wayne's prefabbed mobile home, a grate covering a crawl space that likely hides some sort of bodily remains, his beat-up old hatchback, and a conspicuously-placed metal pole stuck in the ground. "I hate to play the contrarian again, but are you *certain* this is the man that killed Danielle? I only need to hear you say it."

"I'm positive. Without a doubt." Shelly nods.

"We have photographs of him stalking another girl, but I won't make you suffer through those," Dan says. "Wayne Taylor is a serial killer, and he did, in fact, murder Danielle Carlisle in cold blood. What do you say now, Marilyn? Are you with us? You can still walk away with no hard feelings if your heart isn't in it."

"Yeah, it's okay, Marilyn." Shelly smiles at her with her eyes decidedly drier. "Regardless of what you decide, you've meant more to me than you could ever realize."

"I brought you here to help us, Marilyn, but I did so with the utmost humility. I do realize how strange we must seem to you, out stalking a vile man as if *we* were the serial killers instead, but I fully believe the intel we've gathered to be correct. Wayne deserves to die and so much worse."

Marilyn gulps wine from the bottle like a thirsty infant and stares at it a moment longer. All her aversions to therapy have led her here. Every one of her murdered friends and family have set her on this path. She looks at Shelly and then Dr. Dan and suddenly feels a swelling of empathy rise for both of them. Shelly, for the great loss of having her daughter taken far too young, and Dan for his immense sacrifice in taking this mantle of serial killer hunter as a mentor for others. She takes another hearty swig. "Alright. I'm in. Let's gut this son of a bitch before he can ever hurt another girl again."

So much for only having dinner.

8

—

SYMBIOSIS

The night air has run dry since Marilyn arrived at Dr. Dan's house, when the condensation in the freezing evening sky felt somehow more joyous, reminiscent of her childhood years when she would watch eagerly through the window on especially cold nights with hopes of snow. The feeling was synonymous with wintertime, and Christmas in particular, when they would have snow days off from school, Mom's special hot chocolate, and a fire crackling in the living room.

The moisture has evaporated, and the air shrouds her in a bitter cold that feels rather bleak by comparison. What could've been associated with the comforting scent of pine trees and burning fire logs now reeks of death and despair, a sort of wafting that brings with it a true shiver instead of hope.

Marilyn drives down the familiar old street with her headlights illuminating only a couple car lengths of space ahead on the road. She inhales the frigid air deeply and takes a sharp right turn down a path she's taken several times already for various reasons. There are no streetlights here nor any other cars creating traffic. She approaches a locked metal gate that prevents vehicles from driving any further.

The moon disappears behind a grouping of clouds that stands alone in the vacated sky. Marilyn exits her car and leaps the gate with her bag in hand to walk the dirt road in the cover of darkness that she's grown all too comfortable within. Rows of stone pillars stand in the grass and display certain indistinguishable information, but she passes by them and knows exactly where to go tonight.

"Hello again, although I do say so with the absolute least amount of niceties. In fact, I wish you many agonizing curses." Marilyn looks down at another patch of grass that stands alone from the other gravestones. The stage and ceremonials are gone. The Butcher wasn't buried but burned instead, yet this is the landing spot where Marilyn kicked her remains into the grass and allowed them to intermingle with all the innocents of the town whose lives she affected in one way or another. "You fucking bitch."

She pulls a wine bottle from her purse, the second one of the evening offered by Dr. Dan that he said she could take with her, having already put her lips on the rim, and she pours a small glassful worth in the grass.

"I absolutely hate you for making me do this, maybe even something more than hate, whatever that word is. Loathe? No, not strong enough. Detest? Maybe times a million. You see, the thing is I have nobody else anymore. Every person I've ever been even remotely friendly with has met their early end at your hands. My family has all died now of natural causes or been murdered by you. I've nowhere to turn to now, but does that reflect more poorly on you or me for being here?"

Marilyn takes a swig from the bottle and wipes her mouth before gazing into the obscured moon's outline.

"I wish I knew *why* I came here. Truly, I do. You were repugnant enough in life that I would've gnashed at your throat with my gritted teeth if ever given the chance, although that level of passion might've voided my apathy that rendered you impotent. We're bound together forever, despite how much I hate it—how much I hate *you*. I wish I would've done it, I wish I would've hacked you to pieces like Shelly is going to do to Wayne, yet it seems my methods were effective in their own way. You're still dead, and I'm not. Not yet, and at least I know it won't be by your hands."

Marilyn takes another hearty gulp of wine, but the acrid flavor in her mouth causes the alcohol to taste as if it's turned to vinegar instead. The blackness of night feels especially dark this evening, almost suffocatingly so, like being stranded in an unnervingly placid body of water and the endless rows of gravestones were sunken ships and drowned sailors at sea.

"I'm lonely. I have nobody, which you sure as shit made sure of. I don't like people. I find them boring, untrustworthy, and difficult to be around, although I can't remember now if I felt that way before you came around or if it's a direct result of you. The few people I found myself even somewhat attached to were all the ones you took from me. Many of them are buried in this cemetery, too, yet here I am talking to you."

She reaches in her pocket and removes the glass vial of preserved ashes and clutches tightly with her fingers wrapped like a vise around it. The grass is clean now and greenish again and free of any more Butcher particles, at least to the naked eye, washed away by morning dew and sprinklers and trampling footsteps. A lifetime of inflicted misery so easily scrubbed from this realm by something as simple as a few drops of harmless water, though the memories of such remain branded.

"I don't even know your real name. How could my life be so irrevocably altered by a creature called the Bardstown Butcher? It's ironic, don't you think? We know nothing about one another on a personal level, yet neither of us ever knew anyone else so intimately. Something about death simply binds people like nothing else, especially when one of those people is the dealer while the other is the recipient. We're bound together for as long as the stories continue through cagey whispers, though I hate it beyond comprehension, and nobody else among the living will understand the impossible complexities that comprise our relationship. I still don't get it myself, despite how hard I try to make sense of what happened. I blamed myself at first, like any normal, shell-shocked twenty-year-old would, as if I could've prevented you from fucking up the party in the first place or somehow fought you off once the blood spatter started.

Nothing but endless coping mechanisms. The house was mired in death, the actual primordial being with its leathery black wings flapping madly to shroud us in their oppressive shadows, and I clung to the only semblance of a reaction I could muster—defiance, and it worked. Yet still I see your fucking face everywhere."

Marilyn stares into the shaded grass blades that are barely visible now, and the mirage of the Butcher's mask coming off seems to mix itself amongst the sprawling lawn. Her uncovered face scowls in a wrinkled frown and twists into something much more agonizing before her necrotized, gunshot-laden head replaces it. The night sky is a peculiar shade of green swirled with the typical black on this particularly starless night. Perfect coloring for a cemetery. She takes another swig of wine and gazes back into the mirage that has plagued her so. It's been present for most of every day since that fateful gunshot, the forever yawning mouth laid agape just as countless others were found. Her friends, brothers and sisters and sons and daughters to others, left pale and lifeless with their eyes in a perpetual state of shock at their undeserved deaths. Her family members, loved ones whom she grew up with, shared blood with, and shared a last name with. All of them gone in a cloud of dust, though the memories of their faces evaporated long ago where the Butcher's still pervades.

"I would give anything to hurt you. To have really cut through your guts and chest and yank on your heart till the aorta snapped and splashed blood on your gasping face. Regardless if we break bread now in death, it's only for me to gloat. To rub my victory in your face, to pray that you suffer so much anguish you'll blow the back of your skull out a thousand more times over in whatever fiery pit you fester in now. I pray that you find yourself in so much pain that repeated self-extinction would feel like the only mercy you'll ever know. But then again, that's exactly what happened. You thought that taking everything from me would bring me down, break me, but I degraded you even more in return. I spat on what little dignity you had left and snatched your self-worth and laughed at it like the pathetic joke that it was. I disrespected the very life right out of you. And I fucking won."

Marilyn stands up and downs the rest of the wine bottle, then drops it over the Butcher's remains and stomps on the glass. It shatters decisively, her mood more of a vengeful moratorium than a happy drunk, as if the broken bottle could somehow be a symbol of the reciprocating grip they'd held on one another for years on end, though Marilyn never would've guessed just how ugly the divorce would be.

9

CONSECRATION

What does one wear on their first serial killer hunt? Particularly a hunt for the benefit of another person who will also be present. Should they dress in synchronicity to avoid being noticed by any watchful eyes? Or would that make things worse? It's difficult to suddenly try caring after so many years without.

She never kept any sort of weapons in the apartment aside from simple kitchen knives intended only for cooking. Being armed would defeat the purpose of an unlocked door, and thus far defense hasn't been necessary. Some people keep guns or baseball bats or other wooden sticks in their homes for security, but they always seemed more like superfluous trinkets. Security blankets. That attitude may have to be adjusted if Dr. Dan's warnings are correct—others may come to prove their worth with nothing to lose but their nonexistent reputations, and her time in this apartment may indeed be limited. Death has begun to seem a bit less like an impending release and more like something to avoid.

Marilyn packs a suitcase full of clothes, mostly all black or dark colors, in the event that she doesn't return home for whatever reason. Death is always looming. Or perhaps she might not leave Dr. Dan's house again. The thought of being murdered, something she long since considered little more than an afterthought, now suddenly strikes just the slightest bit of discomfort in her gut. Something that some might call fear, but she isn't *afraid* of dying. It just now sounds sort of unappealing instead of like nothing. She shouldn't die yet.

And Shelly deserves this. She deserves justice for her daughter and to achieve closure by her own hands. Marilyn would've continued to suffer atrocity after atrocity for as long as they would happen like an impartial observer trapped in her own life. How many massacres before she would've finally made an attempt to stop them herself? A grieving mother should have every right to walk into the home of their child's killer, no matter how old the kids were, and do *whatever* they like with them, no holds barred. That should be the law of the land, not the law of man—it's only right. The more brutal the revenge, the better. Marilyn smiles at the thought, a rare expression that forces her facial muscles to creak into position.

She packs what few family photos remain on the walls and shelves into a cardboard box, and she tapes it shut and stores it in the hallway closet. Memories of dead people who were once related to a girl who could justifiably be assumed dead by quality-of-life standards have no use anymore. They're only reminders of a past life that isn't coming back ... it *can't* come back. Besides the point, she might never return to this apartment again herself. It was never anything more than a stopgap living arrangement regardless.

Marilyn reaches for another photo of Tara and herself and pauses. They both appear young, or at least younger, and Tara seems *happy* while Marilyn glowers. The two of them went to a carnival not long after meeting in an attempt to get acquainted as brand-new roommates, and Tara insisted on buying the ridiculously expensive picture to hang in their apartment. It would commemorate the start of a great friendship, she said at the time. Marilyn forced a smile externally but knew inside that using the F-word meant that Tara had volunteered herself for death row.

"I'm sorry you got caught in the crossfire, Tara. I should've pushed you away for your own safety, but instead, I stood by and allowed it to happen with my silence. My apathy. Perhaps I'm just more comfortable talking to the dead these days than the living. It seems we have more in common, anyway."

She flips the picture downward as the memory of the Butcher wearing Tara's skin crosses her mind.

"Sometimes I wonder if I've buried my emotions deep enough to never see the light of day again instead of simply never feeling them at all. I believed for a time that I was invulnerable, that maybe I had been one of the lucky few not to suffer such pettiness as *emotions*, that hopefully I had evolved past normal human needs. Now, a part of me fears that it was all a facade, a mask caked on so thick that even I couldn't tell the difference anymore. I fear that I only know how to live in the face of death, that the instinct to survive is the only thing that drives me forward. And now, the only true threat I've ever known is gone, and thus my north star with it ... or perhaps that's only my self-made persona speaking for me. Am I still that catatonic twenty-year-old girl scared to death sitting on Dalilah's sofa, surrounded by dead friends with no hope to live? Or am I simply stuck between games of cat and mouse, hoping a more worthy competitor will rise to the occasion soon? Maybe this is all just a game ... Come and get me, killers ... Catch me if you can ..."

"We'll enter the trailer through this window back here." Dr. Dan taps a blown-up photo emphatically where a thin screen covers the kitchen window. "Shelly and I double-checked the latch before—he never locks it. One of you will need to slip through and open the front door for us to enter. I don't believe I'd fit."

"I'll do it," Marilyn says.

"I hoped you would. If something goes awry, I know you'll know what to do."

She nods. "Is Wayne going to be there when I enter? Or should we do it when he's gone?"

"It's in our best interest if we ambush him. He'll likely be more aggressive if he walks in the front door and finds us, or worse—he might run away. That could blow our one good chance to end him. Serial killers are surprisingly risk-averse in regards to their own survival, and I doubt he would return for quite some time in that case, if at all."

"Marilyn, he's going to kill again. We know it," Shelly adds. "We can't let him escape ... for my daughter's sake and the next girl's, too. I don't want anyone else to suffer the kind of pain I've been through."

"I'll do everything I can. What happens once we're inside?"

"We confront him," Dr. Dan affirms.

"And if he gets violent?"

"We do expect some pushback, but frankly, that's why we waited for you, Marilyn. We'll follow your lead in there. You know how to deal with these people."

Just one of them, she thinks as she nods again. "Are we going to be armed at least? I'm afraid I won't be much help otherwise if things go south."

"But of course. How else do you propose we kill him?" Dr. Dan laughs and walks to his kitchen counter then comes back with a lengthy chef's knife. The swirling on the blade looks fancy as it somehow shimmers brilliantly even beneath the dimmed dining room lights. "It's Japanese Damascus steel with a birchwood handle. Birchwood always was my favorite." He places the knife on the wood table with a dull clink and smiles at it. "Although it *is* ironic that this tool, which has been used to prepare my meals and keep me alive by extension, will now be used to take another life that will in turn save many others. Life's a riot, eh?"

Shelly sniffles from the other side of the table with tears flooding her eyes and streaming down her cheeks. "Thank you both so much for doing this. I can never repay you for avenging my poor Danielle."

"Don't worry about it, Shelly. I'm happy to help," Marilyn says.

"We all fight for the same side," Dr. Dan adds. "The side of righteousness. When a wicked beast threatens one of us, he threatens us all. Or at least I wish more people thought that way. They'd rather stick their heads in the sand and hide from evil until it inevitably knocks on their door. Then they're the broken ones left mourning an innocent life lost too soon while their families and neighbors continue to pretend as if none of it exists. But we know this all too well. Don't we?"

"Yes." Magma boils in Marilyn's core. "I, too, sometimes wish I could hide from all the malevolence in the world, but it seems to be dead set on seeking me out. And I accept it. I enjoy flipping death the middle finger."

"Where there's life, there's hope. And we mustn't ever lose hope in the good fight, for life follows with it. I'm so incredibly proud of you both for making it this far. Sometimes you simply don't realize how much pain you're in until the thorn is removed. We adapt—that's our survival instinct at work. But it's only when you finish that long walk through hell that you realize how much good was always waiting on the other side. And that's why we continue to fight against insurmountable odds to get there." Dan's eyes visibly sharpen.

Marilyn fidgets her hands, feeling as if her feet are caught with one on each side of the dividing line between life and death. Like she should already know how to make the proper decisions herself if it weren't for the darkness that's long since shrouded her. It's a stain that won't wash off, a mark that's burrowed much deeper than surface level. Perhaps the Butcher, and Wayne after her, were blinded by familiarity through the eyes of a recognizable adversary. Perhaps whatever festers behind Marilyn's many masked layers is as rotten as they are, and it makes them uncomfortable. "That's why I'm here. To keep fighting that fight. Although honestly, I haven't felt much hope in a long time."

"Yet you still have life," Dan says.

"Yes."

"Life perpetuates hope, not the other way around," he grins. "Besides the point, would you really have joined us if you didn't have faith in life? I believe that you *do* have hope, even if it might be buried beneath other complex feelings. Understandably so."

Marilyn turns to stare into Shelly's bloodshot eyes which glisten now as the lids scrunch from her smile. If only they knew what feelings those were. "Of course. Anyway, the knife?"

"Yes, you'll take the knife with you into the house in case anything goes sideways. Once we have Wayne cornered, you'll pass the blade to Shelly, and she will end him for good." The doctor smiles wildly and punches his right fist into his left palm. "You know, Marilyn, we've been rehearsing this plan for months, but I never thought we would have a third with us to make it happen, let alone that third being *you*. Anyway, you take the blade with you for safekeeping until we're by your side. I hope we can do this quietly enough, but three of us with weapons should be enough to neutralize him with ease. We know that serial killers crave control over both their victims, of which Wayne will never have another again, and themselves. We're going to snatch that right away from him. This will be a thorough conquest."

Shelly's sniffles turn to cackles and the hard-earned crow's feet of her persistent suffering fold upon themselves and darken. She stares at Marilyn for an unusually long amount of time with no sounds but that of her several breaths being inhaled sharply and expelled from her nose. "Yes, it will be," she says at last. "Thank you so much for giving this to me, Marilyn. It's the only thing I want anymore."

10

PROVISION

They progress along the forest floor with their six footsteps eerily soft and silent as if they were born to do this. To hunt. Not a single twig snaps nor does the fallen foliage crunch beneath their weight. The only proof of their presence comes from the white clouds of breathy condensation into the witching hour darkness, though even those are measured and muted.

A purple sheen shrouds the forest in an almost mystical blanket of winter atmosphere. The jagged and seemingly dead trees carry a thin layer of silver frost on their appendages, yet those, too, stand unnervingly still. What little bit of light remains from the crescent moon above pokes through in patches that they stealthily avoid.

Dr. Dan walks ahead of them, insistent that if something were to go awry, he should be the one to take the brunt of the punishment as a brief opportunity for them to escape. He holds up his right hand and turns to face them with a grim expression that hides unbridled joy behind it. "This is our last chance to speak," he whispers softly with the misty condensation of these words partially obscuring his face. "Any noise from here on could blow our cover, and we can't take even the slightest of chances. Are you both absolutely clear on the plan?"

They nod.

He steps forward and places a hand on their shoulders, then he grins. "Good.

Let's go heal you both."

Marilyn reaches underneath her jacket and grips the birchwood handle with her hand as steady as a surgeon's. Dr. Dan made a leather sheath that is now affixed to her belt to conceal the blade. She looks at Shelly who stares back and nods again, her eyes dark and brooding but radiating an absolute assurance in all that's about to happen.

They walk onward in a single-file line as detailed in the plan to be less visible from afar. Dr. Dan envisioned every possible scenario and thought of multiple ways to pivot should any of them actually happen, and then he even made backup plans for the most unpredictable situations from there. Marilyn asked what they should do if shit absolutely hits the fan, goes full FUBAR, to which he replied, "Don't you worry about that."

A three-on-one armed ambush should be as easy as shooting fish in a barrel, he added, yet Marilyn knows all too well that those damned serial killers are the definition of unbridled chaos. Wayne might still be awake, even nearing three in the morning, or he might've finally made a move on that next unlucky girl. Anything can happen with these wily bastards.

You defied death, Marilyn, and it seems to have no answer for you. Tara's voice whispers with the wind through the barren trees. Dan and Shelly march silently ahead while Marilyn follows in the rear, suddenly turning her head far more frequently to ensure that there won't be an ambush from behind. *You defied death* ... and yet they continue to face off. Marilyn seems to be more of a conscientious objector than any sort of glorified rebel as the public has made her out to be. Maybe she really is an imposter? Just the next hapless idiot who lucked her way into fifteen minutes of fame because of circumstances beyond her control.

It seems to have no answer for you ... The same could be said of anyone living. Death hasn't taken any of them yet either, but they carry on nonetheless as if the frigid touch isn't overshadowing at all times. Tara ran into a buzzsaw that she unfortunately couldn't avoid, but Marilyn is determined to protect Shelly from doing the same. It's personal now.

Wayne's dilapidated mobile home comes into view through several more rows of twisted trees, its stilted foundation incredibly fitting for the surroundings, and there isn't a neighboring home in sight. Nobody to hear him scream.

Dr. Dan holds up a clenched fist without turning, and he freezes in position as he scans the landscape for movement as he said he would. Shelly reaches into her coat and removes a tomahawk hatchet, specifically chosen as the same weapon that was used to murder her daughter. Marilyn never released her white-knuckle grip on the knife handle, and it wasn't until they stopped walking that she noticed the burning sensation in her forearm muscles. Now is not the time to let up, not when Wayne could be lurking the forest doing whatever odious activities a killer would be doing at this hour. Like hunting prey for the slaughter.

Shelly has been still as a gargoyle statue, seemingly staring at the raised fist for what feels like several minutes in anticipation for the all-clear signal to continue. Marilyn's eyes have been staring anywhere but, anticipating an ambush in equal parts impatience and excitement to finish the job. The longer the night lasts, the higher the chance that the deed never gets finalized at all. They can only stalk a serial killer for so long before he catches on—Wayne is certainly not the highest status killer on the totem pole, but even the dumbest of them have a distinctive reptilian sense of danger. Each minute that passes only tilts the odds back in his favor regardless of how the deck is stacked. She presses her left hand against her heart yet feels nothing. It must beat somewhere in there, though her pulse seems to have come to an icy trudge.

Dan lowers his hand at last and takes a single step forward, then pauses ... before taking one more with the same level of predatorial care not to alarm their prey. Wayne's trailer is shrouded in darkness, both inside and out, and his rusted old truck is parked outside as they'd hoped. All good signs. Shelly follows Dr. Dan's step with one of her own and crunches a small twig into the soft dirt, causing him to drop to the ground before the sound has even fully reached Marilyn's ears. The two women follow the motion behind him and press themselves into the earth as flat as they can. He pulls his jacket above his mouth to hide the condensation and motions for them to do the same. *"We likely only have one shot at this,"* he'd said while planning. *"We can't take any chances. It's possible that Wayne may even pick up on something else we failed to prepare for."* Though Marilyn doubted that. Dr. Dan is more meticulous than anyone she's ever met, neurotic in all the ways only a shrink could be.

A full ten minutes of suffocating silence pass, the three of them all releasing micro shivers without movement as the cold overtakes them. Marilyn bites her lip to avoid the noise of her teeth chattering. The purple starless sky above is both oppressive and freeing, on one hand feeling like the lid of a tomb and on the other seeming like a means of escape.

Dan taps Shelly who taps Marilyn in turn. They rise in synchronicity and resume their single-file line to complete the final stretch. The forest density thins considerably the closer they get until the earthen floor beneath grows less and less spongy and turns to concrete. They're on the edge of the driveway.

Shelly and Dan step aside and allow Marilyn to walk ritualistically between them. They both nod, and she finally releases the death grip on her knife blade as she steps forward toward the house with a rush of euphoria surging her system. The window—she's stared upon it countless times through many different photos, but now is the time to finally climb through that threshold and do something righteous. It's situated on the back wall of the mobile home and leads into the kitchen, out of view from the driveway or the improbable pedestrian.

She can't remember if she nodded back or even looked their way again. The call of the window was too strong, a gateway to all the things she always wished she could do on her own. Rise up, fight back, be more than a defiant spectator just once in her life, even if it's only a one-time experience. Marilyn slows her approach as she gets closer to the window, realizing she'd been walking at a normal pace, lost in excitement and unaware of her surroundings. The house still doesn't illuminate as she gets closer, another one of Dr. Dan's good signs, although a serial killer wouldn't give their position away so easily as to flip on a light whenever they hear a little bump in the night. Then again, they wouldn't typically be the hunted.

Marilyn presses her fingers into the glass, both as hard and as softly as she can, and she carefully slides that kitchen window open with the measured approach of a seasoned assassin. Dan and Shelly stand just out of sight around the trailer's corner or else she would signal them a thumbs up to assure that all is going well so far. They'll have to wait until the door opens.

She pauses for thirty seconds as instructed by Dr. Dan with the balmy, rancid air of the mobile home blowing through the opening and striking her in the face. No sound. She stifles a wince and vaults herself into the hellhole of rotted flesh stench and ammonia of rat urine. Half-eaten cans of meat and sausages line the counters next to grubby plates in stacks with movement on the highest of them that she can only hope to be maggots. A plastic gallon of milk shines next to the sink with the purple remnants of moonlight illuminating it to reveal that the contents have long since separated into a white skin and murky, watery liquid beneath. And she can only guess at what rests beneath the molded floor, which is already coated in trash and food wrappers, empty liquor bottles, and unidentified stains. Still no sound.

Marilyn slides her feet across the linoleum kitchen floor as planned to avoid creeks in the hollow foundation. She keeps one eye on the dark hallway where a bedroom door is shut as she tiptoes past an old tube TV, piles of putrid clothing, and excrement that hopefully belongs to a pet. Only five more feet to the front door.

Another odor strikes her as she passes beneath a blowing vent, a scent so strong, so acrid, that it could never be forgotten. Death. Decay. Biological matter that has ceased to function as such. Marilyn knows the smell and she knows it well, but she's never encountered the stench this concentrated in an enclosed area. Wayne is hiding bodies, or individual body parts, inside the ducting. Maybe even some of Shelly's daughter.

She grits her teeth and grinds them in the darkness with the slightest ember of rage kindling in her chest. She places a hand over her heart again and exhales slowly. Still nothing. Not a palpable heartbeat or twitch or quiver. The same lack of sensation she felt during all nine run-ins with The Butcher, and the same depths of emptiness that carried on after eight of those meetings, too. She's ready.

The dented doorknob squeaks slightly as she turns it, and she pauses for only ten seconds this time to wait for safety with her sense of fabricated fear waning rapidly. A part of her lingers in the shadows with her teeth bared for conflict, just hoping for that bedroom door to burst open. *Come on out, Wayne. Come the fuck out.* Nothing. Not a single sound, no lights, no sign of life—all part of the plan, no doubt, but she could end the entire hunt right now with a simple slice through his Adam's apple. Maybe a stab instead? A knife through the heart? But what would that do to Shelly? She deserves her vengeance more than anyone else, a grieving mother with the very will to live snatched right out of her.

Marilyn blinks hard in the blackness with her eyes burning from the multiple sources of rancid stench. She pushes the rickety door outward gently enough not to make another sound and stops halfway from fully open yet the purple night sky pours in all the same. That should be enough to alert Dr. Dan and Shelly.

She looks up at the heater vent and notices that the ceiling surrounding it is coated in some sort of mold or grime. Or blood. Maybe all three. Wayne must enjoy breathing in the scent of decay. Their silent footsteps approach on the concrete outside, noticeable only to Marilyn who studied the patterns for hours so she could fall in line between them.

Dr. Dan grabs the door with his gloved hand and swings it open fully with a smile that sours rapidly. "Marilyn! Turn around!"

A metallic crack rings inside the house, and she hits the hollow floor with a thud, trying her damnedest to ward off fate just once more with defiance, with willpower, or some other form of *fuck you* as her thoughts grow fuzzy. She looks up at Dr. Dan through double vision as he pulls a revolver from his coat and fires. The gunshot pierces her already ringing ears, and the wet sound of flesh tearing is the last thing she hears before succumbing to the blackness.

11

METAMORPHOSIS

"Marilyn. Are you with me now? Marilyn?" Dr. Dan pats her face gently and drips water onto it. Her first thought is feverish hope that it isn't water from the putrid sink.

Fluttering visions of his smiling face, either still or once again, flood her clouded vision second. "What happened?"

"My worst fear. Hidden cameras." He steps aside to reveal multiple outdated monitors with fuzzy, live CC footage streaming on them. One records the outside of the bedroom, while another shows the front door. The third points directly at the kitchen window.

Marilyn wipes the aura from her aching eyes and forces several more blinks. "He knew we were here."

"Worse. He knew we were *coming*. Probably saw Shelly and me scouting the place when he was gone, if I had to guess. He's probably been waiting for an attack of some sort, staying up all night every night in anticipation of this very occurrence, I imagine. But he didn't expect this."

She squints to force her eyes into compliance. Dr. Dan holds a long silver revolver in front of his chest playfully like a child pretending to be a cowboy. "You shot him?"

"I shot him. But only through the shoulder for now, far from anything vital.

He's tied up and waiting for the rest of his punishment, but you're still integral to the process. Are you okay to continue?"

"Yes. He mostly hit me between my shoulder blades. Might've gotten just a little bit of my head."

"And with a shovel, no less. Far less impactful than a bat or something else just as solid. I never did say he was one of the smart ones," he chuckles. "You remember the plan?"

Marilyn stands and catches herself on the corner wall as every impulse within tells her to lay back down and quit, but the thought of already being on the grubby floor once is repulsive enough. "Yes. I'm ready. Where's Shelly?"

"With Wayne. We tied him to a chair and gagged him, although he likely enjoys the latter. Are you sure that you're okay?"

"Good enough to finish the job. I'll rest later."

Dr. Dan nods. "We left him in the living room since it seemed much easier to move you into the bedroom to recover. I wasn't so sure you'd be getting up after that one, but who am I kidding? You're Marilyn Soroka."

Her vision closes to that of a small tunnel, either from impact or adrenaline, and she stares into his eyes in the increasing darkness until only the irises and pupils are visible. Bluish light flickers from the static of the television monitors. "It'll take more than a shovel to kill me. I'm ready."

"You're going to do great. Let's get to it—Shelly must be eager." He turns and opens the bedroom door to reveal the same dark hallway, now with a piercing light reflecting from the end of it. The living room.

Marilyn takes a shaky step behind him and quickly finds her footing, feeling more confident with each successive stride. Another killer will meet his end tonight, and the world will be a better place for it. They walk forward with the light growing so bright that it appears to carry a ringing with it inside Marilyn's head. An ambience of flashing light emanates from the center of the room where a humanoid silhouette sits in the form of a pulsating black mass—Wayne.

Shelly's face lights up as they enter the living room, but she only nods in return. She holds the tomahawk's blade to his throat, though his mouth is taped and his arms and legs are bound by steel chains and locked to a metal folding chair. *We will take no chances*, Dr. Dan said during planning. And he meant every bit of it, right down to the failsafe of bringing a gun to a knife fight.

"You can remove the tape now, Shelly," Marilyn says.

Shelly rips the strip from Wayne's lips without the slightest reaction from him.

"Yeh fin'ly made it," Wayne snarls with a yellow-toothed grin, each of his teeth as vivid as corn kernels in the dark. "The town celebr'ty. I been waitin."

Marilyn ignores his goading and steps forward. She blinks slowly to fend off the lingering dizziness and drifting attention and fetid smells. Her eyes strengthen and focus on his rotten appearance in the blackness before disengaging to a momentary state of rest. There's only one shot to kill Wayne, and it's now.

"Ain't I one lucky sum bitch? Norm'ly I'd a been stalkin y'all. Now all's I gotta do is kill y'all here, nice and easy."

"Shut up, or I'll shoot you again," Dan growls uncharacteristically. "Perhaps a kneecap this time."

Wayne smirks again but stays silent and shifts his focus back to Marilyn.

She opens a manila folder that had been previously stored in Dr. Dan's bag, and she removes a crime scene photograph from it to hold in front of Wayne's face, which feels like the sort of miscreant, inbred features that should've been behind the Butcher's mask. "Do you recognize this woman? Her name was Danielle."

"Course. Prettiest lil bitch I ever saw." He spits on the floor. "Though she was even prettier in pieces. Even gave her dead mouth a big ol' wet kiss."

Marilyn remains stoic. She can't see Shelly's face clearly in her peripheral vision, but the expression appears to be one of rage and resolve instead of sorrow. Full of fury ... Wrath.

I even sliced her face clean off her skull and wore it like a bloody masquerade mask! She sees the Butcher in the darkness holding Tara's freshly-peeled and dripping face dangling before her own, her trauma-soaked eyes gleaming with playful derision through the jagged holes. *I cut that bitch's face off to see through her eyes*! Marilyn feels a knock in her chest for the first time in the presence of a serial killer.

"Fuck you," she says at last. "We're going to hack you into little chunks for what you did to Danielle. Then you'll be fed to the wildlife and forgotten like the insignificant waste that you are."

Wayne's expression morphs into something far less joyful. He attempts to free himself from the chains with a burst of energy to no avail, and he releases a primal bellow of perhaps frustration or pain from the gunshot wound pressing against the restraints. His jaw hangs agape to reveal the golden mustard teeth again as a new pungent stench hits Marilyn's nose, and she can't be sure if it's from the decay in the house or his mouth. Then it curls upward sharply at the corners like gift wrapping ribbon. "Go on then. But flip me them famous fingers first."

"You don't deserve them. We've already beaten you. With ease."

An ethereal ringing in her ears accompanies a return of tunnel vision. The noise isn't quite mechanical but emanates from somewhere deeper—somewhere within. The pitch is persistent yet faint. She sees a lavish living room with an ornate fireplace and pottery and exquisite furniture around it. White everything. There's a group of young adults, barely drinking age, and they're laughing loudly, so loud that it's audible above the blaring music, and they're drinking beer and taking shots and having fun. There's a fondness to this vision that Marilyn recognizes as friendly, perhaps even more loving than that. They dance and sing and revel in their togetherness before it's snatched away from them at the snap of a finger. They enjoy themselves too much with a few too many beers, to the point of eventual oblivion when survival would come to call.

A figure cloaked in black slips through a bathroom window undetected and unopposed—the Butcher. She stealthily stabs a partygoer in the back of the neck at the edge of the living room before anyone else notices. Chad. There's a crunching sound as the blade meets bone and cartilage and Chad falls limp, grasping helplessly at his throat for breath but it does not come. The rest of the party catches on slower than they should, probably in shock or hoping the stunt is nothing but a prank, but bedlam ensues eventually regardless. The young adults run in circles and crash into the decorations and splash blood all over the white furniture as they're slaughtered, all too panicked to think clearly and a bit too inebriated and disheveled by the surprise to escape. Flesh is slashed and her friends are gutted and dismembered and beheaded in record fashion. Marilyn sits on the couch watching, already accepting of her fate as yet another victim of this masked assassin, an emaciated wolf set loose in a sheep enclosure, a shark swimming through a school of hapless fish. Eventually, all falls silent except for the music blaring still, and the partygoers are all dead except for Marilyn. She stares into the black velvet face covering with a swelling of absurdity rising in her gut, being the last person to live despite her lack of action. There's only one descriptor for the feeling, something of a mix between hatred and non-compliance mixed with nihilistic freedom. *Fuck you* is all she can mutter with a laugh, and both of her middle fingers immediately spring upward in one last act of defiance. The figure pauses, the black cloak painted with shimmering red spatter, the knife blade stained and dripping, and she runs—leaving the college-aged girl alone and still as stone and confused until the turn of the morning light.

Marilyn blinks hard and shakes her head in Wayne's living room. She looks over at Dr. Dan, who stares back with a face of great concern, but he nods for them to proceed as planned. She only needs to finish the ritual and pass the rest off to Shelly. But Dan was indeed set on showing Wayne the error of his ways as only Marilyn would know how.

"We're on to you," Marilyn seethes. "On to how you've been stalking your next victim recently, and we know that you were going to strike soon. Well. Fuck you for that, too. That's another life saved to go on and live and prosper and do great things, and she'll never even know how close she was to losing it all.

What about the next girl? And the girl after that? A butterfly effect of only good things that will come with your death." She grabs the knife at her belt with white knuckles, and she glances over at Shelly who nods, too. They're ready. Wayne must be eviscerated.

I cut off her face to see through her eyes. The Butcher peels the skin just below the scalp with the sound of separating sandwich condiments on the bread spreading from the meat. The exposed skull of Tara's forehead precedes her bulging eyeballs still stuck in their sockets.

A wedding. The attendees are dressed in white floral dresses and black suits, and they cheer with great bravado as the bride and groom appear at the edge of the long carpet rolled out on a picturesque cliffside. The first atrocity of the day occurs as the Butcher slashes the bride across the lower back first, this time with much more urgency as she stabs her half a dozen times in quick succession about the spine. The groom tries to fight back, likely still cemented by shock, but he, too, is stabbed multiple times through his bleach white dress shirt, and he falls. The audience scatters like the young partygoers as the shadowed figure steps forward to kill as many as she can. Multiple attendees escape this attack, sprinting and jumping from the ledge along this cliffside wedding, though others still die on the rocks beneath upon impact. Marilyn stands in her lilac dress on the steps, one of the bridesmaids, holding a bouquet of moist flowers that will only die in a landfill eventually like everyone here, like every single organism along the east-to-west axis. It's over for the audience.

Marilyn notices the same black outfit approaching her, and she tosses her flowers lackadaisically in a last-ditch effort to bestow them upon a deserving recipient. They land flat on a dead girl's chest, a family member of the bride that didn't quite make the bridal party, a girl who will never make good on the bouquet's promise. The Butcher wields two dripping daggers as she approaches Marilyn, who stands still in contempt again of performing the fearful charade. Everyone in the party has either fled or is dead, the delicate lilac dresses painted with red arterial spray as they lay horizontally or slumped in their seats, and the black tuxedos shine beneath the sun with glistening streams of sanguinary adornment running down them. The Butcher steps forward wearing her black cloak and mask, and she stares with searing hatred palpable through the fabric, a type of rage so strong that Marilyn can even feel it in the present moment.

"You expect me to be *more* afraid the second time? Fuck off," she says to the Butcher, who pauses with what must be a thousand burning questions swirling beneath her shadowed covering. *I cut off the face to see through their eyes.*

Marilyn shakes her head again in present time to see Wayne's expression drooping quickly. She unsheathed the kitchen knife at some point during the flashback but how long did the fugue state last? He stares at the blade as if his fate were transcribed upon it.

"We demand your life, and your suffering, in return for killing Tara—I mean Danielle. Shelly is going to cut you limb from limb for what you did to her daughter, among several other young girls." Marilyn attempts to swallow, but her throat instinctively closes as the sounds of her friends' and acquaintances' anguished screams from the party and wedding pierce her ears. "Any last ... Any last words from you?" She forces her eyes shut as a fresh wave of ringing in her ears brings with it further visions of death and pain.

Wayne begins to fret. "Just make it quick, alright?! Danielle or Stacy or Tara ... None a them meant any more to me than the rest a them other bitches, but stop starin' at me like that!"

"Nothing will save you now," Marilyn broods, caught between past and present. "Not your apologies, your tears, and definitely not your whiny begging. You killed my friends ... my family! Divine intervention couldn't save your piss-poor life even if God himself entered this shithole of a trailer and tried to take you from me. You will die tonight. And it's going to fucking hurt." She looks at Dr. Dan who stares back with a furrowed brow, and then she turns to Shelly, whose face is so full of boiling hatred, so full of unrestrained malice and unrelenting enmity, that she couldn't possibly have heard what Marilyn said. "Do you hear me, you fucking swine?! Never again will you be allowed to haunt my nights." She steps forward and lands a right hook where his lips meet at the corner of his mouth, and a few rotten teeth propel from his gums and chatter across the floor like a rolling of the dice.

Wayne remains looking down at his lap with a thick bloody string of spittle descending from his lips that reaches down past his pot belly, resembling a beat dog that understands when the fight has already been lost.

Marilyn blinks through a dark aura that radiates inward. She sees an intimate night with a close friend from high school, though they had grown apart by that time during their college and young adult years. Marilyn had gotten a job while Rose struggled to find work. They sit on couches facing one another just like she and Wayne in the present moment, just as she and the Butcher did in her final moments. Rose reached out before in search of a helping hand after a stubborn string of bad luck, as she had seen Marilyn in the news after two horrific massacres and realized that she was back in town. Rose doesn't wish to talk about the tragedies but instead about her own struggles with work and relationships. Marilyn goes along willingly, also hoping to use this relative stranger for her own benefit—to resume a sense of normalcy. Having someone living to talk to instead of visiting fresh gravesites, listening to mundane human complications instead of screams of death and pain, empathizing with a sort of friend for a change instead of trying to sympathize with the dead—it's refreshing. Marilyn fakes a smile and nods, just as she faked every typical emotion since that first Butcher visit back at the college party. The well has run dry as if that one event damned all input and forced her to stuff the very notion of survival down into the pits of her bowels like the fear of death itself. Rose continues to jabber mindlessly about her last boyfriend and work and all sorts of trivial manners that couldn't hold a candle to Marilyn's struggles. Still she nods like a dutiful friend, or an excellent actress pretending to be one, remaining motionless even as the front door lock is picked and it swings open unsuspectingly as an uninvited guest enters their grievance session.

The Butcher lunges forward, no doubt hoping an ambush of a smaller group would be more successful, and wraps her black-gloved hand around Rose's mouth. Rose attempts to scream beneath it to no avail, and she's eventually stabbed through her eyeballs and the bridge of her nose several times to muzzle the concern. Marilyn stares at the black mask with a blank expression that suggests she couldn't care less either way as her friend shrieks—and perhaps she simply can't, given all that she's seen.

"I've grown tired," Marilyn says to the Butcher once Rose crumples. "I'm just so tired of your endless games. Kill me now or be done with it forever. I hope to never see you again, one way or another."

I cut off the face to see through their eyes.

Wayne's living room is silent aside from the ringing that has burrowed deeper into her head, like a drill bit, and a touch of throbbing that escalated from background noise to encapsulating waves of syncopated drumbeats. His greasy, stringy hair bleeds into the Butcher's surprisingly well-kept presence with her jet-black ponytail now hanging over their shared shoulder. The screams of her victims replace the ringing, and the pain of their sorrow falls upon Marilyn like some great stone block from above. "Shut up. Stop your talking before I gut you."

Dr. Dan steps forward, but she shoots him a look with a face that doesn't quite feel like her own. He stops and steps back, though with no less concern than before.

The Butcher leans her head back and laughs, bound to Wayne's chair by metal chains and repressed trauma from both sides of the chasm. "I killed your family, Marilyn. Your pregnant sister, her husband, everything they held dear. You may have evaded my knife, but I left you destitute nonetheless. You tell me who lost?"

Years' worth of buried rage begins to burn in her core, where it festered and metastasized like cancer for nothing more than a performative demonstration just to spite the Butcher. Playing dress-up as some sort of anti-hero who drove a serial killer to suicide when in truth it was only a matter of time before that gun ended up in one of their mouths, by one hand or the other. "I said shut up! *Shut the fuck up!*" Marilyn grips the birchwood in her palm that has begun to perspire. "We're going to kill you now so nobody ever has to hear you again!"

"You want to hear how I killed Tara? I figured you would want to know since you were present for the rest. She was buying something nice for you or so she said when she got in her car. I was waiting in the back seat and strangled her with a wire while she begged to be freed. It was pathetic. I sliced that cute little face of hers clean off like deli meat and put it on my own with the fresh blood still hot and sopping wet. It dried quickly in the frigid night air and sealed upon my skin like an adhesive. Finally—I could see through the eyes of someone *important* to the infamous Marilyn Soroka. That's why I had to cut off the face ... to *be* her. To see you just once through her eyes."

The room goes dark with undulating waves of blackness that crescendo and cease and rise again. She drops to one knee, and she can't hear whether Dr. Dan and Shelly have said anything further to her. Absolute silence, surrounded by viscous cold air as if she'd been buried alive. Echoes of her fall rebound off the walls and return to her with the shrieks of her many lost friends, classmates, coworkers, and family, but instead of feeling sorrow, she feels ... excitement. An adrenaline rush.

Don't you wish you could've seen it my way?

"Marilyn, get up!" someone shouts from the ether. "Chad is dead! We have to run away before he kills us!" The voice belongs to Jocelyn Estevez, her college roommate. Marilyn distinctly remembers watching the horror from the sofa as Jocelyn desperately tugged at her with her gushing wrist.

Cut off the face.

"Marilyn!" another screams. Roger Bennett, the matching groomsman with whom she walked down the aisle as a bridesmaid. She vividly recalls Roger reaching out a hand to pull her from the stage once the carnage began, and he was stabbed in the armpit artery that bled out quickly in spurts among the white decorations and layered wedding cake.

See through the eyes.

"Marilyn, I can't even explain how much I've craved your friendship since we last spoke. I feel so much better already." Rose's last words before she was muzzled and her eyes were pierced to leave seeping black holes in their place.

She feels hands sliding some sort of covering over her face. It's soft yet suffocating and musty. *The Butcher's black mask.* She rises and unsheathes the Damascus blade and steps toward the shadowed figure in the darkness with the Butcher's face. No light permeates except that which shines upon her from crown to chin. There's a final sound of cackling followed by a gunshot and then the sound of sawing. Sawing through sinewy flesh and tough skin and bits of hair and lips.

"Marilyn?! In God's name, what have you done?!" Dr. Dan exclaims, his voice suddenly piercing her senses.

Marilyn falters in and out of consciousness in lucid intervals with visions of Wayne's face alternating with the Butcher's as she slices the last few inches. She peels the skin like spreading a sloppy sandwich and presses the hot blood against her own face to allow it to adhere in the rancid air. Dr. Dan covers his mouth in terror as Shelly releases a bellow, and Wayne howls agonizingly in his restraints with his eyeballs protruding at the center of his red and raw flesh.

Marilyn turns and stares at them with wide eyes peering through Wayne's sockets and both her middle fingers raised to the sky. "I cut off the face to see through his eyes."

12

EXPOSITION

Marilyn's eyes flutter between open and closed, between lightness and dark, as an aura of moving visual disturbances clouds her vision. She sees only white in what little clarity she can muster. "Where am I?"

"Oh. Sorry, let me get you a pillow."

"Dr. Dan?"

"Yes." He props her head up so she can see the room. See him. He returns to his seat and sips a glass of wine and stares at her all the while.

"What happened?"

"Excellent question, Marilyn. *What happened*?" He sips again.

"Jesus, my head. Can I have one of those?"

"Probably not a good idea."

She takes a deep breath through the pounding and swimming and spinning in her brain. "I don't know. The last thing I remember clearly was when Wayne hit me, and then it all turned cloudy. Why?"

"Hm. Just as I feared."

"What? What did you fear? I've been a pretty good goddamn sport, Dan. I'm obviously not in the mood for brooding shrinkisms." She tries to push herself up but can't move, and she feels something sticky on her face holding the skin in position like liquid latex. Wayne's dried blood. "What is this? Did you strap me down?!" She looks down and sees what appear to be blurry leather straps restraining her across the torso and legs, pressing the vial on her necklace into her chest.

"Unfortunately. I had to be sure that your ... *episode* was over."

She closes her eyes and takes a deep breath as if imagining the situation to be yet another face-off with a monster. The warmth of composure washes over her. "What are you so afraid of?"

Dr. Dan sighs accompanied by a long sip. "That your subconscious was acting for you. This is what we would call a problem, given the circumstances."

"I don't understand, Dan. What happened?"

"Try to think. See if you can put yourself in the same headspace as in Wayne's trailer."

"I was obviously concussed. You remember him bashing me across the fucking head, don't you? Whatever you think I did wasn't actually coming from me."

"Oh, but it did, and that's what's concerning." He sets the glass of wine down carefully on an end table and walks toward Marilyn. "We hear the same thing from drunks who absolve themselves of responsibility for their actions when they were intoxicated. *It wasn't me; it was the booze.* No. That's the *real* you coming out, unfiltered and unchained. That big, bad monster you've been trying to pretend doesn't exist, even when it roars behind whatever flimsy door you've hidden it. Eventually it breaks free and reveals itself. We call that the third face."

"Doc, please. I'm already hurting enough."

"You asked. There's an old philosophical saying that every person has three faces. The first is what you allow the world to see—the safe performance you give on stage or in all those interviews you clearly don't want to do. It's friendly enough to fool the average person, but I can see the gaping cracks in the mask. The second face is what we show our loved ones. No offense, but you don't have any loved ones anymore. Thus, the monster was itching to break free. The third face is when we reveal our true selves, maskless, in our most private of moments, and only to ourselves. This is the innermost self, hidden even from our closest friends, and it reveals our most intimate desires, thoughts, and fears. Your third face took control of you in that trailer. No pun intended. Concussed? Maybe, but your actions revealed a hell of a lot more about what goes on deep inside that brain of yours. There are demons, to put it lightly."

Marilyn bites her lip and jerks her body beneath the leather straps, knowing full well that nothing will come of it. "I'm all ears, *Dan*. What did my monster do?"

"Think."

"I can't."

"*Think.*"

Marilyn closes her eyes tightly at first then allows them to relax. Blackness. Oblivion. Peace. Like floating in a warm pool on a soothing summer day. The waters are placid and pacifying like a cocoon. Like a womb. Then those waters turn choppy.

The pounding in her head returns worse than its previous apex with a throbbing in the back that couldn't be matched by an entire drumline. Pain, but more than the obvious physical agony that she suffers, more than a simple body is designed to endure. Agony of the like that should be reserved for those submerged for eternity in a lake of fire. Screams—fear, helplessness, despair. Sixty-four fallen voices that descend into darkness as if being buried alongside the secrets of their demise, secrets that nobody else has been forced to bury.

The Butcher's face. Both masked and unmasked, the blackness of her public appearance behind the dark cloak to hide her true face laid bare beside the barely human representation of the true self. The haggard face of perpetually repressed desires, thoughts, and fears. The face she only allowed herself to see for years on end, the face she inevitably couldn't stand anymore and blew out with a bullet in lieu of suffering it again. It's both mocking and inviting. Fearful and cheerful. Human and demonic.

The mouth opens wide like an abyssal void and vacuums all happiness and pain alike inside it. Marilyn feels actual fear for the first time since that college graduation party, and it feels awful. Her heart tries to burst free from its cage and her lungs feel gashed.

She sees herself standing in the blackness, naked and exposed, appearing quite unlike her physical body that the whole world sees every time she makes a public appearance. She's emaciated and angular, her skin clinging to bone like stretched plastic wrap sans muscle and fat. Her bent limbs and digits are positioned unnaturally and crooked as if she'd leapt from a building to escape this wicked world herself, and her skin is pale with decrepit patches of gangrenous rot like some exhumed corpse years after burial.

The Butcher approaches bare as well holding something folded in her hands and reaches for Marilyn. They stand still in position until Marilyn sidesteps.

Marilyn brushes her thin, sweat-matted hair back and stands upright with her joints creaking and popping. She releases a muffled cackle from behind Wayne's ill-fitting face affixed to her own, the blood from his excoriated skin running and dripping around the edges and seeping into her open mouth to add a wet gurgle to the laugh.

"Don't you see?" the naked Butcher asks her. "*You cut off his face to see through our eyes.*"

Marilyn's eyes burst open as if she was defibrillated, and she screams. The bellows don't sound like her own, tinged with echoes of lost loved ones sacrificed for her unwanted legacy. But they are her screams. She feels the vibrato against the bruise on the back of her neck and throughout her fractured mind. She shrieks with terror beyond human comprehension as if she'd had a walk through hell itself and returned to convey the experience.

"Let me go right now, Dan! LET ME FUCKING GO!"

He shakes his head gravely with the wine glass held beneath his nose. "No can do, my friend. You need this."

"You don't understand! I have to get away! I'm just like them! I killed Wayne!

I killed him!" Marilyn thrashes underneath the leather straps but moves very little. Her eyes dart around the room from either the concussion or panic or both.

"Shh. You're safe here. Try to relax. I know it's tough, but you're experiencing a tidal wave of repressed trauma that I'm frankly surprised took this long to manifest. I won't let anything bad happen to you."

Marilyn's struggles slow, and she closes her eyes again to escape one form of torture for another. The darkness of her true self greets her.

"Take a deep breath in. Hold." Dr. Dan's voice carries from a distance as if shouting into a cavern. "I believe in you, Marilyn. Now release."

She focuses on her gangly figure laid bare adorned with Wayne's dripping facial skin akin to the Butcher wearing Tara's. Run. But there's nowhere to escape to.

"Deep breath. Hold. Release."

The creature steps forward and smears the blood across her chest with her tongue wagging mockingly through pursed lips. The lanky being reaches out and cackles.

"Deep breath. Hold. Release."

The mad laughter falls silent. The space is both vast and suffocating with frigid air that seems to be laced with nerve gas. Marilyn stares at her creation. "I'm not afraid of you anymore. Do your worst," she says either out loud or internally though she doesn't know which.

"Deep breath."

Her liver-spotted taut skin rehydrates and transitions back to normal. The contorted body parts crack and straighten.

"Hold."

The creature peels the sopping backside of Wayne's face from her own and allows it to plop on the floor like a slice of bologna. She's young and pretty but badly beaten with black eyes and a bruised throat and a diagonal jagged stab wound through her sternum. These injuries fade away as well.

"Release."

A newly-adult Marilyn Soroka stands stone-faced and unburdened by the blood that coats her upper body. She wipes her eyes clean and returns the fiery gaze, her hair wet and matted with red streaks like fresh dye.

"What do you see now?" Dr. Dan's smooth voice echoes in the void.

"Myself. But not quite me."

"Good. What does she look like?"

Marilyn shifts as much as she can against the leather straps and falls calm again. "Young and covered in blood. She's staring at me."

"Stare back. Don't be afraid."

The blood begins to dry and dissipate. Young Marilyn's face softens as if a thorn was removed. She smiles.

"What are you seeing now?" Dan asks, his voice feeling considerably more present.

Marilyn's eyes open, and she stares at the ceiling with a sudden interval of clarity. "She was smiling. Unburdened. Full of life."

"Well done. You've finally met your true self."

13

RESOLUTION

There's a knock on Dr. Dan's ornate wooden door, the door to a home in which Marilyn now inhabits as some sort of vagrant it seems. A halfway home for serial killer survivors, a sanctuary for all things broken and fucked up and destitute. Should she answer it herself? Is that normal?

Fortunately, Dr. Dan answers, having obviously invited this guest since Marilyn doesn't have anyone to call. They speak briefly at the door with mumbled niceties and small talk before entering the foyer outside of her guest room. It's Shelly. Fuck.

The situation will only be more awkward the longer she waits to join them. Or maybe she can pretend to be asleep instead and avoid the situation altogether? No. She's never been able to run from her problems. It's better to rip the bandage off quickly and inspect the state of the wound.

The bedroom door opens with an unnecessarily loud creak that startles Shelly. She turns her head quickly.

"Hi, Shelly," Marilyn whispers as she stands in the doorway sheepishly.

"Hi, Marilyn. I'm glad you're doing better. That was quite a knock you took."

Dr. Dan nods toward her with an inkling of comfort. They must've spoken since the event, and the gesture seems to reaffirm that everything is okay between them. "Come sit with us, Marilyn. Shelly and I will only be having a quick conversation about her recovery, a topic of which I'm sure you'll be able to contribute."

Marilyn nods and follows. She would rather face Wayne or the Butcher again than speak to Shelly now after what she did, but it seems there's no other choice. Or at least not an escape that makes any logical sense.

The three of them sit at the dining table once more where a communal bottle of wine and three glasses await. Several seconds of silence pass in unbearable anticipation.

Marilyn clears her throat and spearheads the conversation. "Shelly ..."

"You don't have to say anything," she says with a glint of a tear in her eye.

"I do. I'm so sorry for my actions. I don't know what came over me."

"You have nothing to explain. I can't even imagine all that you went through before we met, and maybe it was a bit selfish of me to ask so much of you, especially so soon after going through a tragic event yourself." Shelly extends her reach and grasps Marilyn's hand with a squeeze of warmth.

"Thank you, Shelly. That means a lot to me." Marilyn nods at her and feels uncomfortable while doing so, as if the exercise of peeling back her armored layers was actually cutting through the skin.

"Of course. I have to admit that I was a little bit disappointed about not killing Wayne myself. I'd rehearsed it over and over in my head, dreamt about it, prayed about it."

Marilyn nods again silently. She doesn't even have the words to express the emotions to herself, let alone to the mourning mother she robbed of retribution.

"But honestly ... I don't know how well I would've done with it. The thought of killing him was only a fantasy for me until it became very real in that trailer. I obviously *wanted* to ... But thank you. Now I'll never have to wonder if I would've made the right decision because you made it for me. My daughter's killer is finally dead, and that's all that matters to me."

Marilyn feels her cheeks heat up thinking about the elephant in the room that none of them have dared bring up yet—dancing in Wayne's skin mask had little to do with vengeance. She must've looked like a fucking doofus. "I'm glad you've found some relief, Shelly. I only wish it went smoother."

"Nonsense," Dan interjects. "We accomplished what we went there to do. The mission was a resounding success. I wish you wouldn't have been smacked over the head, but we did well."

Marilyn bites her tongue but reminds herself she's supposed to be trying this whole *truth* thing. Feeling feelings she thought the receptors of which had long since atrophied. "We can't just pretend I didn't carve his face off first. The same thing the Bucher did to Tara."

He clears his throat. "I wasn't *pretending*. Maybe sidestepping. You were concussed and clearly not in a good mental state."

"And you said that a concussion could bring out a person's true self."

"I did. I acknowledge that what we saw was ... highly unusual, while also objectively knowing it was a legitimate trauma response. Again, a rather unusual one, but strangely not the weirdest I've seen. It's part of your growth—your recovery, and it was entirely necessary to work out the kinks." He nods.

"The kinks."

"Indeed."

"It's okay, Marilyn. Really." Shelly squeezes her hand for support. Marilyn had forgotten they were still attached at the digits and pulls free.

"I don't mean to be problematic, but are you shitting me? I cut a man's fucking face off and slapped it on my own, and you're both acting as if nothing fucking happened!"

"Yes, exactly." Dan nods. "I mean yes to the first part. It definitely happened. I don't want to speak for Shelly, but I think we both agree to accept you for all that you are, including the many idiosyncrasies of being Marilyn Soroka."

"And doesn't that fucking scare you?!" She tempers her tone, suspecting Dan just might have a tranquilizer dart at the ready based on how many other tricks he's pulled from his cardigan sleeves.

He shakes his head with a twisted smile.

"No, Marilyn. You don't scare me." Shelly clears her throat and looks back and forth from doctor to patient. "You've never hurt an innocent person. You released mountains of anger on a deserving killer. That's all I know. That's all I saw. Then you delivered justice."

"Well fucking said, Shelly." Dr. Dan slowly claps with purpose. "You're fine, Marilyn. So fine in fact that I've made the decision we're going to continue our work. I know that might seem counterintuitive considering your reaction with Wayne, but I think I fear for your sanity more if you don't have something to focus on. That apartment of yours is a ticking timebomb, and you'll be much safer here with me. I'll know the warning signs next time when you're pushed too far. I'll do better as well."

Silence overtakes the room, the type of silence that would befall a monastery or a library or a cemetery on a frigid night next to the grave of a certain someone. The type of silence only spoken amongst the dead.

"Okay," Marilyn says at last, followed by a deep breath. "I'm in. And I'll be more honest with you moving forward about what's going on inside my head. It's obviously not a strong suit of mine. I can barely even admit my feelings to myself, but I'll try."

"That's all any of us can do," Dan says.

Marilyn sighs, imagining fatal danger to calm her rising emotions. "So, who's next? What do we do from here?"

Shelly's lip quivers as her eyes dart back and forth between them, visibly filled with questions and racing emotions and heavy thoughts. "I'm sorry ... I can't continue. I wish I felt differently, but I'm simply out of my league. I had nothing left to live for when we went after Wayne, but something feels different inside me now ... Peace, maybe. I'm sorry. I don't feel that hatred anymore."

"Don't be sorry, Shelly." Dr. Dan stands and approaches her then places his hands on her shoulders. "Be glad. Marilyn and I devoted ourselves to helping *you*, not the other way around. You owe us nothing."

Marilyn nods a single time in staunch agreement.

"I know you did. That's *why* I feel this way now, like I'll never be able to repay you for your sacrifices."

"Shelly ... As your psychiatrist, seeing you through to a full recovery is my greatest joy. You're free now—go enjoy a life of freedom from all that's plagued you. You've earned it. Marilyn and I will carry that candle."

She nods several times hurriedly. "Thank you both, from the bottom of my heart. I don't know how I can ever return the favor, but I promise that I'll be ready to do it if the time ever comes. Excuse me for a moment." Shelly stands and hurries away to the restroom and shuts the door.

Marilyn waits for quiet before speaking again. "And what about you, Dr. Dan? What is it that plagues you enough to keep this operation going?"

He walks from Shelly's seat toward the bar with the heavy heels of his fancy Brogues echoing beneath the floorboards, and he pours a hefty glass of single malt instead of wine and noses it at length. "Justice." He takes a sip of the nectar with a faraway gaze and swirls the glass with slow sophistication. "Or lack thereof."

14

REVELATION

"What if we get caught?" Marilyn says, sitting on the other side of the walnut desk in his home office like some everyday patient. A fire crackles in the fireplace, ablaze with a certain sense of life and energy that the rest of the office lacks.

"That's always a possibility."

"You aren't afraid?"

Dr. Dan stops scribbling on his notepad and sets the fountain pen aside with an implied sigh. "How many incredibly capable men and women lost sight of their true purpose because of underlying fear?"

"A great many, I'd imagine."

"Exactly."

"So, you're okay with being caught? Being thrown in jail?"

He stares at her again with a sense of exasperation beneath the surface, yet his face remains stoic and he doesn't sigh. "I accept the idea of it, yes. There's no such thing as a life free of risk or consequence, especially not a successful one. The thrill-seekers risk disaster and the sedentary risk disease. Nobody gets off this ride alive, Marilyn, and definitely not unscathed. We should all choose the path of higher fulfillment and accept the potential hazards as byproducts of our happiness. Otherwise, life would be dreadfully meaningless, as you've already experienced."

"Which basically means you're fine with us getting caught as long as we serve our purpose."

"Basically, yes. As long as we do everything in our power to prevent any mishaps, the rest is out of our control. Happenstance. Acts of God."

Marilyn has never been the fidgety sort, yet she twiddles her thumbs regardless. So many questions. "I'm fine with it, too, when you phrase it that way, but I have to admit that I'm suspicious of your ability to twist words into a more palatable phrasing to meet the end goal."

Dan raises his open palms with the pen between his fingers in a gesture of surrender. "You got me. Pretty spot on, really. Part of my profession is to sway patients in the direction of progression, even when they seem so dead set against it or otherwise unable. Like yourself. It's part of the job."

"But you love it."

"I don't hate it. I find fulfillment in doing this, like we talked about before."

"Psychiatrist pedagogy, yes. But there's more to it for you than being a good shrink." She pauses and taps her index finger on the desk. "I saw your face in Wayne's trailer. You looked ... like a different person."

He chuckles. "As did you."

"Touché. Except we've uncovered the reason why my true self came out. What's yours?"

"Are you trying to use reverse psychology on me? Jesus, no wonder you hate shrinks."

"Maybe." Dr. Dan sighs deeply and rubs his eyes and brows then pushes his notebook aside. He drops his elbows on the desk and places his palms together as if praying with his index fingers pressed against his lips. "You're a unique patient of mine, Marilyn, especially since it was me that sought *you* out for treatment. A special project, if you will. Thus, I feel like we need to be entirely honest with one another."

"Yes, I've been rather open. The whole state knows my story now. Probably other states, too."

"I was referring to myself. My wife was taken from me about ten years ago. Some piece of shit savage not unlike Wayne, although I've run out of derogatory words to describe my hatred for him. Maybe the words simply don't exist. He broke into our home one night when I was out of town attending a work conference, and he stabbed her seventeen times in our bed while she was still asleep. I felt like a coward, like I'd failed her, like I should've been there to sacrifice myself or at least die beside her together in our dreams. Maybe we wouldn't have even known that it happened and could've spent an eternity together uninterrupted. Countless doubts plagued me for years, obsessing over infinitesimally small details that I could've done differently to save her life, but then the truth hit me—evil is an unstoppable force as old as time itself and none of us can change the inevitable. At least not once it's happened."

Marilyn remains silent in a momentary loss for words. Should she grab his hand like Shelly did to her? Maybe hug him? Gross. "I'm so sorry, Dan. I couldn't even imagine."

He smiles. "Yes, you can."

"But not a wife."

"Yes, well, you and I have been brought together, regardless. I learned about your death-defying escapades years ago, and it laid the framework for where we are now. You inspired me to take action and go after my wife's killer, consequences be damned. *Miles Forsythe.* The stupid bastard offed himself once police made a move on his property, so I suppose I wouldn't have gotten him either way. But it was your defiance that inspired me to finally go on the offensive."

She shifts from tapping the desk to touching her fingertips together in unison. "So, Wayne was your first try?"

"He was, and it was a revelation. Years of planning, prep work, research, and vetting patients finally paid dividends like I couldn't believe. Helping others similar to me take vengeance always seemed like a fervent pipe dream I wouldn't be able to achieve since my target was already long gone. But we did it. *You* did it. And to tell you the truth, I would've sliced Miles' fucking face off, too, and probably a lot worse, if I ever had the chance. We're doing a good thing here."

"A good thing that's also highly illegal."

"Yes, there's also that," he says. "Although I would argue that laws are a construct of man, and men are flawed, so why wouldn't the laws be? It's basic algebra. If A plus B equals C, then C minus B equals A. So many people struggle mightily with that concept."

"I agree that we did a good thing for Shelly, but how are you so sure that we can trust these willing patients of yours? What if the pressure becomes too much for them and they eventually blab?"

"A leap of faith, I suppose. Something I take to some degree with all of my patients, hoping they're willing enough to be treated, yet it doesn't always work out that way. Some are unfortunately too broken to accept help. They're misguided and untrusting of authority figures, which I'm often lumped in with for whatever reason."

"I haven't the faintest idea why someone wouldn't trust you. Not the slightest." Marilyn deadpans the joke to a smile from Dan, though she can't be sure if it's genuine. "I meant because you're a therapist, not because you're a bad guy. You aren't bad for a shrink."

"And you aren't bad for a literal mental patient. I wish everyone I see could be as easy to work with."

"Easy? I always thought of myself as a pain in the ass."

"You are. By normal people's standards, at least, but most of my patients are severely disturbed emotionally and carry a type of trauma that I'm beginning to believe is incurable—though the young and naive version of me would've argued that everyone can be saved. Anyway, aside from the occasional facial skinning, you've been the model patient." He winks.

"Am I really even your patient? All we've done is stalk and murder someone together."

"Ouch, easy with that. Never know who's listening. And legally speaking, yes, you *are* my patient, Marilyn. The type of patient who falls under confidentiality and privilege laws. The type of patient should even a subpoena or any other outstanding legal warrant require me to testify against, you will be said to have been following my every order as a condition of treatment. You get me? This is to protect *you*, not me."

"Yes, I get it." Marilyn bites her bottom lip and pauses. "But you aren't worried about it?"

"No."

"Not at all?"

"Not at all. My life is meaningless if I'm not helping others like yourself. Should I ever get caught, and it very well may happen, I'll accept full responsibility and serve my sentence knowing that my actions were a noble sacrifice toward a greater cause. This is my life now. I have no children to look after nor relatives to disappoint."

A moment of silence hangs heavily between them with Marilyn at a loss for words and Dan continuing his scribbles on the note pad. It's the awkward type of silence like a moratorium where neither side knows how to say what they're thinking even though the thoughts run rampant.

Be human, Marilyn. Try it out. "What was your wife's name?"

"Excuse me?"

"Your wife's name. You've told me so much about her now, but I don't even know her name. I'd like to know more about the person that drives you to start doing *this* during middle age."

Dr. Dan stops writing once more and sighs. "Vivian. Her name was Vivian Hudson, although she kept her maiden name professionally so we wouldn't be confused for one another. Dr. Vivian Sinclair, she was always my better. The best psychiatrist I ever knew. We met in medical school and started dating then even though she was two years ahead of me, and we never looked back. Sometimes I wonder what she would think of my activities now." He chuckles with an underlying sense of lingering sorrow and taps the bottom of his pen on the pad several times.

"I obviously never met her, but I think she would be proud that you're so committed to helping people. That's what psychiatrists do, right?"

He raises an eyebrow at her then releases a belly laugh. "Typically using vastly different methods, but yes, you're right. She was always a staunchly moral woman, but her keen sense of justice might've supported these activities. Impossible to say now. The dead will always be trapped in the past where they left us, their memory captured in a snapshot of the moment, fading over time like a waning shadow until the darkness inevitably erases it for good. Besides the point, that was a different Dr. Dan that Vivian loved back then. She probably wouldn't even recognize who I've become, the galvanized shell of a man left behind by *Miles fucking Forsythe*. It's funny ... after all this time and unfathomable agony, I can still smile when I think of Vivian's memory, but the very mention of *Miles'* fucking name still makes me feel—"

"Broken."

"*Enraged.*"

Marilyn's head swims through the mirrored scenarios, her own inadequacies and suppressed emotions and fears and dead desires, the polar opposite of his hardened resolve. Never once throughout years of being a victim, a perpetual target, did she ever seriously consider fighting back. The Butcher was an inevitability, a walking death sentence, but she was also still a living threat. Miles never even gave Dan the chance to hunt him down.

"There's a storm of wrath that rages inside me," he continues. A beast lurks, much like what's in you, and it only grows hungrier as time progresses. The fire, the fury, the absolute *hatred* I hold for Miles, the Butcher, and anyone else like them. It's become an obsession, really, the type of thing that I think about every day, that I dream about, or rather, lose sleep over. I *have* to do this, because I don't want to even think about living in a world where husbands and wives and children will come home to find their loved ones murdered like I did. This is my duty. My true purpose."

She pokes at a hole in her jeans, chewing on the revelation of what very well may be Dan's true face. "Then why were you so shocked when you saw what I did to Wayne? Isn't that what you wanted?"

"Yes and no. I had to be sure you hadn't gone off the deep end, which could've potentially compromised our mission. Of course, I *wanted* to see that and so much worse happen to him, but there still needs to be some semblance of control over our desires." He scoots the rolling chair closer to the desk and gazes deeply at her. "Do you know what I saw in you beyond the media spectacles and hero worship? I saw a lone wolf that had been injured and abandoned by the pack. I saw a natural survivor that the crowd celebrated for being different. And you're wondering what the problem with that may be? When the crowd dances as one, the collective unit eventually notices those who don't join in the charade. They turn their attention against you in an antagonistic manner and wonder why you aren't doing exactly as they did. I knew I had to intervene before they turned on you, to preserve your legacy as a hero while protecting you from the eventual downfall. You're too important to the work ahead."

Marilyn returns the stare quietly, mulling over Dan's monologue until the revelation flattens her like a steamroller. He doesn't do this for the patients. He's lost his desire to fix anyone. He only wants to take out the world's trash, and in some convoluted manner of perverse reasoning, maybe he's actually curing the killers, too, by forcibly removing the monster within them like an exorcism. Saving them from themselves. He's using her to get the job done, but that's just fine. She's using him back as a life raft for healing, for hope. Maybe they aren't yet close enough to reveal their honest intentions, maybe they never will be. Or maybe the *true* face is always just one layer deeper than what's exposed.

15

INQUISITION

Dr. Dan left the house early to meet with what Marilyn assumes to be more run-of-the-mill patients at the office. Maybe he also treats people with so-called normal conditions like anxiety and schizophrenia, although there's no shortage of people left broken in the wake of the Butcher's conquest, let alone her murderous colleagues. The mental health industry must be booming.

Marilyn wanders the house which feels too big to be a suburban abode yet too small to be a mansion. It feels entirely foreign without Dan there, as if she was drugged and mistakenly woke up early in a strange place. The strange place that now happens to be where she lives. She feels like a vagrant in the home with her own thoughts despite his repeated insistence otherwise.

Or maybe she's a prisoner since the outside world is apparently somehow less safe than when she was a serial killer's biggest crush for the better part of a decade. Feeling trapped is nothing new, though she never acknowledged it, but her body and flesh have kept her locked away wherever she's gone for years. Life could be a hell of a lot worse than rotting away in some posh house with too many bedrooms. Even if some new killer finds her hiding out here, it wouldn't be the worst place to die.

Closed doors line the hallway like one of those funhouse mirror attractions, each one seeming to stretch further upward with an all-encompassing sense of overwhelm. What does a bachelor need with all these rooms?

The office door awaits at the end of the hallway, the only room she's been into other than her own, and she pushes the cracked door open to slip inside for a drink of the good stuff that Dan didn't offer the night before. There might be hidden cameras in the books or plants or somewhere else like some dramatic TV show, similar to Wayne's trailer, but it doesn't matter. He told her to be comfortable and make herself at home in his house, and this is ironically, a fucking shrink's office, where she currently feels the most at-ease. Yet something within tells her she shouldn't be here. It's more a product of her own ability to be comfortable.

The room was dimly lit the night before, akin to an old den from a forgotten time, devoid of technology and brimming with nostalgia. The fireplace is now dull and gray and cold in between bookshelves lined with what appears to be novels and textbooks alike, both leather-bound and paperback on the left half and all hardcovers on the right. He's a meticulous man, almost annoyingly so, a foil in every way to Marilyn's methods of masterfully riding chaos like surfing waves as they rise and fall.

The office is spotless, as is Dan's walnut desk. He even took the notepad he was scribbling on with him, in which he probably wrote that she's simply a lunatic just trying to blow off steam. Every pen is lined in a neat row with equal spacing between them, every stack of paper aligned without even a single sheet out of place, every bit of equipment from the wireless phone to the desktop computer left deliberately in particular positions.

Marilyn pours herself a heavy glass of scotch, aged eighteen years, and plops back in the same leather chair she sat in the night before. She swirls the glass of amber nectar and takes a long sip with a deep sigh. "Dr. Dan, you've been holding out on me."

She noses the liquid in the glass with thick notes of dried fruit, vanilla, and cinnamon invading her sinuses, and they linger for a full ten seconds or longer after the sniff. She cracks a smile and takes another sip with a rich harmony of sherry, nutmeg, and chocolate warming her tongue and throat. The whisky settles in her stomach with a satisfying burn that warms her from within amongst the bitter cold of a harsh winter morning sans fire. She would love to light one, but it would be a dead giveaway that she was in there. Or maybe Dr. Dan truly wouldn't care as he says.

Marilyn relaxes into the cushioned chair with her arms growing increasingly more numb from both the drink and being pressed against the armrests. The tingling extends throughout her extremities with a sort of emptiness and weightlessness that makes her feel alive. She takes another sip and floats beyond her body sitting in that chair, beyond the chains of baggage and burden that have plagued her entire adult life. This small, square room has become a beacon of comfort from all that beguiles her, a place where Dr. Dan's guidance extends far beyond the words that he speaks when they're both physically present together.

She reaches over her shoulder and grabs a random book to thumb through. *Getting in Touch With the Inner Self*—how fitting. The printed words on the pages swim amongst each other like those proverbial chaotic waves she's so fond of surfing. She returns the book to the shelf, unable to focus on reading, and stares blankly before her eyes pinpoint on a pair of grey filing cabinets in the corner of the room. The silver push locks extend from their latches, indicating they can be opened.

Marilyn carries the whisky glass with her, sipping along the way, and sets it down atop the left cabinet. She slides the first drawer open carefully as if someone in the empty house might hear her snooping, then she looks around one final time for any signs of camera lenses glinting in the light. Nothing is visible.

There's only random paperwork, receipts, and procedural nonsense in manila folders, but there must be some sort of cryptic organizational system knowing Dan. All three drawers in the left cabinet look the same, so Marilyn shifts her focus to the right and finds exactly what she's searching for immediately.

The top drawer reveals patient files beginning with the As, from Alvarez, Anderson, Armstrong, and more, then into the Bs. She removes the manila folder for Laura Alvarez with a twinge of guilt like she's reading someone's private diary. Something about doctor-patient confidentiality or some other such moral principles. They're far beyond the boundaries of legalities and the laws of man now, and the new book of morals seems to be in the works as they go. The information in these files is vital to understand exactly the type of people she'll be working with, who she'll be fighting for, or so she tells herself. Research. Development. Growth.

Laura Alvarez lost her mother when she was eight-years-old. Rosalinda Alvarez, murdered at the age of thirty by a killer named Roberto Gonzalez in the greater Los Angeles area. Dan's notes say that she struggled with her mother's death for the rest of her life and finally sought professional help at age twenty-nine. *Delayed onset survivor's guilt?* his handwritten annotations say at the bottom of the page. Rosalinda was stabbed through the back of the neck with a ten-inch blade, consistent with a string of other killings committed by Roberto, who snuck up on the women in dark, secluded locations. Laura lost her battle at age thirty, ironically the same age that her mother died, by self-inflicted gunshot wound. Suicide.

Marilyn neatly restores the folder in its rightful place and pulls out the file on Erik Anderson. He lost his twenty-year-old daughter, Sarah, in an incident of strangulation by an unknown perpetrator. *Victor Holloway suspected. The Phantom Strangler.* He was apparently never found guilty of his murders. Erik had already been separated from his wife, Sandra, though she severed all contact with him once Sarah was killed, and he never heard from her again. He made it two more years before his sorrow and rage turned inward. Dead at forty-five due to drug overdose. Suicide.

Hannah Armstrong. Lost her twin sister, Heather, due to blunt force trauma after leaving her server job at a restaurant late one night. Felix Quinn was suspected of the crime after a sequence of similar murders took place in the area.

A fellow college student. Hannah jumped from a local bridge into a shallow pool of runoff water before Felix would be arrested only a few months later. Suicide.

Marilyn downs the whisky and begins to sweat profusely despite the bitter temperatures. She thumbs through the B files beginning with Baker.

Leslie Baker, aged thirty-six. Fifteen-year-old daughter found drowned with signs of foul play and eventually ruled as a homicide. Gunshot wound to the skull. Suicide.

Bernard Bennett, aged fifty-two. Eighteen-year-old daughter found dead with at least two dozen stab wounds. The killer's name was Ed Freeman, and he was caught and arrested immediately after. Bernard died of a heart attack induced by acute onset stress. *Presumably due to Mary's death.*

Katherine Caldwell, aged thirty-nine. Husband found disemboweled. Katherine drove her car into a lake. Suicide.

Tanya Caldwell, mother of Katherine's husband. Suicide.

Richard Dixon. Suicide.

Amanda Eaton. Suicide.

Zyra Ford. Suicide.

Marilyn slams the drawer shut and slumps against another one of the wooden bookshelves that line the room and slides to the floor. This life is a death sentence, the weight of survival seemingly a zero percent chance of success. Surviving the killer's attack only exacerbates darker, harder-to-understand feelings within, the disturbance of a cancerous mass that soon spreads and eventually kills through a different method. Then why doesn't she feel the same? The ins and outs of being a serial killer survivor, the weight of existence bogging her down, the thoughts of countless friends and loved ones slain by the Butcher's hand, and in front of her, no less. *Tara.* Yet she's never once thought about finding a way out. Life has always seemed like an inexorable amusement park ride that mostly lacks amusement, regardless of circumstances. It doesn't stop until it does. Have to ride the lightning until the storm inevitably passes.

It's not *entirely* unusual for a long string of people whose lives had been utterly shattered to seek ultimate relief in the worst of ways, but something about it does seem a bit peculiar that so many patients of the same doctor would meet the same fate. Some may even call it a bit fishy, or maybe this is what happens to normal people who experience tragic death. Will Shelly eventually end up falling into the same stygian depths? Or is she truly healed of the darkness that swarmed her mind?

Marilyn slides open the second drawer down in which the folders begin with Ls and end with Zs, and she closes it again without bothering to rifle through what she assumes to be more suicides. She opens the bottom drawer and sees that the folders are organized from A to Z. The survivors.

Doug Adler lost his niece whom he had legally adopted after her parents died in a car crash initiated by a drunk driver. He found her in his home brutally bludgeoned with several different skull fractures, including the orbital socket with a dislodged eyeball, internal bleeding, and a perforated lung. Felix Quinn's last murder before his arrest. Doug is listed as currently AWOL after failing to make his last appointment and not answering any phone calls. Presumed alive.

Slightly encouraging, if only wishful thinking.

Rebecca Archer lost her daughter. Beheaded and burned. Brianna, aged seventeen. Unknown suspect still on the lam. Rebecca is listed as a current patient—maybe that's who Dr. Dan met with this morning. She's undergone intensive psychotherapy and a cocktail of various medications, but she's listed as currently stable. Maybe they were all considered stable at one point in time until the teetering tightrope gave out.

Anna Benson lost her younger brother. Don was killed by Mike O'Malley at the age of thirteen. At least two dozen stab wounds to the arms, legs, and abdomen, with the final thrust plunged into his heart, and the knife was left there. Marilyn winces at the crime scene photos and turns her head away until she can flip the page—a highly unusual external reaction from her. Mike was found stabbed to death in a similar manner, and his death remains unsolved. *Revenge by the family?* Dr. Dan's notes were scribbled hurriedly. Excitedly. Is this what laid the foundation for their work today? Young Donny Benson's accidental sacrifice may have saved dozens of people or more down the line, the butterfly effect of one death impossible to quantify against the lives of many others.

Marilyn leans back cross-legged and rubs her tired eyes as a faux-sense of dizziness smacks her. Overwhelm, lingering fatigue and brain fog from the concussion, the feeling of projected helplessness—the combination of such causes her to feel *dizzy* in the traditional sense, although she's at a loss for the proper words to accurately describe her thoughts and emotions. Something doesn't feel quite right regardless.

Saving lives and chasing bad guys and girls seems entirely over her head, like something every child fantasizes about at one time or another but never pursues in reality. Cops and robbers and other games like that. Marilyn also wanted to be an actress and the president when she was a little girl, yet some things suddenly seem fucking ridiculous once the darkly depressing curtains of adulthood are drawn.

Marilyn Soroka—serial killer *prey* to *predator*. She laughs.

Then the front door squeaks open.

16

———

INEVITABILITY

Marilyn pushes the drawer inward gingerly and leaves it maybe half an inch short of closing to avoid that *click* sound from ringing out. She shuffles quietly back to the leather arm chair and crosses one leg over the other with her hands clasped on the top knee in an illusion of innocence. *Shit, forgot the glass on the cabinet.*

"Marilyn? Are you awake yet?" Dan sets his keys down somewhere in the foyer. His fancy Brogues clip clop across the marble floor. There's no escape now.

"Yes. I'm in here." The office door is still cracked, and it should allow enough sound to leak out and lead him in. She brushes her pants to look somehow more presentable. Innocent. *Smile.*

Dr. Dan pushes the door open and steps inside with a look of surprise on his face. Maybe more amusement than surprise. "Oh? Are you going to start treating my patients for me now? I could use a relaxing vacation."

"Sorry ... I feel comfortable in here. I hope you don't mind."

"I don't. I told you before to make yourself at home. Anything you need is yours." He glances at the circular end table between the two leather chairs where the bottle of whisky sits half-corked. "I see you *have* helped yourself."

Marilyn quickly looks at the bottle, and then to her glass on the cabinet with

98

miniscule remnants of amber liquid inside it. She can even see her lip imprints and fingerprints on the rim when the light strikes the glass right. She feels her cheeks warm up from either embarrassment or the alcohol. Maybe both. "Yes, well ... you left me curious after cracking into it last night. I had to see what the fuss was all about. I also didn't expect you home so soon."

"Marilyn, I kid. I mean it, the house is yours. I wouldn't move you in here just to hold you hostage nor if I didn't believe it was absolutely essential for your safety. If the office is where you feel most comfortable, then please spend as much time in here as you need. And I don't have another appointment for a few more hours. I like to eat my lunch at home whenever possible. Feels safer."

Dan settles into his own leather chair and loosens his tie with a deep sigh. He glances sideways quickly enough that Marilyn isn't sure whether she actually saw it or not, but he would've looked directly at the filing cabinet.

"Anything else you want to talk about? Anything on your mind? I've got time," he continues.

Honesty. Be human. "I looked through your patient files."

"I know."

She scoffs. "Cameras? I knew you would have something hidden somewhere."

"You didn't shut the drawer all the way. I always shut my drawers. Compulsion." He swivels his chair and pushes it closed with the side of his shoe and smiles. "Not to mention your glass left on the cabinet. There's nothing there that you shouldn't see. It's important for you to fully understand the type of people we'll be working with. What stuck out to you?"

She feels hot again. Despite his affirmations, she feels like a child in school being taught some sort of life lesson instead of being disciplined. His demeanor is like a parent explaining how they aren't mad, only *disappointed*. His grin and cadence suggest otherwise, but Marilyn still feels dirty both from getting caught and the content in those files. Like reliving the dozens of Butcher murders in real-time except through a clinical lens. It's all so sterile. Human lives, shattered dreams, suicides—nothing but data. Specimens.

"A lot of your patients …"

"Dead, yes."

"Suicides."

"Yes."

Marilyn sighs and rubs her eyes with her index fingers. "And that's not strange to you?"

"Not in my line of work, no." He leans back in the chair and rests his right leg atop his left knee. Neatly pressed black slacks, as always. "But I can see how someone outside of the field would find it unusual. Many doctors deal with terminally ill patients. Believe me, many of them are looking for a way out. Peace and relief in whatever form it comes. I consider my patients as such, too. Those affected by serial killers will be broken forever with a staggeringly high rate of substance abuse. And yes, also suicide. My goal is to make them as comfortable as possible for as long as possible, to the best of my ability, although true recovery in the traditional sense is nearly impossible, between you and me. This is why I believe that you're an anomaly."

"Doesn't that bother you? That recovery is essentially hopeless?" Marilyn shuffles to grab her glass and helps herself to another serving of eighteen-year-old single malt. Dr. Dan doesn't seem to mind.

"It used to. For many, many years, it used to. It ate me alive. I drowned myself in booze and excuses and lies to bury the failures I felt so deeply. I swore an *oath* for Christ's sake, a commitment to my patients' collective wellbeing that I couldn't deliver upon. It gnawed at me, yes. But it was like being tasked to repair a shattered window and pretend that the glued-together pieces weren't still entirely splintered. At a certain point, I suppose it's inevitable to build some sort of callous just to get through the day. Otherwise, I might've just become one of *them*."

"I get that, I really do. And I'm sure you're right, but then why bother? Why continue trying to solve an impossible puzzle? Why put yourself through the torture?"

"Well, that's life, isn't it? We're doomed for failure from birth ... our very existence is a death sentence. Yet we fight anyway, and we do so with blinders on as if we'll be the first one to finally crack the code. And like I said last night, this is my true purpose. All of the agony suffered by both my patients and myself is worth the effort if I can discover a way for even one person to be saved ... for their lives to return to what they were meant to be. This is where we are now: no more half measures in treatment. No quarter." Dan pauses and squints his eyes toward Marilyn and the end table. "If we're going to keep talking about such heavy topics this early in the day, then I'm going to need a drink myself. Would you mind?"

Marilyn looks at the half-empty bottle and the second glass beside it. She nods and pours with a heavy hand then walks it over to his desk. "Wouldn't want you missing out on all the fun."

"Thank you." He sips the whisky slowly and exhales with a harsh air of relief. "I hope you realize, Marilyn, that the many suicides of not only my patients, but of those who for whatever reason never sought treatment, or couldn't face themselves in the mirror anymore, or who couldn't bear to fight another day after losing their loved ones ... I hope you realize that the tragic loss of those lives, numbers we can't even fathom, were a direct result of the same people we're hunting. It's not our fault, it's *theirs*, and extreme problems require extreme solutions. We're doing the right thing." He nods and sips and nods again. "We're doing the right thing."

Marilyn taps her leg anxiously, knowing they're in too deep to doubt the process now. Shelly seemed genuinely relieved, like a cancer patient in remission with a new lease on life. Maybe there were others, too, like Rebecca Archer, that Dan was able to give a second chance to. Or maybe she's an empty shell still living and breathing with very little actual life left inside her. "Don Benson. What about him?"

"Horrific tragedy. I couldn't even imagine."

"But his killer, Mike O'Malley. Was that you?"

Dan pauses with the glass at his lips and the visible side of his mouth curls into a sharp smirk. The type of smirk that Wayne brandished when he was mocking them in his trailer. "No. But I wish it was. Oh, how I wish it was."

"So, Mike was found coincidentally stabbed in the exact same way as Don?"

"People break, Marilyn. Occasionally, when you push enough buttons, you accidentally come across the wrong ones to fuck with. That was the Benson family. But no, I don't know for certain that they did it, although it was strongly implied by Anna. That was the seed that blossomed into our work. Speaking of, are you ready to continue?"

"Yes, I'm ready."

"Excellent. Because I have an appointment with our potential next partner tonight."

17

ILLUMINATION

Marilyn hasn't seen the cityscape under daylight since the Butcher's funeral. Death day. It's depressingly bleak, morose, and not at all the rainbow-soaked paradise of happy people living their lives free from the Butcher's wrath that the mayor alluded to. Little do they know how many beasts walk amongst them in their day-to-day lives. The neighbors they avoid at the mailbox or when waiting for an elevator. The coworkers with whom they can pretend to be something entirely different than who they are in their private lives. The strangers they pass on the sidewalks as they all stare at their phones like walking phantoms. Maybe they do know subconsciously and it's the cause of the gloom. Another monster is always lying in wait.

Dusk will be upon them in an hour or so, with encroaching darkness set to descend on the citizens for another night of underlying uncertainty. Ribbons of pink and goldenrod yellow have begun to weave throughout the gray-blue city sky, the only bit of beauty in this godforsaken hell hole.

Homeless people fill the filthy sidewalks in decrepit, crusty-looking blankets and box forts like livestock hogtied for the taking. How many of them have disappeared without a trace? With nobody to miss them or search for them or even report that they're missing? Nobody's avenging them when they die, nobody's visiting a crackpot psychiatrist to work through their deaths. There's no Marilyn and Dr. Dan duo hunting beasts specifically to save their lives.

Maybe it's a condition of their lifestyles like some occupational hazard that so-called normal people face in their jobs, too. Why is one death more or less significant than another? The answer is obvious even if the pill goes down sideways and jagged like swallowing a Lego brick.

The buildings stand tall and stiff like gravestones jetting from the ground, a necropolis of lost souls seeking validation from their careers as if their job titles serve as a fitting epitaph for who they were as people. And Marilyn used to be one of them, living in a stupidly expensive and undersized apartment in the center of town, trying desperately as it seems in retrospect to hide in plain sight. That was until Dr. Dan *rescued* her or jettisoned her from one hazardous lifestyle to the next.

They pass by a generic coffee shop, Thanks a Latte!, and speed into another red light. It turns green after an eternity of waiting, and they turn into the office building's lower parking structure. The shifter and the emergency brake click into position.

"Are you ready to get back in the saddle?" he asks. His face has once again morphed back into the good doctor's, Daniel Hudson M.D., like a goddamned chameleon changing shades to get the most of whatever situation he finds himself in.

"Ready as I will be. Let's do this."

Dan's actual office is located on the third floor of a building dedicated to mental health treatment of different sorts—otherwise considered a fucking *nightmare*—complete with a receptionist and seemingly useless security in the main lobby. It closely resembles his home office, minus any visible whisky and with fewer books, and the leather chairs for patients are made of a generic cloth upholstery. No fireplace, either.

"Hello, Debra. On any other day, I'd ask how you've been since our last meeting, but I'd like to cut straight to the chase today and discuss the reason for this meeting. It's my pleasure to introduce you to my good friend Marilyn Soroka. She'll be working with us on your case." Dan flashes a wide smile and clasps his hands proudly on the same model of walnut desk as in his home like he just resolved the entire process with one statement.

Debra gives her a once-over with a side-eyed glance. Her expression is steely, her eyes glazed over like wet stones, a far cry from Shelly's weepy and emotional demeanor. She's about thirty with short, dark brown hair and a strong jaw as if she'd kept it clenched since whatever murder brought her here. "I know who you are. I've seen you on the news. Big fan, by the way."

"Thank you. It's a pleasure to be working together."

Debra nods. Her hands twitch on the arm rests like someone who's desperate for a smoke. Maybe something stronger.

"Do you remember the times we've discussed your sister's murderer in depth, Debra?" Dan asks in his doctor voice.

"How could I forget? *Victor Holloway.* That son of a bitch deserves to burn a thousand times over."

"The Phantom Strangler—and yes, he does. Remember you said that you would do anything to make that happen? That you would pull the trigger yourself if given the chance? Do you remember that?"

"Of course, I do. I'd cut his heart out and stomp it into the dirt if I could." Debra nods again with her eyes aflame, appearing eerily like Dan's when he was talking about his wife's murder.

"Good, very good. That's why Marilyn is here today. She's going to help us get close to the Strangler and let you do the rest."

Marilyn's eyes widen as Debra turns to her with an equally shocked expression. They lock eyes with a million words spoken between them. "That's right, Debra. We can't say too much about it at the moment, but I'm going to help you make that happen."

She glances rapid fire back and forth between them as her expression softens from the hardened outer shell to reveal the second face, the one only shared with loved and trusted ones. "You are? You mean we're going to finally—"

"Yes," Dan says. "Although, for all our safety, we'll go over the sensitive details in my home office. You get me? Can never be too careful in a city setting."

She nods once more with a smile forming on her face.

"I've thoroughly vetted you, Debra, both your personal life and characteristics, and I've gotten to know you incredibly well through our sessions together. I believe you fit the mold for a patient who might benefit from this sort of intensive treatment. Think of it as a special, invite only, type of program that Marilyn and I conduct with those who display a certain profile. This is, of course, a rather sensitive matter. Nobody else can know."

Debra lights up even more like a child who was just told they would be going out for ice cream. "Of course. I have no one else to tell. You can trust me, Dr. Hudson."

"I know. Like I said, thoroughly vetted." Dan winks and turns his attention to Marilyn. "Tell her a bit more about the program." He raises his eyebrows quickly as if to pass along all the things she should and shouldn't say without explicitly telling her what those things are.

"Right." She turns toward Debra and forces herself to relax, to come across as less inhuman like the media might portray. Less foreign. Less alien. "Deb—is it okay if I call you Deb?"

"My sister called me Deb. But yes, you can call me Deb, too."

"Okay. Deb, I wish I could tell you that I can't imagine what you've gone through in losing your sister, but unfortunately, I can. My own sister was taken from me, along with all my closest friends, acquaintances, and my recent roommate, but this isn't about me now. I want to help you get the closure that you need, that you *deserve*. We've had a one hundred percent success rate in recovery for previous patients who went through this same program." She swallows hard, burying the sort-of lie knowing that they've only ever tried this once so far. A half-truth at worst.

"Thank you, Marilyn. And thank you, Dr. Hudson. I can't tell you how much this means to me. I won't let you down."

He bows his head dramatically like a magician after the final act. "We won't let *you* down, Debra. This will be a major relief for you, the type that pharmaceuticals just can't deliver. You'll feel like a new person once it's done. All three of us will."

"I can't wait to give that bastard a taste of his own medicine. It's all I've thought about since we found Cassie gray in the face ... her eyes blood red and veiny, her neck bruised with purple handprints. I've seen Victor in the same sort of fucked-up shape in my dreams, and that image has stuck with me ever since. I just didn't know if I had the strength to do it on my own. Thank you."

"Now there's three of us," Marilyn says. "And we can absolutely do this together. You're not alone in the darkness anymore, Deb. We're your strength now. We're the justice that you crave."

Dan listens with a look of gratification plastered across his face as if they were talking about hunting down Miles Forsythe, as if all the same sort of dreams he's had about killing him would come true by eradicating Victor. But they won't, and Marilyn knows it. The Butcher's unceremonious exit from the mortal world only opened a hidden door that she never realized was waiting beyond the facade of protection disguised as trauma, a door that held her doubts and regrets and fears at bay like the embodiment of some beastly entity chained away. A door that can never close again once the hinges are broken.

"Excellent," he says at last. "This is going to be great. My place tomorrow night? It's the only place we can feel safe having this sort of conversation. I'll text you the address."

18

EVOLUTION

No dinner tonight for Debra's visit, but Dan ordered a fresh cheesecake to be delivered—the best in the city, he said—and promised plenty of wine to ease their weighty discussion. She's scheduled to arrive at six o'clock, only fifteen minutes away, and the lavish house seems somber for the time being, with the exception of Dan's muted typing behind his closed office door.

Marilyn wanders the halls aimlessly, still feeling like a short-term guest in her new home, like it was some shady overnight motel instead of a mini mansion. She and Dan haven't discussed any plans to transition back to living separately, be it in the apartment or otherwise, although she would much prefer to live alone again at some point when he deems it safe (even if safety is at the forefront of his concern alone).

The kitchen and its many cabinets still feel off-limits despite Dan's insistence otherwise. Marilyn virtually tiptoes across the marble floor like a burglar trying to steal a sip of juice from the refrigerator before the sleeping occupants notice. This is very much a *her* problem, likely stemming from childhood when the Soroka sisters were meant to be seen and not heard, essentially ordered by their father to treat the house as his alone. He never directly *forbade* them from eating the food he stocked in their minimal pantry, but it sure as shit felt like an executive order. *Times are tough,* he would always say, *and the world ain't what it used to be.* He wasn't the *worst* alcoholic son of a bitch out there, yet it often seemed so when they were young. Especially when he ran away after Mom died.

"Marilyn, are you almost ready? You look lost." Dan and his wicked sense of humor startle her. She had been too distracted by his non-existent rules to notice the office door opening.

"Yes. I was just thinking about … things that don't really matter anymore, honestly."

"Well, we're all prone to daydream every now and then. It's good for your recovery, as well, and in this case, I mean your concussion protocol. You still aren't totally out of those woods just yet."

"I'm feeling better," she nods, not knowing exactly if *better* refers to the head injury itself or the mental lapse that caused Wayne's face to be sliced off his skull like deli meat. The two might be related. "Are you ready?"

"I am. I typed up a quick report showing similarities between Shelly and Debra's symptoms and cases, detailing the positive results we were able to obtain from Wayne's death." He straightens the stack of papers on his kitchen counter, probably still nice and warm from the printer. "Shelly asked me how you were doing, by the way. We had a follow-up appointment this morning."

Be human, Marilyn. "That's nice of her. Like I said, I'm doing much better now. How is she?"

"Great, she's excelling in recovery. She insists that we won't need to continue meeting for much longer, but I want to keep an eye on her for a few more months to be sure." He clears his throat into a closed fist and eyes Marilyn intently for several seconds before speaking again. "Listen, all those suicides … We're off to a good start here. I just hope that our work can drastically reduce those numbers."

"I hope so, too. And I'm glad she's doing better—I'm glad we were able to give her the relief that she deserves." It seems almost too good to be true. Years worth of deep-seated trauma erased in a momentary outburst of rage that she didn't even perpetrate. It doesn't make sense. The Butcher died by her own hand, decidedly not Marilyn's, and yet her death still hasn't delivered this instant sense of relief.

"We did, and the evidence points toward a full, and most importantly lasting, recovery. I don't want to speak too soon or come across as hyperbolic, but it seems that rehabilitation is entirely possible with our established methods. I never would've imagined it to be possible." He shakes his head with an expression of shock, maybe perplexion, adorning his face.

Marilyn's mind swims through the possibilities, drowning in the thoughts of what she could or couldn't have done to right her own ship. Wayne's death didn't make her feel any better either, a proxy revenge kill of rabid emotions to avenge her great many friends lost throughout the years. But this is supposed to be a service performed for the benefit of other people who can't directly defend themselves. Then why doesn't she feel more positive about it? Dan already admitted to having his own hidden agenda in taking revenge. Why is he able to heal if she can't?

A knock on the double doors breaks Marilyn's concentration, and it's a welcome distraction. It must be Deb since the cheesecake was already delivered around four o'clock, or right around the time they returned home from the city office. *Ready up. Game face on.*

Dan bows his head halfway and turns on one heel to welcome her inside. Debra enters like a fish out of water, an identical expression on her face as the first time Marilyn walked into the elegant house. She seems to have never seen something so nice, suggesting a lower-middle class background, at best. Maybe that information will be helpful in the investigation, or maybe not. Marilyn feels like she's still grasping at straws herself.

"Debra, welcome." Dan motions her inside in a swirling of déjà vu reminiscent of when Marilyn first visited, and Shelly sat waiting at the dinner table.

"Hi, Deb. Happy to see you again. Have a seat," Marilyn says, patting the table in front of the seat next to her. The act of relating to others is growing more routine, if not forcibly normal.

"Thank you both." She walks through the foyer with her flip flops clapping her heels, appearing somewhat lost as if already in over her head. Or maybe Marilyn is only projecting.

"Before we dive into the nitty-gritty of our meeting, would you like some cheesecake? Best in the city." Dan slices a shiny, stainless cake knife through the dessert in eight equal portions without waiting for an answer.

"Uh, yes. That would be great."

"Perfect." He places a plate in front of their seats, followed by wine glasses that he fills one by one.

Debra places a hand over her glass before Dan pours. "No, thank you. I'm actually in the program."

Dan raises his eyebrows, almost dejected, and retracts the wine bottle. "My apologies, I wasn't aware."

"I never told you. I, uh ... haven't told anyone outside of my meetings, either. I'm still a bit embarrassed about it."

"You're free to feel whatever you like, Debra, but I can assure you there's no need to be embarrassed about addiction. Definitely not here. The three of us have certain shared experiences that ninety-nine percent of the population couldn't imagine. Substance abuse is a natural byproduct in that sort of healing process."

Debra nods with a worldly gaze focused on something from another plane of existence. A thousand-yard stare. "I agree. My sister's death sent me into a spiral that was at first only helped by booze, but honestly, I was only addicted to feeling numb in whatever form that relief took."

"Many of us have been there a time or two with various vices, but I applaud you for working through it." Dan nods. "Do you feel better now?"

"No," Deb says.

"No?" Dan's eyes glint with a semblance of a repressed smirk, something that could be misconstrued as a predator sensing an easy target, brief enough to maybe not have happened at all. He sips his glass of wine slowly and methodically. "And why is that, Debra?"

Her jaw visibly tightens with knots forming beneath her ears, and her expression turns grave as if she'd just witnessed a murder stuck on loop. "Because," she says with a steely voice that threatens to crack, "*he* is still out there ... living ... killing ... and I can't fucking stand it anymore. The drinks and drugs only helped me not think about him for brief periods of time, but they never let me forget him. I'll never be happy until he's dead. I'll never feel *relief.*"

"So, that's what you want?" Dan takes another sip with the same sort of reptilian flash in his eyes, a sense of serpentine satisfaction. The apex predator's will to power. "You wish Victor Holloway *dead*?"

"No. I *need* it. And it needs to be done by me."

Marilyn opens her mouth to offer her own experience, her jaw hanging slack like a bloody-soaked maw wiped clean, but she stops herself from speaking with the words bottlenecked inside her esophagus. She wishes to at least warn Deb of the risks involved in serial killer hunting, occupational hazards, the darkness that might swarm her like a horde of hornets as it did Marilyn, the feeling of emptiness once you finally rid yourself of the one thing that gave your life meaning ... Yet she remains silent. It might hinder the mission. Dan might not agree.

"Excellent," he says at last. "Excellent, Debra. You've come to the right place. You've found the perfect doctor to facilitate that sort of radical treatment, and there's no one better to walk you through this process than the inimitable Marilyn Soroka."

Marilyn feels like she should be blushing or smiling or playing coy, but any semblance of appraisal only brings about another oppressive wave of apathy. So she nods instead.

"Thank you." Deb is stoic, steely, entirely focused. There isn't an ounce of doubt in her expression. "What do you need from me? I'll do whatever it takes to make this happen."

"I'm glad to hear that, but we have a few ground rules to cover before the action begins. First, and most importantly, you can't trust anyone outside of this room. Nobody else can know the details of our work, and this rule doesn't become null and void once the fucker is dead—this goes to the grave. Do you understand?"

Debra agrees.

"Second, we can't discuss our work anywhere outside of my house. Nowhere else, not my city office, your house, some random coffee shop on the corner, nowhere. *Nobody* can be trusted. Although, that shouldn't be an issue since we don't talk about the work away from each other. Don't talk about it, don't write about it, don't even think about it outside of my home." Dan smiles sharply with his curled lips seemingly concealing a veiled threat.

Debra agrees again.

"And finally, we follow the plan to a goddamn tee, a *goddamn tee*, unless I, for any reason, need to change it on the fly to protect our safety or the work. Once we're at the kill site, anything Marilyn says goes. To use a sports analogy, I'm the coach and Marilyn is the quarterback. The coach creates the plan, but once it's game time, the quarterback is in charge of execution. Got that?"

"Yes, Dr. Hudson."

"We're going to be in a pressure cooker environment. There can be no mistakes, or we may be seriously injured. Even worse, we might fail. You don't mind a little pressure do you, Debra?"

"No, Dr. Hudson," she says without changing her expression. "I have nothing to lose, so there's nothing to fear."

He scoffs. "That's good, because Marilyn and I don't have anything to lose, either. This is going to be a rousing success."

Marilyn has been unusually quiet since Deb arrived, listening to the ground rules herself with fresh ears, having missed out on the introductory prep work with Shelly. It almost sounds like a cult. Though maybe it actually is. A charismatic leader, check. Authoritarian ideology, check. Isolation from outside sources, check. She glances at Dan as he returns the gaze, his boyish features betraying violent promises of restitution in the name of justifiably righteous vengeance. It's like he's playing cops and robbers on the school playground, riling up his team for a decisive victory against their less-competitive classmates. Only the stakes are life and death instead of schoolyard clout. Win or go home for good.

"I won't let you down, Marilyn." Debra repeats the promise from earlier that day in the city office. "You've been a hero to me since my sister died. It was … actually you that inspired me to get sober."

Marilyn looks quickly down at her wine glass with a twinge of guilt. So many others must have felt similarly, like she was some savior, some messianic figure, all the while she was simply waiting around to die. "I know you won't, Deb. I won't let you down, either. We're going to find Victor and do to him what he did to your sister tenfold."

Deb smiles at last. Then she takes a bite of cheesecake.

Dan stares at her, swirling his wine slowly, his eyes slightly squinted and gleaming. Ready for his next meal.

19

CONFIRMATION

Dr. Dan has been animated and talking for several minutes straight without interruption, writing and drawing on one of those giant notepads made for artists with a permanent marker and acting out the motions dramatically. "First, we need to learn Victor's daily routine. Does he work? Where does he live? Where does he like to go, and at what time? All serial killers are creatures of habit. They're compulsive slaves to routine." He glances down at the table and straightens his three markers used for crafting the plan.

"He works evening security for the insurance company where my sister used to work. Pathway Insurance," Deb says.

"How did he get away with the murders if you know so much about him?" Marilyn asks. "Wouldn't the police be aware of that, too?"

"Faulty warrant and lack of evidence. He supposedly burned his fingerprints off in a foundry accident as a young adult, so they were never able to create a case. Victor also never even made contact with anyone at work to suggest a connection, which was proven by the security cameras."

"Or maybe he destroyed the evidence, working in security himself," Dan suggests.

"Likely. Cassie told me she had a strange feeling about him, that he would follow her to the parking lot after her shift to *protect* her from weirdos. Then she disappeared."

"I know that's odd, but how is it hard evidence that Victor Holloway is the murderer?" Marilyn asks. "What we have is circumstantial. And once again, shouldn't that information have been given to the police?"

"It was over a phone call—no concrete proof. She called me from the lobby so I could stay on the line while Victor followed her. She disappeared the next day."

"He's the murderer." Dan scribbles something not immediately visible on the massive pad with his marker squeaking as he writes across the paper. "A police friend and prior patient of mine confirmed that at least three other murder cases were closed because of the bad warrant. Same murder method, same profile of young women, same partial prints found at the crime scenes. None of it usable."

"I know he did it," Deb says. "Every woman in the building thought he was a creep. Just look at him."

Marilyn intends to argue the point, that finding someone creepy isn't necessarily causation nor correlation to find them guilty of serial murder, a crime of which carries the consequence of frontier justice when Dr. Dan is involved. But she does not. She remains quiet and bobs her head up and down, determined to find undeniable proof while vetting him.

"Yes, let's have a look at Victor Holloway, *The Phantom Strangler*. Hideous little shit." Dan clicks a remote to turn on his almost absurdly-large monitor mounted in the corner of his living room, then he clicks a few more times to cycle through the first couple slides of the presentation. "There he is."

Debra's face hardens as she inhales sharply through her nose. She taps her flip-flopped heel on the floor, appearing as if she'd just been shown the crime scene photos instead.

"It's okay, Deb. We're doing this together," Marilyn says softly, doing her best to try and feel normal person feelings again. She turns and faces the monitor again to study Victor's mugshot and sear his image into her brain. He actually is an ugly little shit.

The mugshot depicts what appears to be a small man with a scrawny neck and oversized head. Kind of like a Q-tip. His ears hang on the sides of his narrow jaw as if melting off his skull, and the transition from his chin to neck is a smooth, downward slope that looks like it belongs on a finger puppet. His eyes are droopy and dopey. Despite his weak features, he wears a flat top haircut in a stark juxtaposition to his less-than-masculine facial features, what some might refer to as reminiscent of a stereotypical child predator.

"Is this the guy?" Dan asks, his voice pointed and direct. "Your sister's killer?"

Debra slams her eyes shut, hard enough to produce crow's feet from her youthful eyes. She's obviously distressed. "Yes."

"Yes?"

"Yes!"

"How bad do you want it, Debra? How badly do you want his life?" Dan slams his fist on the coffee table with a thunderous echo like a muted gunshot. His face turns again.

"That's the only thing I want! I swear!"

"I don't *believe* you, Debra. How will you kill him if you can't even *look* at him? Open your eyes and gaze upon your prey. Open them right now!"

Debra shakes her head no.

Dan turns to Marilyn and nods at her. She hesitates while interpreting the direction, yet the message is clear. "Deb, you can do this. You have to."

She shakes her head again.

Marilyn slides over to the couch beside her and wraps an arm over her shoulder. The action feels horrid, like two magnets repelling, but Deb needs the support more than Marilyn needs to feel comfortable. "Listen to me. You don't have to be brave just yet, but you do need to at least fake it until it's real. He'll smell the weakness on you immediately inside that room."

"I can't do this, Marilyn. I'm not strong like you."

"You are. Open your eyes and look. Do it."

"I can't. I just can't." She shakes her head forcefully, causing tears to be expelled from her cheeks.

"Do you trust me, Debra?" Dan interjects.

"I do, Dr. Hudson."

"Okay." He stands and saunters toward the couch with his typical, purposeful walk as if something else was forcing him forward. He stops just in front of Deb and bends down to whisper into her ear: "I'm terribly sorry about this, but it's necessary for your recovery. Doctor's orders."

Dan pulls her from the couch as she screams and struggles and fights. He walks her toward the monitor, his hands resting gently on her shoulders yet firm enough to keep her in lock step. They stop once they're maybe a foot away from the massive screen.

"Look," he continues.

Marilyn watches from the couch without objection, knowing herself that true evolution is rooted in otherworldly suffering and often must be coerced. The true face will force its way to the surface under extreme duress. She takes the unspoken cue to leap up and help hold Deb still.

Dan reaches a hand over her head and hooks his index and ring fingers beneath her eyebrows, pulling them upwards until the seal of the eyelids breaks and Deb gives in to the pressure.

"Keep them open, Deb," Marilyn whispers.

The mugshot lights up her face from such close exposure, the reflection of his features imprinted upon her dancing eyes. Deb gazes into the photographed face of the man who forever altered her life's trajectory as they all three stand silently in the screen's glow. She stares still, and the silence of her confirmation seems to echo in Marilyn's mind with the weight of her pain bearing down like a cluster of black clouds.

"Can I trust you to work with me now?" Dan asks.

Debra nods.

He releases his grip and reaches for the remote, then clicks a button to flip the screen to the next slide. It's a picture of a young woman lying on the ground, her face blue and gray, and her eyes deeply bloodshot with brick red veins thick and vascular across the whites. *Must be Cassie.*

"No! Turn it off!"

"You can do this, Debra. You said you trust me."

"I do, but—"

"And you told me I can trust you. Remember?" He leans closer to stare into her face from only half a foot away, the reflection of the crime scene mirrored from her eyes into his own. "You don't want to betray your team's trust already, do you?"

"No, Dr. Hudson."

"I trust you with my life, Marilyn," he says. "Do you trust me with yours?"

Marilyn nods. "I do."

"Do you want to kill Victor Holloway, Debra?"

"Yes!"

"Then I need you to swallow your personal feelings for the good of the work. Your emotions will get us all killed. Look at your sister. Look at her and bottle that venomous rage you feel for later."

Debra visibly relents and drops her shoulders as Dan cycles through slides featuring photos of suffocated corpses in various colors of death, while the images flicker continuously in her glossy, wide-open eyes and leave the impression of ligature marks across the irises. Several slides of Victor replace the bodies, causing her to wince and tremble, yet she stays focused on the monitor.

Marilyn softens, realizing that regardless of whether or not Victor killed Cassie, he's guilty of killing others. He deserves to die, and Deb deserves peace. She'll rot from the inside out, likely turn back to substance abuse, and probably end up immortalized as another folder in Dan's suicide cabinet. Either Deb or Victor will wind up dead because of this situation, and Marilyn knows which team she's choosing.

The slideshow comes to an end with a black finale across the monitor. Deb's shadowed image remains in the center of the screen like a drowned victim underwater, which she gazes into for several seconds in harrowing silence as if eulogizing her past self.

"I'm sorry to have put you through that, Debra, but this is an essential part of the process. We must fracture fully to be put back together again. Otherwise, it's only a temporary fix."

Deb doesn't speak at first, though her body language creates a ripple that reaches Marilyn's core. She's despondent, similar to a great many nights when Marilyn stood staring blankly into a wall-mounted mirror, unable to recognize the enigma of a womanly figure staring back until the shape of her melted into some amorphous, black mass.

"It's okay," she says at last. "I'm committed. Whatever you think I need to do, I'll do it."

"It's not about random punishment for punishment's sake, Debra. Your trauma recovery comes first, but we can't kill Victor Holloway until you're ready. Which, clearly, you aren't yet."

"No, I guess not. I really thought I could do it ... I fantasized, dreamed, and obsessed over killing him for a year."

"We all think we're ready until the moment meets us face-to-face." Dan glances at Marilyn. "But that's what makes us different from *them*. They kill for fun, for pleasure, while we do so unwillingly because it's what's right. We're martyrs, if you're willing to go that far—sacrificing ourselves for the greater good, so all those occasionally ungrateful people out there can sleep soundly at night without the same fears the three of us carry."

Debra listens intently without saying another word, just like Marilyn.

"You did well," Dan continues, "and I'm proud of you. I'll go get you some tea before we continue." He saunters into the kitchen, more floating than walking, whistling all the while as if the world is suddenly devoid of atrocities.

The room feels shockingly empty without his presence, like a desolate night sky without its north star for guidance, like a sailboat lost on the blackened sea. Marilyn clears her throat, which sounds like someone shattered glass in the middle of a library.

"Did he do that to you, too?" Deb asks.

Marilyn scoffs. "Not exactly. My killer was already dead."

"The Butcher, yes. Like I said, I've been a big fan of yours for a while."

"It seems like many people were, even though the fandom still doesn't feel earned even now. I doubt it ever will."

"Well, you should be proud," she nudges. "I wish I had even a tenth of your courage, not only to fool the Butcher so many times, but to face the public attention that was packaged with it."

"You *are* courageous, Deb. I couldn't imagine the strength necessary to take up sobriety through the worst period of your life. And what we're doing here—it's not for the weak. Trust me. It took a ton of bravery for you to even accept the ... *work*."

"Yeah." Debra taps her foot nervously on the ground. She looks down at the rapid up-and-down motion as if the energy of it will generate answers. "Marilyn? Do you think we're doing the right thing?"

Normal people would comfort someone after such a question, after what she just experienced, maybe offer a reassuring pat on the back, or some sort of embrace in a showing of solidarity. They would say overly-nice things to prove that they care, bordering on saccharine and dripping with maraschino syrup. But a simple "yes" is all she musters. "Yes, I believe we are."

"I mean—don't get me wrong, I believe that Victor deserves to die, and I can't wait for that to happen. I guess I'm just not sure about implicating you both with me. It feels wrong."

"Deb, we brought this idea to *you*. We're aware of the risks, and I wouldn't be here helping if I didn't fully agree with the cause."

Debra's left foot begins to tap opposite the rhythm of her right. The syncopation sounds like a drum pattern that increases in speed. "Maybe you're right. I'm okay with whatever happens to me, but I still hope the two of you get out alright."

"This is a team effort. We'll do it together." This time, Marilyn forces herself to return to the couch next to Debra, and she places a hand on her reciprocating knee to calm the anxious movement. "We're in it together," she reaffirms. "You don't have to carry the weight alone anymore." The words escape her lips like a renegade missile without a clear target. She could be talking to any of the three of them in the house.

20

EUSTRESS

"Victor Hollaway, the Phantom Strangler, so named because his suspected victims all died by asphyxiation of some sort, although they weren't bruised or damaged, and no traces of fibers were found in their airways to suggest suffocation." Dan steps aside to reveal the same mugshot of Victor Holloway with his flat top and tiny neck and big head. *Hideous little shit.*

Debra stares at the screen now with a cold, detached demeanor, at least externally, the mask of the first face hardening quickly like papier-mâché. She sips her tea and eyes the mugshot with renewed vigor.

"It seems that he uses some sort of plunger device stuffed in the airway to induce asphyxiation," Dan continues. "He inserts it into the mouth of the victim and forces it down their throat until they stop kicking. Nasty little bastard."

"That's how Cassie was found. She had asphyxiated, though the investigators said there wasn't enough evidence to clearly determine how it happened. That's what I'll do to Victor. I'm going to choke him to death the same way so he can know what the victims' last few seconds felt like."

"Excellent idea. I'll see if I can find you a tool that will do just that." He scribbles something on his notepad, presumably about the plunger. "Any second thoughts about the kill before we get too deep? Any concerns?"

Deb shoots Marilyn a quick side-eyed glance. "No. I'll be ready."

"Good. Marilyn and I will be right behind you in case, for whatever reason, you find yourself suddenly less than ready when the time comes. Marilyn has experience in dispatching serial killers. She'll know how to help you."

Deb turns fully toward her now with a face that suggests more admiration than shock. "So, it *was* you that killed the Butcher. I knew it."

"The Butcher killed herself, just as it was reported. I only antagonized her into doing it, and accidentally, at that."

"Oh. Then who did you kill?"

"His name was Wayne Taylor, another nasty little bastard. We broke into his trailer during the night and killed him." *And sliced his face off and stole Shelly's revenge and descended into temporary psychosis.* "It was really more of a team effort. I wouldn't have been able to do it alone."

Dan chuckles. "Marilyn's only being modest, Debra. We were all there together, but she's the one who navigated the way inside, led the charge, and eventually buried that knife in his chest. She's the real hero."

Her face feels like it flushes internally with pins poking and prodding her skin. *Hero.*

"Wow. I'm glad you're on our side and not theirs." Debra forces a weak laugh. "So, um. How did it feel?"

"Which part?"

"How did it feel to take out the trash?"

"It felt … I don't know, it felt good, I guess." Marilyn clears her throat to buy some time. Humans share experiences with one another. *Be human.* The truth is, she didn't stop to annotate the experience while it was happening, having been in a losing battle with her own monster within, trapped in the waves of concussion, yet the feelings flood her senses as she thinks back on the experience. "It felt right, like I was doing something that *had* to be done. In that moment, I felt like the real me, I guess you could say. Like I was meeting the true Marilyn for the first time."

"Wow," Deb says again. "I can't wait to experience that feeling."

Dan stares at Marilyn with the slightest hint of a squint. "Marilyn is only being the model of humility again. Go on, tell Debra how you really felt. What was it like?"

She shoots a look at Dan so venomous it makes him smile. "It was the best and worst fucking thing I've ever done. I felt so unhinged in the best way possible, like dropping a thousand pounds of dead weight from my shoulders that had been holding me back for years. But I also felt exposed, raw, naked. And I fucking hate that feeling." She gives Dan a sarcastic half-curtsy from her seat.

"That wasn't so bad, was it? Much better. You don't have to hide anything here, Marilyn. Same goes for you, Debra. I understand the topics we're going to cover are typically referred to as *taboo* by the normies out there, but I encourage you to speak your minds before those thoughts fester into something far darker." He glances at Marilyn again with a glint in his eye that says, *like cutting their faces off and wearing them.*

"I don't understand, Marilyn. Did you regret killing Wayne? Why did you feel so bad afterwards?" Deb asks.

Shame, embarrassment, loss of control. Maybe a bit of concussion. "Because I didn't murder him out of vengeance ... I did it because I *wanted* to. He wasn't mine to kill. Then I immediately felt like one of them, like the Butcher left a part of herself inside me, like I wouldn't ever be able to control myself again. I hated that I liked it so much."

"I'm sorry, Marilyn. I can only imagine what you've had to deal with by yourself for all these years. Seems like it finally made its way out. Hopefully for the better." Debra begins to tap her shoe again and twiddles her thumbs. "Do you think that's going to happen to me?"

"No," Dan interjects matter-of-factly. "Not at all. There are many things that make Marilyn unique compared to the rest of us survivors." The *us* hangs heavily in the air, causing Deb to furrow her brow. "Most normal people—no offense, Marilyn—experience *distress* when dealing with grief. Distress can lead to things like negative thoughts and emotions, substance abuse, self-harm, suicide, or anything else that is generally considered detrimental to your well-being. Marilyn doesn't feel distress. She experiences something called *eustress*, which is generally associated with growth and motivation, and typically leads to a positive outcome. Even if she doesn't realize it."

Marilyn raises her eyebrows until they feel like they're about to scrape her hairline. "I'm sorry, what?"

"Yes." He turns toward her with his partly smug, partly self-righteous face like a true shrink. "How the hell else do you think you survived the death of sixty-four loved ones and acquaintances without absolutely fracturing? The grief causes you to grow, to rise to the occasion and laugh in death's face. It's *normal* to fall into substance abuse when grieving. No offense, Debra."

"None taken."

"Doc. I partially skinned Wayne alive then wore his face like an absolute psychopath—like one of *them*. How does that equate to *growth*? Seems more like regression to me." Marilyn glances at Deb, who wears a justifiably shocked expression. Marilyn shrugs.

"Tension and release. Any time we experience stress, whether distress or eustress, there will inevitably be a release of some sort to blow off steam, so to speak. You've been under an inhuman amount of tension for an unusually long period of time, so it seems reasonable to me that your release would be ... substantial. And it was, indeed, gloriously substantial."

"I thought you said *eustress* tends to be positive?"

"I did."

"How is what happened to Wayne *positive* aside from the fucker being gone? How did the Butcher's killing spree lead to a *positive* result for me?"

"You're alive, aren't you?" Dan taps the table with the sort of impatience a parent would feel for an impetuous child. "And you've adjusted rather well, or well enough. You rose to the occasion and did whatever you had to do to survive. And here you are. Most people crumble when they feel their life coming to an end, they beg and plead and turn into pitifully sobbing prey. Not you. The former is distress, but you flipping off a serial killer with all sincerity, the pain in the ass that you are, is *eustress*." Dan continues tapping his finger, seemingly playfully, challenging Marilyn to look inward when the path to clarity is murky at best. "Debra, what would you do if Victor stormed through the front door right now and killed me in front of you?"

"I ... I don't know," she stammers. "I would probably try to run."

"Exactly. Distress. Marilyn? What would you do?"

She rolls her eyes with a groan. "I'm guessing I would flip him the bird and call him a short little dickhead."

"Exactly. Eustress."

Debra stifles a laugh with one hand over her mouth.

"Remind me why this matters, Doc?"

"*Tension and release*. It's the foundation of life. What do we do when we have a long and stressful day at work? We come home and have a drink to unwind. It's also used extensively in music for effect. Without the release, unfortunate things tend to happen."

Marilyn nods unenthusiastically. "So the murders didn't cause tension?"

"I have a theory that your tension stems from the media attention rather than the Butcher herself. You needed a release from the spectacle that your life became once the public caught hold of your story, which eventually led to Wayne's facial scalping. Correct me if I'm wrong."

Marilyn wants to scream, laugh hysterically, cry, anything to deflect the attention away from her. This is exactly why she's always hated shrinks, the way they pry into every nonsensical facet of her life, the way they try desperately to find deep meaning in meaningless moments. Yet she relents. "You aren't wrong."

"Of course not. Debra, let that be your first lesson about taking a human life, no matter how heinous that person may be. There are consequences in such a powerful release, consequences that can carry with you for the rest of your life if you aren't fully prepared to understand the weight of life and death. Marilyn, I'm sorry this lesson was at your expense."

Dan turns to face Marilyn with that same glint in his eye and a slight smirk that could be interpreted as many different things. Thoughts that she's his one true project and the rest of the patients are only scapegoats to achieve a certain end goal. Thoughts that Debra and the rest of the patients to come are horribly equipped to step into the role that she and Dan seem destined to fulfill. Continued thoughts that she's broken beyond repair despite what Dan says, and this is the only path she's fit to follow now.

"So," Dan continues. "Are we ready to continue?"

21

RECONNOITER

They stand outside what appears to be an abandoned industrial factory, a sprawling mausoleum of a structure with weather-worn windows high on the building and stained concrete cloaking whatever nefarious activities happen inside. The rusted chain link fence surrounding the property has long since depreciated into a virtually useless barrier, with the mounted barbed wire now a jumbled bramble of dull edges.

The building is dark, inside and out, with peculiar shadows under the moonlight cast upon various crevices like the sneering, mocking eyes of the lost souls that remain trapped within. The ledge of the roof seems like there should be a gargoyle statue perched upon it to warn away unwanted visitors.

"This is the last location signal I received from Cassie's phone before it went dark," Deb says as she scans the exterior. "I'll never forget how I felt that night, knowing that it was up to me to rush in there and save her. I felt guilty for the longest time, thinking that if I had moved quicker, if I hadn't hesitated, maybe I could've done something about it." She turns to face them now with a glazed look over her eyes. "But I know that's not true because I called the police, and they found nothing here."

"What makes you think this is where Victor lives?" Marilyn asks. "Maybe it was only the kill site."

"It's both. I used to drive here on those nights when my mind decided to be my worst enemy, usually with the help of a bit of booze," she chuckles weakly. "I would stand right here and hate myself for not being strong enough to run inside the factory, even if it wouldn't have mattered anyway. It's the point that I chickened out in my moment. Anyway, one night I heard a car pull up, and I jumped in the bushes to hide. Luckily, my car was back by the main road where we parked tonight, or I might've joined my sister sooner than I'd like. I saw his giant basketball head bouncing up and down as he walked inside, alone, then he never left as long as I was here."

"You're probably right. If Victor doesn't live in the factory, he must still spend an awful lot of time here." Dan presses his phone against the chain link fence and snaps a few pictures from different angles, then he records a short video of the property. "Either way, this place is probably our best opportunity to get him."

Deb agrees. "It's completely abandoned. I've never seen anyone else here, and I spent more nights than I'd care to admit standing right by this fence."

"It's all part of the process, Debra. We can't change the past, but we *can* manipulate the future. Cliché, I know, but I'm giddy being here." He takes more pictures of the fence, the roof, the front doors, and more. "Do you remember there being a way through the fence? This rusted old thing shouldn't be hard to get through. I also brought bolt cutters just in case."

"Someone already cut a hole in the fence." She points to a panel at the corner of the property where a section remains peeled back. "I crawled through there the last time I was here. Finally got the courage to walk up to the door."

"That's great, Debra. I'm proud of the steps you've taken thus far."

"We're going in?" Marilyn says. "Seems like a death trap."

"Not us. I'll go alone to scope the place out. Just from the outside this time." Dan walks toward the opening in the fence and kneels down to where a small piece of ripped fabric clings to the sharp edge of the intertwined metal. "Interesting." He snaps a quick photo.

"Looks like part of a shirt sleeve," Deb adds.

"Couldn't it just belong to some teenagers who snuck in here to smoke pot?" Marilyn asks.

"Anything's possible, I suppose. Can never be too careful." Dan tugs on the piece of cloth and stuffs it in the back pocket of his slacks. He's dressed too nicely to be a predator. "Ladies, would you mind pulling back the fence so I don't lose a piece of my clothes, as well?"

"We should go with you. What are you going to do if someone's hiding in there?" Marilyn glowers at him as Deb opens the chasm single-handedly.

Dr. Dan smiles and pats something firm inside his jacket, implying it to be the revolver. "Never leave home without it. Besides, I'll be less noticeable by myself." He slides through a bit too gracefully for a psychiatrist and pops up on the other side.

"And what if something happens to you while we're out here doing fucking nothing? You could be killed."

He shrugs dramatically. "I'll just give them two of these." He flips both middle fingers toward them as he walks away backward. "Worked for the great Marilyn Soroka." His footsteps decrescendo as he shuffles around the building and out of sight.

"He's such a pain in my ass." Marilyn spits on the ground then kicks the dirt.

"Oh? I didn't realize there was tension between you two."

"There isn't. He's just a pain in my ass."

Deb scoffs. "The way only a man can be, right?"

"Something like that. I think we might just be too much alike in a lot of ways, but he also probably saved my life." Marilyn stares at the side of the building where Dan circled around the back. She feels a scowl staining her face that Deb doesn't deserve to stare at. She might really start to think there's actually some sort of malice to the expression. "Anyway, he's good for us, even if I hate to admit it."

"He is. *Both* of you have been so good to me." Deb bites her lip, and condensation escapes the tiny corners of her distorted mouth. "Listen, Marilyn … I know that you don't like to hear stuff like this, but I really might not be alive right now if it weren't for you. You gave me hope and strength to continue fighting for another day. Otherwise, I might've been—"

Just another suicide.

"—well, I might've done something horrific to myself. Something permanent. So, thank you."

Marilyn thinks about the horde of faceless and nameless people out there—anonymous to her, at least—that had every right to become another folder in Dr. Dan's cabinet. Those who never would've sought help, maybe out of shame or misguided pride, had she not sauntered onto all those TV interviews feeling like a fucking idiot, though still a shining light to every person who made up that cacophony of screaming voices. A beacon of hope. An icon.

"My pleasure, Deb. I did hate it for a long time, being some sort of *hero*, but I think there was some small part of me that realized it was important. I'm not sure I would've capitulated to the dog-and-pony show otherwise."

"Well … Thank you. Really. I've already found some sort of peace just being with the two of you. I don't *need* to kill Holloway anymore, but it would just be the cherry on top, you know?"

Yes, I know. The Butcher's death offered some reprieve, at least a temporary cease-fire on Marilyn's life. Though the darkness remains, swallowing everything in its path like some cosmic force, a torrential hurricane of death. That's not Deb's problem. "I'm happy for you, Deb. We're going to bring this little son of a bitch down, and then you can ride off in the sunset in true peace."

True peace. Something Marilyn will never experience. There will only be more like Deb and Shelly to be helped once Victor has been dealt with, a never-ending assembly line of work to be done.

Deb lunges forward in a full embrace, shocking the indomitable Marilyn into a form of living rigor mortis. She stands upright and stiff as a board with her arms down by her sides. Deb pulls away.

"Sorry." She chuckles awkwardly and flicks a tear from her right eye.

Headlights illuminate the dirt road leading into the factory, interrupting what could've been a cathartic moment for Marilyn, if only she knew how to experience one. "Shit. It's Victor." She yanks Deb's arm downward until they're both flat on the dirt.

"We need to warn Dan. Should we call him?"

"No. Too much noise." Marilyn pulls out her phone with the screen angled toward the ground and types *SOS* to Dan. She eyes the crevice in the chain link fence and points toward it. "Follow me. And hurry."

They military crawl through the opening and remain below the sightline of Victor's headlights until the humming of the car's engine ceases. Marilyn raises an index finger to her mouth then slowly mouths: *do exactly as I do.*

Deb nods.

They could take Victor there, ambush him at the front door and outnumber him, shoot him if they have to. Or they could be picked off one by one in foreign territory like invaders entirely unaware of the landscape they inhabit.

Marilyn slides the chef's knife from the sheath hidden beneath the back of her jacket. She stands up tall once they reach the building, followed by Deb doing the same.

They lean with their backs against the concrete blocks, listening to the sounds of Victor's car door shutting and the beep as he double clicks the lock button on his keychain. Marilyn looks down and notices the slight outline of a footprint in the dirt pointed toward the exit.

She points to the rear of the building and mouths: *move to the back.*

They slide along the mortar, their jackets making the slightest scratching sound against the concrete's textured surface. Footsteps pound the dirt from an indiscernible direction, causing Marilyn to raise the knife to her chest in a striking position. They grow louder before stopping completely.

Marilyn turns with her chest and the knife toward the building and holds up her left hand in a gesture for Deb to stop. Silence.

Dan leaps around the corner with the silver revolver pointed at head level. Marilyn jabs the blade a few inches forward before pulling it back.

"I almost shot you," he whispers just a decibel above being inaudible.

"Yeah, well, I almost gutted you, so we're even."

"Where is he?"

"Walking toward the door, last we knew. We could take him now. Be done with it."

"No," Dan says sternly. "Stick to the plan. Go back to the car, and if he follows, *then* I'll blow him away."

Dan moves to the left side of Debra and motions for them to follow, stepping gingerly in the dirt to avoid suspicion. The front of the factory is dark, suggesting that Victor made his way inside without realizing they're outside stalking him. Moonlight reflects forebodingly off the revolver's nickel finish. Dan reaches the corner and pokes his head around it methodically. He gives them a thumbs up.

"Go," Marilyn nudges. "I'll hold the fence open."

"I'll do it. You go first. I'm the one with the gun."

"Exactly. You can protect us coming through. I'm the quarterback, remember?"

Dan nods, appearing ready to argue. Marilyn steps out from safety and slowly pulls the metal barricade back with a sound no louder than the cold wind blowing through it. He carefully maneuvers beneath the peeled-back section, followed by Marilyn as Deb takes her place.

"Come on, Debra. We need to go," Dan beckons, keeping his revolver raised toward the factory like a safety blanket.

Deb stares at them from the other side of the fence, her eyes welling up with tears in the icy darkness. She removes a silver dagger of her own from her jacket pocket. "I'm sorry. I need to do this on my own. Thank you both for everything, but I can't have you getting hurt for me."

22

AVIDITY

Debra sprints headlong for the front door and slips inside before Dan and Marilyn can make it back through the rusted chain link fence. Her shoes pound dirt with reckless abandon and little concern for who hears them.

Come and get me, killers ... Catch me if you can ...

"Oh, fuck me," Dan says as he scratches his forehead with the revolver's hammer, the silver barrel pointed to the crescent moon. "I didn't see that one coming."

"Doc! We have to go after her!"

"What about the plan? Just give me a second to think about—"

"Fuck your plan!" Marilyn grabs him by the lapels of his duster jacket and does her best to pull the larger man toward her. "Deb just threw the plan out the window. Are we going to do the same to her?"

His brow furrows both contemplatively and with a bit of that predatorial fire. "No, I suppose not. You take the lead, and I'll be right behind you for backup."

Will he cut and run? Leave them both for dead? Maybe shoot Deb and Marilyn in the back of the head for putting his life at risk? Marilyn shakes off her untrusting nature, the great abounding pessimism she has toward the human race as a whole. She nods.

"I'll hold the gate for you and then slide through after. I'm small enough to fit."

Dan nods in return and slips back under the gate. He dusts himself off then extends a hand to help Marilyn stand up. He grabs her shoulder with a father's warmth. "Safety first, you hear me? We'll do everything we can to get Debra out of here alive, but our continued work depends on our survival. We can't take any more unnecessary chances."

"Yes," she says, immediately feeling wrong about it, as if Deb's life is suddenly expendable to justify the means. "We'll make it out."

He removes his hand and motions toward the front door. Marilyn walks quickly and quietly along the multi-colored concrete building, stained from years of rust runoff and moss and weather damage, peering back periodically to make sure Dan is still following before deciding to simply trust that he'll be there.

The thick and heavy steel door is still ajar when she gets there, and it makes an echoing creak through the front room as she opens it. The scent inside is pungent, like a mixture of mildew and water damage with metal shavings and machine oil, although it smells nothing like the malodorous carrion collection inside Wayne's trailer.

Nuts and bolts and metal shards and remnants of shredded boxes line the ground, the cardboard no doubt torn up by rats, evidenced by the wafting of ammonia that strikes her. There are a handful of scattered machines that appear non-operational and several other mis-colored shapes on the concrete floor where large machinery once was, where it would've whirred to life in the factory. The overhead lights dangle unlit, and the factory is only illuminated by the moon shining brilliantly through the high-mounted windows.

Dan's footsteps follow behind as quiet as a librarian's, but they're still there, trotting in synchronicity with Marilyn's every time she trudges forward. Nothing immediately catches her attention beyond the main room, not a sound or light nor movement. There's a hallway in the center of the front room that leads somewhere deeper into the bowels where Deb must be searching. Where Victor must be hiding.

Without turning around, Marilyn motions with her index and middle finger for them to progress down the hallway now that the front room has been deemed clear. She curses internally at Deb, wishing for a happy ending to the situation that involves the three of them escaping unscathed through the gap in that rusted old fence. She also wishes for a gun of her own and preferably one bigger than Dan's revolver. No offense, Dan.

The hallway leads to a series of nondescript doors shrouded in darkness, likely offices, storage, and restrooms once used by the factory workers in their previous lives, people who are most likely dead now. The thought is chilling in the eerily desolate building where the echoes of days past are imprinted upon the textured cement walls, the fiery atmosphere of a bustling manufacturing workplace still somehow felt in its mausoleum-esque state.

A faint noise reverberates from somewhere up ahead, sounding like the light footsteps of a below average size woman like Deb. They're rapid in pitch and hurried as if she's either sprinting to or from someone else with purpose. *Will she scream for help if she needs it?* Marilyn wonders before realizing that Deb won't be expecting any cavalry to call for.

She turns to face Dan, feeling somewhat aimless in her approach. He nods confidently, his eyes damn near glowing a dark red in the blackness like a predator closing in on its next meal. He performs the same gesture that Marilyn did with his index and middle finger, suggesting that they push forward. Run toward the danger.

The hallway opens up to a second massive room of rustic and missing machines stretching from wall to wall. No sights or sounds, nor movements. More frantic footsteps echo with a second set close behind. Deb's either the meat or the carnivore now. Dan drops the hammer of his revolver behind Marilyn, the sound of which carries across the room like a single strike on a drumhead.

Marilyn picks up her pace, the footsteps behind her indiscernible, and rounds the only available corner into a series of smaller rooms where the dim light of a fire dances with a dull reflection on the concrete walls. There's a brief yelp, neither immediately discernible as masculine nor feminine, followed by the wet squelch of flesh being penetrated by something sharp. Marilyn has heard the sound too many times to mistake it.

She takes off running, the sound of pounding footsteps be damned, and dashes down the hallway where the fire's soft orange light flickers. Muffled screams and sounds of struggle enter earshot as the light grows brighter. They run into a third identical evacuated room in which a furnace used for heat-treating and forming metal roars and blazes. Deb stands at the center with her own bloody knife pressed precariously against her throat, her eyes pleading for help even if she doesn't know how to ask.

Victor hides behind Deb, his beach ball head craned to peer over her shoulder, standing the same height as her with a slight advantage from his flat top haircut. His other hand bleeds through a puncture wound, the skin appearing burnt around the wound, and seals her mouth as she continues to moan behind it.

Dan raises his revolver and fires a warning shot dangerously close to Deb's shoulder, and the slug whizzes by Victor's bulbous head and strikes a concrete wall with a showering of stoney debris. "Let her go, Victor, or the next one goes through your forehead. It's an easy target."

"This fuckin' whore stabbed me!" he shrieks, shaking Deb's body hard enough to draw blood beneath the knife's point.

Marilyn notices the red-soaked hole in Victor's shirt just beneath the inner half of his collarbone, a mere two inches away from leaving him bleeding out in this grimy shithole. *Atta girl.* "And how many women have you hurt to deserve being stabbed? You *hideous little shit.*" She steps forward confidently, feeling her heart skip a beat yet she knows it's not from fear.

Victor's face contorts as he snarls weakly for a serial killer. Then an awkward smirk curls across his lips as he turns his head toward Deb. "Ahhh ... You even brought the bitch!" He kisses her on the cheek, and she whimpers through his bloody fingers. "So, the rumors *are* true."

"I'm not in the mood for your shit, Victor." Marilyn unsheathes her Damascus blade by its birchwood handle as a flutter of electricity traverses her chest, and she feels that great snarling alpha wolf rising inside, rabid with bloodlust, baring its teeth for carnage. *I cut off the face …*

Dan eyes her with the gun still trained on Victor, his finger resting firmly on the trigger, seemingly waiting to see which of the predators will strike first—fallen angel or savage demon. "Let Debra go. You're outnumbered, Victor, there's no way out of here for you."

He sneers with his corroded, thin lips reaching from ear to ear. "Am I? You think this ends with me?"

"It never ends. You fuckwits just keep crawling out of the woodwork like cockroaches, but nothing needs to happen to Debra. Let her go so we can talk," Dan says.

Victor slowly removes his putrid hand from her mouth with the knife still digging into her skin. "Go on, slut. Go on, I want to hear them beg. Tell them to beg me for your whore life."

Deb remains silent and stoic, even when Victor digs the knife's point deeper and the blood runs down her chest, glistening in the fire light. "I'm sorry that I got you both involved in my mess. I never wanted any blood on your hands because of me. Don't forget that the work must be completed."

Victor plunges the serrated blade longways through the base of Debra's throat with a savage smile and cranks it to the side as another shot explodes from the revolver. It rips through the top of Victor's left shoulder, and he yelps in pain like a tiny dog suddenly fearing for his life. But Deb doesn't scream—she releases a gurgled moan as the color drains from her face and the blood gushes down her front from the open wound. There's peace in her glassy eyes, an expression of serenity that Marilyn hadn't ever seen from her before.

Marilyn charges with her knife pointed outward, intending to tackle Victor and make him suffer as much agony as his little body can handle before his heart gives out. *Open his chest and carve out his heart ...*

Victor shoves Deb forward into the sprinting Marilyn, who skids upright across the slick, dust-coated floor in an attempt to stop. She collides with Marilyn off-balance, and the blade accidentally plunges into Deb's ribs as they fall backwards with the dead weight of the limp body sandwiching her against the concrete. Deb's chin rests on Marilyn's upper chest, propping her head up and stretching the wound.

Two more projectiles whizz through the air above. One of them strikes a wall and the other flesh, causing Victor to yelp again as he lumbers away. "Death to the world!" he screams as there's the sound of a heavy door slamming shut, followed by the click of an industrial lock. Marilyn doesn't move.

She stares up into Deb's listless eyes as the last of the light inside them fades, the dull gray-blue spheres holding all of her life's secrets, now slipping away into obscurity to take her story with them. The stab wound releases one last pump of warm blood onto Marilyn's chest and neck, and the crimson liquid drenching Deb's shirt creates a sticky bond between them. Her final breath is expelled into Marilyn's open mouth, the death rattle injecting new life into Marilyn to find Victor and slowly saw his big fucking head off.

Dan rushes to her side and gently pulls Deb from atop Marilyn, who immediately runs for the locked door in vain. She pounds her fists and kicks it, already knowing that Victor got away with another one, for now. He cackles faintly from somewhere on the other side of the door before the sound disappears altogether.

She returns to Deb and kneels, the front of her clothes drenched in blood as if she'd bathed in it.

Dan shakes his head gravely and closes Deb's eyes. "Looks like we lost our first game, kid. One and one on the season."

She nods, drowning in her thoughts on recovery as the shackles around the lurking leviathan of her true self grow tight enough to fracture, the chains already pulled taut and stretched to their limits. "One and one," she repeats.

"That's right. Can't win 'em all, unfortunately." He scratches his forehead with the revolver's barrel this time and turns his attention to Deb on the ground. "I'm sorry, Debra. We did our best, given the circumstances."

"We did our best," Marilyn whispers to herself. Did they really? Did they really do everything they could to save her? Did Deb do everything in her power to stay alive? She should feel wrong for thinking Deb foolish while her corpse is still warm, but it wasn't the wisest decision to go renegade. Unless she only wanted to die regardless.

"*Help me!*" A muffled male voice screams, hidden somewhere in the room, accompanied by knocking on the walls. "*I can hear you out there! Oh God, help me!*"

23

EQUILIBRIUM

The knocking in the walls continues to grow more urgent, increasing in speed and intensity. "Might be a trap," Marilyn says. "You heard what Victor said about this not ending with him?"

"I did, but do you really want to just leave the poor schlub trapped in there?"

"I don't *want* to, but I'm also not looking to die."

"Hm." Dan rubs the stubble on his chin. "Since when?" He winks, then walks to the door closest to them and knocks. Nothing.

"Over here! Please, God! Help me!" The muffled voice shouts again, sounding obviously panicked, but also distressed, as if something horrific has already happened to him. Yet he lived.

"Coming. Take a deep breath." Dan walks to the next door and tries the handle. Locked.

"Yes, I'm in here! I need out right now! Right now!"

"It's locked. Step away from the door, please." Dan pauses and glances back toward Marilyn, who only watches from Deb's side, inadvertently standing in the puddle of her blood. Her hands are soaked in it. "Are you clear?"

"Yes!"

He aims the revolver at the door handle and shoots twice to break the seal, then he kicks it open. A haggard man, half-dressed with cindered clothes revealing heavily burnt skin, bursts from the opening and dashes to the fire side of the room. He holds an old drill bit in his hand and swings it at them defensively from afar.

"Easy, friend. We're not here to fight you, but it would definitely be rather one-sided if you don't calm down." Dan holds the revolver with both hands, keeping it aimed downward with his finger on the trigger.

The man pivots to face Marilyn. His body quivers when he focuses on Deb's dead body, his eyes darting back and forth between the corpse and Marilyn's bloody clothes. "You're part of them! I knew it!"

"Keep calm. We're not here to hurt you." Marilyn sheathes the chef's knife and steps forward with her hands raised. "Victor Holloway killed this woman, not us. She was our friend."

"These are the same games *they* used to play." His voice shakes along with the drill bit, his charred skin revealed fully from the light of the furnace. "They would only let us out for their own entertainment, my ... My wife and I. Just to t-torture us."

"What happened to her? Where's your wife?" Dan asks.

He points the quivering bit backward toward the oven. "They ... They burned her in the oven." His body convulses as tears stream from his one unaffected eye. "I can't talk about this anymore! I have to get out of here!"

"My friend ... I have a gun. If we wanted to hurt you, it would've happened already. We only want to help you." Dan digs into his pocket and pulls out his wallet. "Here, have a look at my card. My name is Dr. Daniel Hudson, and I'm a board-certified psychiatrist."

"What's your name?" Marilyn drops her arms and takes another step forward gingerly. "I'm Marilyn. Marilyn Soroka."

"I know you. I've—I've seen you on TV before."

"That's right. You know me, so you know we aren't dangerous. I told you my name, now tell me yours."

"F-Fred. It's Fred." He takes a deep breath and slowly lowers the pointed bit.

"My wife's name was Helen, and they killed her. Brought me out of the room to watch, pressed my face against the furnace to smell her flesh burning, to hear her skin sizzling, then *he* threw me back in that room."

"I'm terribly sorry," Dan says. "My wife was also murdered by one of these savages. That's what we're doing here—we came to help people like us. To cleanse the world of killers, one by one." He reaches in his back pocket and walks a flask over to Fred. "Here, you look like you could use it. I figured at least one of us would need some whisky tonight. Doctor's orders."

Fred eagerly unscrews the cap then pauses, staring into the narrow hole.

"Fred. We have half a dozen different ways to kill you in this room alone. It's not poisoned," Dan chuckles.

He guzzles the liquor with only a few small pauses and exhales and groans. The burn of the whisky can only pale in comparison to that of his skin or any of the other horrific things he's witnessed in this room. "Do you have any water?"

"In the car. We're going to have to find our way out there eventually, Fred."

"I don't know what to do, I ... I don't know who I can trust."

"Likewise, friend." Dan releases the drum on his revolver and removes the five spent shells, replacing them with fresh bullets as he speaks. "You see, Fred, I find myself in quite a predicament, as well. How do I know that I can trust *you*? I don't know what you've seen us do, and we can't risk you running to the police and involving us in a murder investigation."

Fred's expression turns from panic to sheer, all-consuming terror. "I didn't see anything! I swear!"

The drum clicks back into position. "I'm in a precarious position, Fred. You understand that I can't simply allow you to waltz out of here to wander the streets at this hour in your condition. Your burns are very likely infected, and you aren't thinking clearly. You understand how that might be bad for Marilyn and me?"

"You're a *psychiatrist*?"

"I am. And Marilyn is here as my patient."

She gives an awkward curtsy in her blood-stained clothes, miming the motion of pulling on a dress that she isn't wearing.

"I can help you, too, Fred," Dan says. "*We* can help you, if only you're willing to trust me."

"What are you going to do if I don't?"

"Haven't decided yet."

Fred raises the drill bit again, his arm shaking like a leaf. "You're going to hurt me?"

"No, I said that I hadn't decided yet, but I assure you that I'll be ready for anything. Say the three of us get ambushed here? Maybe Victor has a trap in store?"

"I have a question, Fred." Marilyn inches ever closer to the man, seemingly without him noticing. "You keep saying 'them,' as in a group of people that killed your wife. So, it was more than just Victor? Who hurt you?"

Fred takes several more rapid and shallow breaths before he sighs, seemingly releasing some tension. "I don't know their names. They killed Helen here in this room, but it was like some sort of ceremony. A group of people, but they wore masks that looked like what kids would wear in some old Halloween movie. Half of them wore black goat head masks on the left side of the room, and they had curled horns coming out of their foreheads. The masks stopped below the noses, so I could only see their mouths, but only one of the people ever talked. She wore a golden Venetian mask, like one of those plain, inhuman faces people would wear to a masquerade. The right side wore simple skull masks."

"Jesus. Jesus H. Christ." Dan wraps his hand over his chin and visibly squeezes his jaw.

"What?" Marilyn asks. "What's wrong with that?"

"It means the little shit wasn't lying. There are more of them, apparently a *fuckload* more, and I just opened the floodgates without meaning to." He presses both hands to his forehead, the revolver pointing upward like a horn. "No, this is fine. We're fine. I'll think of a new plan, and we'll live if we stick to it. They can't come out of the shadows, or they'll be caught by the police. That will play to our advantage."

"But we hunt them in the shadows."

"We do. That's why the plan has to be lock tight. This is the life that I asked for repeatedly, years and years of plotting and formulating to get here. We will succeed." Dan turns back toward Fred, his movements jagged and suggesting unrest. "So, what happened with you?"

"I ... I already told you that they burned me. Pressed my face and torso to the scorching hot metal of the furnace."

"Yes, I know that, but why didn't they throw you in with Helen? Why are you still alive?"

Fred winces at the mention of Helen. "They don't kill people using the furnace. They murder them in this big room with two semi-circles surrounding the victim, goats and skulls on opposite sides, *then* they throw them into the fire. I only saw the goats handling the bodies ... *killing them*. The skulls did everything else. They presented the weapons, cleaned up the mess. Everything else."

"And why do they throw corpses into the furnace? To hide the evidence?" Dan says.

Fred shakes his head no.

"For some sort of pleasure those twisted fucks crave?"

Fred shakes his head again.

"Speak, Fred. What the hell is the meaning of this?"

He takes a deep, vibrato-laden breath and slams his eyes shut. "They were sacrifices. Their bodies were burnt as sacrifices, and they recited some sort of prayer while it happened."

"Sacrifices to *whom*, Fred? I'm losing my patience."

Fred bows his head and breathes in deeply again. "To *Death*."

"They were already dead. I still don't understand why they were burned."

"They were sacrificed to *Death itself*, like ... like some fucking deity that they worship, and they would say a prayer—Prince of Death, Prince of Fire, Prince of Satan. That's all I remember. Then they tossed the bodies into the furnace and chanted while they burned. They got close to the fire and inhaled the smoke deeply."

"How many people were killed in front of you?" Marilyn asks, eyeing the massive, ash-laden oven.

"Five. The woman who spoke said that I would be the last of my group, and she said they kill in sixes."

"Cute. So, we're dealing with a cult of serial killers who think they're fulfilling some dark purpose to a malevolent deity."

"I'm afraid it's a little bit deeper than that, Marilyn," Dan says. "These are people that likely walk among us in our day-to-day lives. We could've even passed one of them on the city sidewalk outside my office. They probably pretend to be normal like the rest of us and befriend people they find suitable for the kill. No offense, Fred. They're united under one purpose, one leader, but it's the delusion that drives them, which makes our situation that much more dangerous. We need to be extra careful moving forward because Victor's going to sing to the group like a canary."

Marilyn nods, deep in thought about this sort of death cult, a syndicate of serial killers. "Maybe not. He might be too embarrassed that he got caught. He might not want to tell them we were here—they might kill him themselves for being a weak link."

"I don't know any of their names," Fred interjects, "but there was one guy that the leader said was new to the group. She made him pay penance. Short guy, bigger mask than the rest."

"That's Victor Holloway. The Phantom Strangler."

"He had to put his hand in the fire along with ... Helen. She said it was because he murdered someone without her approval, that it was his last chance before he would be their next sacrifice."

Dan paces the room and scratches his chin. "Then we need to find the little piggy before he squeals. That might be our way out of this mess without an overwhelming defeat. Anything else to add before we get out of here, Fred? Anything at all that can help us."

"I'll try to think back, but it's all so … It's just so fuzzy. I remember six of them on each side, six goats and six skulls, plus the leader in the middle. She watched as the victims were stabbed to death."

"Thirteen total," Marilyn says.

"Yes."

"And you said that only the goats killed people?"

"At least while I was here." Fred claps a hand over his good eye as if they were all being murdered again in front of him. "The skulls presented them with the blades and assisted with the process. Acolytes, I think she called them."

"So, really only six killers for us to worry about."

"And six snitches that might be watching us around the city," Dan sneers. "We really need to get out of here before we get ambushed. We can talk more back at the house when Fred is feeling better."

"You're taking me with you?"

"I'm afraid I must insist. We'll think of a plan for you when we're in a safe place."

Fred hesitates before nodding, appearing utterly defeated.

"Take the revolver, Marilyn," Dan continues. "We can't just leave Debra here to be another sacrifice. We'll bury her beneath a tree in the woods. Somewhere peaceful." He squats down and grabs one of Deb's wrists before hoisting her lifeless body over his shoulder, the damp blood already leaving imprints on his duster jacket. "And drop the drill bit, Fred. We don't need you having acid flashbacks in the car, thinking Marilyn and I are your real enemies. Remember, we're going to take care of you. But I can't do anything for you without mutual trust."

24

RECKONING

"Any last words?" Dan asks.

Marilyn stares down into the bottom of a rectangular, six-foot deep hole where Debra lies in an eternal, tranquil sleep that was more than earned. She still wears the same bloody clothes, which Dan thought was a fitting testament to the way she died—as a warrior standing up for what little righteousness remains in this world.

Marilyn doesn't *do* death, and she never has. Her mother died several years before the Butcher showed up unexpectedly like a parasite and wouldn't leave. She was just sixteen at the time, and she excreted every bit of liquid in her body from her eye sockets until only the equivalent of dry heaving from her tear ducts occurred. Her face and forehead pounded, and she felt utterly shameful for how weak and vulnerable the experience left her. That was the end of emotions for Marilyn, long before her closest friends were butchered en masse in Technicolor red against that bleach-white furniture. Nothing else could ever compare again, and her tear ducts calcified long ago.

Dad had always been a shell of a human long before Mom died, but the years of watching her wither away due to cancer finally did him in years before death actually came in a physical sense. Painkillers and beer took hold of his soul till they wrung him dry in the end, about the time Marilyn was entering her junior year of college. Even then, the outcome felt like something she and her sister expected since they were young kids. It was a release for both Soroka girls, but the biggest release was that of the jaws of their father's vices, having finally let *him* go since he would never have been able to do the same.

Deb's death hurts in a different way, the only life she ever truly felt responsible for saving. Her petite frame lying at the bottom of this earthen hole feels like the only time she's ever actually *failed* to save someone, instead of being the inadvertent survivor of a mass tragedy event where others died by happenstance. Deb didn't want them to carry the burden for her, to involve themselves in a situation that was hers alone in which to be the martyr, and in that sense, she prevailed. Even still, the thoughts and emotions and associated words of such elude Marilyn as she reminds herself that the dead can't hear their eulogies. *Try*.

"I'm sorry, Deb. I wish we could've stood here together, the three of us, talking over Victor's grave about how we rid the world of another evil bastard. Instead, it's you … although I believe you finally found some sense of peace in discovering the strength to avenge your sister, regardless of the outcome. And I respect the hell out of that."

"Beautiful, Marilyn. Debra would be thrilled to know that you would be the one to bury her." Dan fetches the shovel leaned against the trunk of a birch tree. The trees surround them, devoid of leaves and shedding bark in the frosty morning air. "I feel bad that I wasn't able to deliver on my promise, Debra, to give you the vengeance you deserved. But it will come, my friend, by my hand or otherwise. Good always prevails."

Marilyn scoffs. "Do you actually feel anything anymore though, Dan?"

"No more than you do." He digs the shovel into the fresh dirt pile and tosses the first scoop over Deb's bloodstained shirt. The second covers her pale face, and the third lands over her matted hair. Within only a minute of shoveling, her body disappears from view like all the rest, nothing more than a fading memory of a snapshot into a person's life, a fictional character that comes and goes whenever something evokes recollection.

Dan pauses to take a break as they share an accidental moment of silence among the dense woodland. "Beautiful spot, isn't it?" he says. The rows of birch trees blow in the wind, their branches dancing nakedly, at risk of snapping from the breeze. "Come spring the leaves will bloom again, bringing with them a new sense of normal. What we see now as endless dead trees will blossom from the harsh winter and grow anew." He tosses a few more scoops of dirt on the pile. "That's the thing with normalcy—it's fleeting, always evolving. Some people accept that, and they grow in whatever new form it takes. Some people struggle with the concept, and they inevitably fall behind in stagnation. But change isn't for everyone, and that's okay, too."

"Yeah." Marilyn looks out through the trees with her hair streaming in the frigid wind. "I still wish we could've saved her."

"I do, too, Marilyn. I do, too. But we also saved another victim simply because Debra ran inside that building, so in that sense, she died a hero. It's the butterfly effect of our every action. We couldn't possibly comprehend the unfathomable amount of good and bad things that result from our actions. It's poetic, really."

"Yeah," she says again. "Doesn't help the failure feel any better just yet."

"There's a question to ask yourself: do you feel bad because Debra died or because we failed to complete the work? It's an important distinction." Dan smiles weakly, undoubtedly fatigued by the long night they had, and he wipes his forehead with the back of his hand to leave a brown smear of dirt.

"I don't know. Both. I feel like we led her to her death, even though I know the truth."

"I don't mean to speak ill of the dead, even less so the very recently deceased, but Debra ran headlong into danger of her own volition. There was nothing we could do at that point—can't say I blame her, but she threw out the plan, and thus, made her own bed."

"I guess so." Marilyn shrugs.

"Don't forget we're serving our true purposes by completing the work. There will inevitably be mistakes made along the way, the proverbial broken eggs lost while making an omelet, but I still believe the outcome to be a net positive. We're doing the right thing, Marilyn. We're doing the right thing." He nods with an air of finality, like a father saying 'and that's that,' then he returns to shoveling.

"Don't you feel the least bit responsible for Deb's death? She would still be alive if we hadn't goaded her into being just like us."

"No. Why would I?" The shovel scrapes both stone and earth with a sharp sound that echoes amongst the trees. "Debra made her decision to join us—we didn't force anything upon her. Besides the point, she had all the signs of a patient who would've soon relapsed, or worse. We gave her closure, and unfortunately, the process didn't go how any of us had hoped. It happens."

"And that's it? Nothing more to say or think about it?"

"Listen, feel free to mourn as you please, but we still have plenty of work to do. Debra is dead, but that doesn't change the fact that her killer is roaming free. We still have work to do," he repeats, head nodding fervently.

Something rises inside of Marilyn, something boiling that expands with steam until the fasteners holding back her true feelings burst. "No, you fucking listen to me for a minute ..." Then she clams up, reverting back to hiding her true thoughts for survival.

Dan stops shoveling again with his full attention focused on her. "Go on. It's good for your recovery."

She sighs. "Can't you ever be not so fucking perfect? So fucking clinical? Try being human for once!"

He scoffs. "That's ironic, coming from you. The truth is, I need to maintain control of my emotions at all times, same as you. I worry about the beast in me, just as you should be worried about yours. We need to keep calm or else we may do something rash based on desire. Our freedom depends on it."

"So, you just lock your feelings away? I did the same thing for years, and trust me, it's a recipe for disaster. Just ask Wayne." Marilyn pauses, biting her lip, then continues to release the acidic word vomit that feels so foreign. It feels dirty. "Deb was our responsibility. She's dead because of *us*, because we couldn't protect her when her impulses took control, because we didn't know how to save her from herself. She never should've been there in the first place. She wasn't ready."

Dan exhales deeply. "It's all part of the process. We also weren't expecting to run into Victor in the factory." He looks downward, where his former patient rests under at least a couple feet of loose dirt. "Of course, I feel responsible for her death, but there isn't a single doctor out there who hasn't failed to save a patient in one way or another. I feel terrible about all of them, but there needs to be some sort of objectivity to prevent us from carrying the burden of things we can't control. I'm sure you can sympathize, being that you've done the same thing so well."

Marilyn copies his gaze, staring down into the half-filled hole, feeling just a bit embarrassed from speaking her mind. This is the exact reason she clammed up for so long, knowing that it's easier to carry the weight of repressed emotions instead of peeling back the layers to reveal her inner faces. Dan seems to understand the feeling just as well, appearing entirely unaffected by anything she's ever said and done.

"Let me take a turn," she says. "You must be getting tired."

"I'm doing fine."

"Still, I feel like I need to contribute."

Dan passes the shovel across the grave and wipes his sweaty forehead again. Another smear. "Knock yourself out."

"How's Fred?"

"Strapped to the bed, just like you were. I gave him some heavy sedatives to knock him out, which should last for at least a few more hours."

A bead of sweat rolls down her temple as she digs hurriedly, wanting to leave Deb behind in the grave along with her own regrets and guilt. "I guess I was wondering more about his injuries."

"He's got an IV of antibiotics for the infection, which had gotten fairly bad, along with a cocktail of anti-inflammatories, steroids, and electrolytes. Poor fucker was in pretty bad shape when we found him. I'm surprised he was able to form a sentence. I suppose we'll see how much of what he said was the truth when he wakes up, although he won't be back to one hundred percent for a while yet."

"Yeah." *Scoop.* "He's the key to where we head next."

"Indeed. Regardless, I've got the basis of a plan ready for us to follow when the time is right. I'll fill you in when I've got all the details hammered out. I imagine they'll be planning for us, as well." He pauses with a faraway gaze that he's worn more frequently recently, the icy breeze seeming to speak to him from another realm as it whistles through the barren tree branches. "I'll tell you one thing ... Whoever these people are, whatever their purpose is ... they picked the absolute worst ones to fuck with. That much is fact."

Marilyn holds the shovel full of dirt over Deb's plot, and she stares at Dan, only he doesn't look back at her. He appears to be focused elsewhere, almost as if he was never actually speaking to her in the first place. The trees waver in the wind again.

"Anyway, I'm going to go and grab some branches to spread over the area, so Debra's grave doesn't look quite so much like a ... well, a *grave*. Do you need any help?"

"No, I've got the rest. It's almost done."

Dan smiles, though his eyes betray the gesture. He's hiding something, some sort of emotions cut loose from Deb's death, even if his act of prestidigitation would fool most normal people. Not Marilyn.

Once Dan is out of sight, she scoops back a corner of the burial mound and tosses Deb's folded patient file from inside her jacket into the dirt hole, then she pushes it down further with the shovel. Deb deserves better than to be just another entry in a neatly-categorized filing cabinet full of suicide victims. She knew what she was doing running into that building all alone, and nothing that Marilyn or Dan had planned for her recovery would've been enough. They only brokered the deal to get her close enough to Victor so that he could end her misery. Suicide by serial killer.

25

OBLITERATION

Dan pops two ammonia capsules and practically shoves them into Fred's nostrils. Fred inhales gutturally as if life had been injected back into him, and he thrashes against the leather straps like a demon under threat of exorcism. The burns on his face almost appear to seer red with rage.

"What the hell is this?! Who's there?" Fred continues to fight and scream, quickly running out of steam as he burns his limited store of energy.

"You'll be able to see again soon. Trust me," Marilyn says.

"Take it easy, Fred. You're safe now, nothing to fear." Dan injects some sort of liquid into the IV line as Fred's good eye opens unnaturally wide and white like a cue ball. "Don't worry, just a mild sedative so you don't go into shock. You'll *probably* be fine, but I have a separate adrenaline needle handy, just in case. You know what, forget I mentioned it."

Marilyn side-eyes him as if to say, *you never gave me any sedatives when I was strapped to the fucking bed.*

"What is this? What kind of quack doctor are you?" he asks with his voice decrescendoing as the sedative takes hold, like watching one of those inflatable arm waving things deflate in real time.

"A very careful one, believe it or not. Plus or minus the quack part."

"Then ... Then let me go if you're such a good guy."

"I can assure you that we'll release you, unharmed, once we hash out a few essentials. Are you in pain?"

Fred makes a sloppy attempt to wriggle his way out but inevitably gives up. "No."

"Exactly. Marilyn and I promise to do what's best for you, as long as those needs don't interfere with our work or well-being. I do have an oath to fulfill. Get me?"

Fred nods weakly.

"Good. This is my house, and you're going to be staying here with us for the time being. I assume you don't have anywhere else to be with your wife gone? No kids or anything like that?"

Fred shakes his head.

"Even better. You see, I feel somewhat responsible for you now, even though what happened to you had absolutely nothing to do with us. In fact, we saved your life and are now overseeing your recovery. A happy coincidence, if you will. Lost one, gained one. You still following?"

Fred nods.

"Before I let you out of these straps, I need you to tell me that you're going to do everything we say because it's good for your recovery. No arguments. Say it."

"I will."

"Okay." Dan approaches the brass buckle on the leather strap across Fred's chest. Then he pauses. "Since you're not yet technically my patient, I also need to threaten you against doing anything stupid. Make a move against either Marilyn or me, and I blow a hole in you the size of the fucking Grand Canyon. And in the interest of being thorough, I need you to understand that nobody knows you're here. They probably already think you're dead. Understand?"

"Yes. I understand."

"Good man." Dan releases the three buckles and steps aside, but Fred doesn't move. He remains in the same position, staring up at the ceiling as though he's already asleep. "Take your time."

"Okay. I will."

"Are you still with us, Fred? You're free now," Marilyn says.

"Yes, I'm just ... just really tired."

"That's good. Whenever I survived a massacre, I slept for a day or two straight. Every time."

"Does the feeling ever get better?" he slurs.

No, she says inside. "Yes," she lies. "Just takes time."

"Fred, I have a few questions for you, if you're able to answer them. The shock of the sedative should loosen up soon." Dan stands at the side of the bed patiently, seeming not to care whether or not the questions do, in fact, get answered. Seeming not to care if Fred is there at all, or why.

"I'm fine now. You can ask me questions."

Dan motions to Marilyn, giving her the floor to ask away. "I just have a few questions about what happened inside the factory. Specifically, about the people that did this to you. You said some things that would seem rather wild to a normal person's ears, but this is right in my wheelhouse."

"I told you everything I know. It was all true."

"I believe you, but I also want to know more about them, and I believe you'll be able to recall more details now that your life isn't in danger."

"Isn't it, though?" Fred pushes himself up in bed with his eyes droopy. He still sits at an awkward angle. "Am I *really* safe?"

"Yes, and you'll be even safer if we know more about this syndicate to hunt them down. You get me?" Marilyn grimaces for only the slightest moment with the corner of her lip curled upward, realizing that she just mimicked Dan.

He sighs. "Yes, I get you. I just don't remember much else about them."

"Think. You said only one of them spoke, but what did she sound like? Did you ever see her face?"

"No, they all wore masks in front of us. Her voice was ... I don't know how to describe it. Rich? She kind of sounded like an actress in a really old movie, which I remember because it made her seem even more powerful. All she talked about was death and sacrificing us to the Prince of Fire, but she never said why."

Marilyn bites her bottom lip with her canine nearly hard enough to draw blood. "And she never hurt any of you directly?"

"No. She only told them what to do, and they always did it. No questions asked."

"So, this woman made them press your face against the furnace?"

"Yes. She told them to force me to experience death up close … And not just dying, she said … but the complete obliteration of a human life. Those exact words." Fred begins to tremble as his face falls pale. He inhales then exhales deeply with a rasp. "They made me stare into my wife's dead eyes as her flesh sizzled, and her hair singed, and her blood boiled into a steamy mist that filled the room. *That's* who you're dealing with."

Marilyn notices Dan's eyes revert back to primordial instinct, his facial expression hardening. It's not a physical change, at least not one that Fred notices, but she's developed a keen sense in understanding who is in the good doctor's driver's seat at any given time.

"I have a proposition for you, Fred, one that I wouldn't normally offer the average person. You see, my wife was also stolen from me many years back now. *Miles Forsythe* was his fucking name, and there hasn't been a day since then that I haven't fantasized about brutalizing the prick with a claw hammer. You're still in shock now, but the day will come soon that those thoughts become unbearable, like a gaping wound that simply won't heal. The adrenaline will cease to numb you, and let me tell you, my friend … the agony you're suffering now is *nothing* compared to what's in store."

Fred wipes his face and attempts to straighten himself again. "Maybe I'm still a little groggy, but what are you saying? You want to kill Miles?"

"Oh, no. I should say that I would gladly give up the rest of my life for five minutes alone with him, but alas, he's already dead. I've missed my opportunity. My proposition to you is that the three of us figure out who these deranged people are, and we destroy them from the inside out. Root and stem."

Fred's good eye opens wide, and he stares at the nearly-snarling psychiatrist with a face of bewildered confusion. Then he looks at Marilyn. "You're in on this, too?"

"I am. Dan and I want to help people like ourselves, people whose lives have been destroyed by the trash that walk among us. Someone has to get their hands dirty, Fred."

He pauses with his mouth agape, one side stuck together at the corner where the skin was burned. "I don't want to do that. I just want to go home and deal with this on my own. Maybe in enough time ... the pain will heal ..."

"There's no healing from this kind of fucked up, Fred," Dan says sharply. "And it's my *job* to heal people like us. Do you know what the expected full recovery rate is for patients affected by serial killers? It's *zero*, Fred. Even if you survive the process, those sights and sounds you experienced are going to fester in your mind like a parasite forever. There's no cure. We can only manage symptoms. That's why the killers must be eradicated, no quarter—the death of an innocent not only kills that person, it splinters through families like broken glass until they all shatter. The savages are a growing cancer."

Fred's face is glazed over, his body language deflated. "I understand that. I do ... But I don't feel that fight in me right now. I don't want to feel anything."

Dan remains stoic, almost alarmingly so, yet his demeanor grows more intense by the second. "There's an old saying by Sun Tzu: If you wait by the river long enough, the bodies of your enemies will float by. I've been pacing and plotting and planning *ten years* for those fucking bodies to find their way to me, and it's the only thing that's kept me going this long. You think Marilyn is doing well after all she's seen?" He turns his head toward her. "No offense, Marilyn."

She shrugs.

"I'll answer for her—she's not. She only plays it off better than anyone else because she's stronger than us. She can compartmentalize the horrific things she's seen into simple historical events without emotional attachment, though that, too, comes with its own cost. Can you do that, Fred? You need us, my friend."

"I'm sure I do, but I just can't do it." He gulps as a tear runs down his cheek, no doubt reliving Helen's murder and burning on repeat. "But I swear I'll never tell anyone about what you guys are doing. I support the idea fully, and they all deserve to die the most painful deaths possible. I just can't join you. I'm sorry."

Dan stares for several seconds without changing his expression. His eye twitches almost imperceptibly, then he walks out of the room without another word, leaving Fred and Marilyn alone in the silence of confusion. He returns with a hefty glass of brown liquid and hands it to Fred.

"You've earned this after all you went through," Dan says. "It's the good stuff."

Fred gulps it down and winces, then finishes the last few ounces with a heavy exhalation that reaches Marilyn's nose. "Thank you."

"Regardless of you working with us or not, I'm going to keep you here for now. I can't send you out there alone in this condition, and I can't afford you going to a hospital and exposing everything that happened. Marilyn and I will resolve that issue. You'll be well taken care of."

"Thank you," Fred says again. "I feel like I don't deserve it."

"That's only the trauma talking," Marilyn interjects. "Like Dr. Dan said, I'm afraid it only gets worse before you'll feel better. The self-doubt, survivor's guilt, the feeling of emptiness ... These are all normal emotions for your situation."

"Sounds like I caught myself a death sentence."

"Life in itself is a death sentence, but your particular situation doesn't have to be. Although you'll have to learn to live with it before the darkness consumes you. And the darkness *is* coming sooner than later."

"Like I said, we can manage symptoms," Dan says. "I've found a higher than fifty percent rate of recovery in patients using a combination of medications, talk therapy, and lifestyle changes, but you have to understand that in this case, recovery only refers to keeping you alive. Some even find things that make them comfortable from time to time, but you'll never feel like your old self again. You need to find a new normal."

"I understand." Fred's face is glistening with streaks of tears rolling from both sides of his eye.

"I know these words sound harsh, but I tell you this as someone who has spent a decade walking in your shoes, not as your doctor. It's your reality now, an unbearably uncomfortable one, and something that Marilyn and I understand more than almost anyone alive. You need to brace yourself for the storm to come, because it can rock you in ways you couldn't even imagine." Dan bows his head to Fred and turns to Marilyn. "I have to meet someone in the city. Are you fine staying here with him?"

She nods.

Dan turns away and walks around the room scattershot, grabbing various items seemingly at random, uncharacteristically unfocused. "Call me with anything urgent. Fred, do you need anything else before I leave?"

"Yes. Can you give me something else for the pain?"

26

TRANSFIGURATION

*B**eg for it. I want to hear you beg for your life, Marilyn.* The Butcher holds Marilyn's head between her gnarled, bloodstained hands and faces it toward the roaring fire.

The malodorous stench of putrefied remains wafts into her nose. Wayne. *Prettiest little bitch I ever saw.* He presses one hand against the back of Marilyn's head and pushes. The smell grows unbearable. *But flip me them famous fingers first before you go.*

Go on, slut. Victor's sultry, rancid breath coats the back of her neck, feeling even hotter and grimier than the furnace and like it left a film behind on her skin. He reaches around her and opens the oven door, revealing smoldering, slack-jawed faces soldered together by their searing, boiling skin. A blister develops into a bubble on one of their cheeks, and it balloons outward to the size of a tennis ball before popping. Pus droplets expel from the wound and land amongst the red-hot coals and sizzle with a new scent of decay.

I'm going to cut off your fucking face, Marilyn. Soon, you'll see through their eyes, the Butcher whispers into her ear. She and Wayne force Marilyn toward the glowing furnace as she grits her teeth and digs her nails into the squalid concrete. Her teeth crack under the pressure, her jaw popping, and she spits out bone remnants that click and bounce across the floor. Her nails splinter and peel back from the flesh as Wayne and the Butcher drag her onward, powerless, anemic in the face of danger.

Burn, bitch, Wayne whispers into her right ear.

Death to the world, Victor whispers into her left.

Marilyn struggles and fights against nothing, her limbs feeling as if they're swinging in slow motion. They toss her into the furnace like a ragdoll, her hands and feet flailing through the iron grate with no contact to slow her descent.

The searing pain of the hot coals against her skin registers first. She smells the smoke of her own flesh burning, then her hair, followed by the voices of those around her.

We were counting on you, Marilyn.

You failed us, Marilyn.

You deserve *to burn with us, Marilyn.*

Victor slams the grated door shut then cackles maniacally, the sound echoing throughout the vacant factory.

Her body slowly turns to dust as the screams of the innocent plead for mercy and dig their ashen claws into the meat of her arms.

Marilyn releases a sorrowful scream while the flames lap at the bottom of her hair and consume the remainder of her living skin.

Marilyn bolts upright in Dan's home office, slumped back against the leather chair with her hands gripping the arm rests tightly. She hasn't had a nightmare since the Butcher first struck, her nights typically filled with sleep deeper than the dead's.

She helps herself to a pour of the good stuff once again and twirls the glass, and she watches the amber nectar cling to the side walls before crawling back into the pool of liquid below like watered-down honey. She takes a sip.

Fred hasn't stirred since Dan left, when he injected a heavy dose of morphine into the IV to leave the ailing man sleeping like one of her loved ones six feet under. Marilyn has already checked on him three times, feeling as if she's caring for the newborn she never had. She leans her head back against the leather cushion with a deep exhale and lingering fatigue. Dan seemed entirely unaffected by any sort of strain throughout the day, even though he's at least fifteen years her senior.

Marilyn's body continues to tremble away the last remnants of panic before it disappears entirely. She takes another long sip then rises from the chair and stretches. There's a dull knock somewhere beneath her feet, sounding like someone fell to the ground. A full-grown man.

"Fred? Are you up?" Marilyn wanders out of the office with the woozy gait of sleep still affecting her coordination. She opens the bedroom door and finds him fast asleep atop the bed, the leather straps missing from where they hung earlier. He's covered by a comforter up to his waist, his upper body burns undoubtedly still feeling too fiery to need any more warmth. "Fred?" she asks in a whisper.

No answer.

She shuts the door gingerly to avoid waking Fred in his fallen state. Another knock, less distinguishable this time, echoes beneath the floorboards. Marilyn opens each of the many hallway doors in succession to find a closet, restroom, and another spare bedroom, in that order. Then there's the basement.

She opens the last door at the end of the hallway to reveal a mostly dark hole into the bowels of the house, only illuminated by a faint light somewhere in the depths. She steps downward slowly, expecting rickety, creaking floorboards, but the stairs are concrete and cold as marble beneath her feet. One voice whispers while another groans as if gagged.

Marilyn rounds a ninety-degree corner in the stairs as she descends into a dim basement only lit by two lanterns that flicker off the walls like the furnace in the factory.

"Dan?"

"Marilyn. I'm sorry, I didn't mean to disturb you." He stands at the far end of a folding table, above a short man fastened to it with leather straps and a rolled-up rag taped in his mouth. Victor. "Since you're here, you might as well help me."

"Dan?" she says again. "How did this happen?"

"I snuck a picture of this little prick's license plate back at the factory before you found me. Sent it to my cop buddy, and he tipped me off this afternoon that a squad car saw him hiding out in the suburbs not far from here."

"I'm assuming you grabbed him from there."

"I grabbed him. And now I'm going to end him. For Debra." Dan open-palm smacks Victor across the eyes and forehead as he squeals with the rag muffling his throat. The Phantom Strangler lies stifled under the same four leather straps that held Marilyn, Fred, and who knows who else in position to receive Dr. Dan's specialized treatment. The straps are tight enough that the edges dig into his skin, and the one fastened over his chest is likely causing him extreme breathing difficulty. Good.

"Dan ... Are you sure you're ready to do this? Let me handle him."

The doctor scoffs and leans his head back eerily in the darkness with his squinted, animalistic eyes still pinned on her. "I'm ready, Marilyn. I've been salivating over this moment for a decade, even if this foul creature isn't *Miles*. He needs to die, and I'm elated to be the one that delivers that justice."

Victor squirms and moans again but stays quiet once Dan slaps the side of his head hard enough to audibly crack his neck when it whips to the side.

"It's not that—he *does* deserve to die, but are *you* ready for what comes next? Are you prepared to open that door within yourself and face the monster on the other side?"

"Yes, Marilyn. The monster is starving. It's been clawing at that door for years now, and I'm more afraid of *not* letting it out than facing it. This has to happen."

Marilyn looks down at Victor, seeing only the bottoms of his shoes and a bit of his legs, then back up to Dan in his ravenous state. "Okay, Doc. I trust you."

She walks forward to stand at the opposite end of the table at Victor's feet. "But if you take things too far, I'll have to knock you out and tie you up, same as you did to me." She glances down quickly to steal a look at Victor's face up close. His eyes open wide.

"Deal. But I can't kill him quite yet, not without the information we need." Dan looks straight down, his and Victor's faces in opposite directions like yin and yang. He appears to be a salivating predator with his fangs bared over a luscious meal prepared for the slaughter. "You're going to die, Victor, you understand me? I'm going to kill you with these hands of mine, and I'm going to make it hurt. Understand?"

Victor nods and winces while doing so.

"Good. I'm going to remove the gag from your mouth, but I don't want to hear any of your fucking screaming or crying or whining. You get me?"

He nods again.

"There's nobody here to help you, nor is there anybody even remotely close, so I don't want to hear a goddamn peep out of you unless I ask a question first. You hear me? Not a goddamn peep."

Victor closes his eyes and nods a third time.

Dan removes the rolled-up rag and places it on the table. "Now that we've established the ground rules, I have a few questions for you, Victor. And I don't want any bullshit answers. Just the truth."

"Why would I cooperate if you're still going to kill me anyway? You really overplayed your hand there, pal."

"Fantastic question. I still haven't decided how quickly I'm going to do it yet, but my mood can be swayed either way. Maybe I'll make it fast and painless with a simple injection. Maybe I draw this process out for days and let you die of attrition, appearing down here periodically to tease you with food and water before consuming them in front of you. Or maybe ..." Dan's face sharpens into something utterly demonic, the darkness overtaking every square inch of it. "Maybe I hand deliver you barely breathing to that factory and tell those dimwitted compadres of yours that you ratted them all out. They'll probably throw you in the furnace ... eventually. I'm sure that every square inch of your body will be charbroiled like an overcooked steak before then."

Victor's face quivers in panic. "Don't ... Don't do that. We can talk. What do you want?"

"I want names. Both the skulls and the goats."

"I can't do that, but I can tell you that the goats are all killers, and the skulls are just helpers. Acolytes. I was a skull in the past and recently became a goat, taking the place of another killer, Wayne Taylor, who recently went missing. Oh ..."

Dan smiles wide. "Oh is right. Marilyn here peeled his face off and killed him herself. It was wonderful work."

She tries to suppress a smile at the sheer absurdity but fails.

"I'm cooperating. No need to do that again." Victor's voice warbles, sounding like one of his many victims.

"We'll see about that. I still need names."

"I can't."

"Victor, we're about to take a ride back to the factory and speak with them directly. Here, let's get those straps undone so we can go." Dan rounds the corner of the table and reaches for the top buckle.

"Don't! Sorry, please don't. What they'll do to me will be ten times worse than anything you can think of."

"Then talk. They won't ever know that it was you who snitched. You'll be long dead."

Victor slams his eyes shut, his mouth stuck in an angular formation as if he might cry. "She calls herself Odessa. That's all she told us, no last name."

Dan covers his mouth briefly, then slides the hand down to grip his chin. "Odessa? You're sure?"

"That's what she said. We had to call her Odessa whenever we spoke to her. Some kind of god complex, if you ask me."

"What's wrong with that, Dan? Who is she?" Marilyn asks.

He shakes his head. "Nobody. Just not a normal name." His face temporarily loses its luster until he peers down at Victor again. "What do you call yourselves? What's your purpose?"

"Odessa called us Famuli Morte. *Servants of Death.* We were tasked with finding people to sacrifice for some stupid reason or another." Victor's face scrunches in the same unpleasantness that he's been a merchant of. "I don't fucking know, man. She was very secretive about the whole thing."

"You mean to tell me you're the innocent victim here? You were *forced* to kill people like a savage?"

Victor pauses, seemingly at a loss for words. "No. Go ahead and kill me now. Get this shit over with."

"In just a moment." Dan reaches into Victor's pants pocket and pulls out his cell phone. He bends Victor's finger back to unlock the device and scrolls through the short contacts list until reaching Odessa, then he presses the call button and turns on the speaker. "We're going to have a quick chat before you go."

"No! Don't do that—she'll know that I talked!"

"You're already dead, what do you care?"

The ringtone on the other end of the line ends as a woman answers. "Victor. What is it?" Her voice is rich, just as Fred described.

"Hello, dear, I'm a friend of Victor's. He's here with me now and would like to have a word with you." Dan lowers the phone and holds it by the killer's restrained head.

"Odessa! You have to help before they kill me!"

"*Who* exactly is going to kill you, sweetheart?"

"That bitch from the TV! And she has a partner with her, some deranged old fuck!" Victor gives one final fit of struggle against the restraints before falling still.

"Ah. Must be them that killed Wayne."

"Hey, uh … sweetheart. Yes, we killed Wayne, but it doesn't end there. We're going to murder Victor, too, then we'll be after you shortly. Go on, Victor," Dan says. "*Beg her*. Beg for your life."

Silence overtakes them for several seconds, and none of the four speak for an amount of time that goes from awkward to tense.

"Well, then," Odessa says at last. "As far as I'm concerned, he's already dead." The line goes dead in Dan's hand, and he tosses the phone onto a desk in the corner of the room.

"Too bad. I guess nobody wants you alive." He raises his head and stares directly into Marilyn's eyes. "What's it going to feel like?"

"It was …" Marilyn's lips curl into a smirk as she searches for the answer. "It was the most powerful thing I've ever experienced. Cathartic."

"Excellent, thank you." Dan removes a stainless blade from the back of his belt and holds it high above Victor's prone body. "Remember, don't scream." He presses the knife longways across Victor's throat, the shiny blade reflecting Marilyn's face back at her from the killer's neck.

"Any last words?" Marilyn asks.

"Prince of Death, Prince of Fire, Prince of Satan … grant me that your infinite power and strength may be the shield and sword of my inner will." Victor's body relents, going limp with his eyes closed to accept the ultimate fate.

Dan presses the blade into Victor's throat. Beads of blood form at both edges of the knife where they touch his skin. "No. You won't die this way." He plops the weapon on the table next to the gag and walks toward another bench before returning with a steel chain. Dan lifts Victor's head roughly by the flat top and ropes the chain around his neck three times before grabbing both exposed ends of it tightly. He looks at Marilyn once more.

She grits her teeth and tightens her jaw. She nods.

Dan's knuckles turn white as he grips the chain and gives it a small tug. Victor gurgles. His eyes protrude from their sockets in fear and regret, which Marilyn imagines stems from being caught rather than committing the murders themselves.

Dan pulls tighter, causing the sound coming from Victor's throat to increase in pitch. More of a whistle than a gurgle. He stares intently downward into Victor's bulging eyes the whole time. "Did you know, Marilyn ... that this fucking savage got away with *molesting children*?" He growls with vitriolic rage, the type of hatred a human shouldn't be able to hold for one of their own. Except Victor isn't human. "That's right. Another little nugget of information passed along from my cop buddy."

Victor struggles against his restraints. He can't speak and doesn't try to. The impending doom beneath those chains grows tighter, like the clutch of the Reaper itself, absorbing his essence into the empty Abaddon.

"You raped and killed innocent women ... Young women, Victor! Women with so much more life to enjoy! All for a cheap thrill ... A singular act of selfishness at the expense of would-be wives and mothers. And then there are the broken families of those victims. I hope you suffer for the rest of eternity, and even beyond that, you savage bastard. Fuck you forever."

Dan brings his hands together in a brief second of respite for Victor, then he yanks on both ends of the chain ferociously. His hands shake from the force, and Victor's body struggles against the straps, though he remains silent aside from the occasional involuntary gurgle. Metallic clinks echo faintly throughout the basement along with the sounds of his heels bouncing off the folding table.

Then there's silence.

Dan releases the chains and looks up into the implied sky with a face of elation, a face of absolutely euphoric pleasure. His inner animal has been freed at long last, the relief of a lifetime, and he breathes heavily with his chest heaving like a snarling wolf's after gorging itself on carrion. He's beside himself—rapturous.

"So?" Marilyn asks. "How did it feel?"

Dan raises his animalistic eyes toward her, the whites of them seemingly black in the basement's darkness as something lively dances around them like hell fire.

"I feel ... transcendent."

27

CONSTRICTION

Three days have passed since Dan killed the Phantom Strangler in what many citizens would argue to be a righteous ceremony. Frontier justice, people used to call it, a group of vigilantes doling out punishments to wrongdoers based on consensus ruling. The city's population, full of exhausted commuters, worried mothers, and protective fathers, would feel that much safer knowing that Victor can never haunt them again. Some might even call what Dan did an act of public service. A good deed.

Of course, the politicians, law makers, and judges would disagree. He would be tried as a murderer himself without regard to exactly who he killed. Many law enforcement officers might even deem Dan a hero in private, whispering over their morning coffee about how someone is finally doing something about the growing violent crime problem in the city. They would never speak up in his defense, though. Those government pensions make sure of it.

Marilyn has tended to Fred in those three days, applying lidocaine and antibiotic ointment to his burns and keeping him comfortable with regular doses of various medications in his IV. He seems likely to make a full recovery, physically, although she secretly worries that the skin is damaged beyond repair. Dan said the burns were easily third-degree. Fred's nerves in the affected area will likely never recover.

She never saw herself as much of a caregiver, or even someone who actually *cares* for most people either way, but playing nurse to Fred has been therapeutic. Apparently, there's more to life than simply surviving, evading serial killers, and subsequently hunting those same killers for justice. Even if this is only a momentary respite, a blip in the radar that allows her to catch a much-needed breath in the middle of life's marathon, it's been nice. Being responsible for Fred's health has made Marilyn almost feel ... *human*.

Dan has mostly been absent since killing Victor. He spent several minutes staring at the unsightly killer in silence, what Marilyn surmised at the time to be an internal struggle with his own monster. She feared he might snap the way she did, that maybe he would brutalize the corpse with his fists or other weapons in a catharsis of repressed rage. Then she remembered the call from the void that urged her to deface Wayne, and she wondered if Dan had any thoughts of dismembering Victor just to prove the point that he had won. That *they* had won. Deb included.

But no, not him. Not Daniel Hudson, MD.

He returned to his uber-professional self after only five minutes of hiding in the valley of the shadow of death, then he immediately unstrapped Victor from the table and told Marilyn to return upstairs in case Fred needed anything. He told her that he would dispose of the body alone so nobody could incriminate her in the off-chance they were seen driving together toward the dump site. Never can be too careful these days, he said.

In one of the few times they've spoken since, Marilyn asked where Victor ultimately ended up, hoping internally that Dan wouldn't bury him anywhere near poor Deb. He was reluctant to tell her at first, again defending the idea of plausible deniability in the event that he had been seen. He told her that she's even more important to the work than he is. But after a bit more prying, he admitted to dumping Victor's corpse behind the factory with a note attached to his chest. *2-1, us.*

That was like kicking a hornet's nest, she told him, not entirely displeased with him doing so. Then Dan, as the good doctor she had come to know, come to depend on in ways she still isn't ready to admit, virtually disappeared. He left notes and sent text messages that he would be in the city meeting patients or running errands or tending to personal matters. He would always ask if Marilyn needed anything, to which she always replied no. And it was true. She's living in a comfortable house for the first time in her life, and she finally has a purpose beyond self-preservation in nursing Fred back to health. Not exactly the type of community outreach Dan had envisioned for his special program, but it's effective for her own recovery.

The few times he *has* been home, Dan didn't speak, didn't eat, only poured himself a glass of the good stuff and glowered like a brooding renegade soldier on the backyard porch. Marilyn didn't bother striking up a conversation—not now, at least. He's likely going through the same things she did following her own first kill, except she had him for support, and all he has is an emotionally destitute human shell by his side. Solitude seems like the best therapy for him now before she makes an ass of herself in trying to help with something beyond her comprehension.

Marilyn knocks on Fred's door with a deli meat sandwich on a dinner plate, all she really knows how to make, and electrolyte solution mixed into a water bottle.

"Come in."

She opens the door and passes Fred the plate and bottle. "Sorry. Dan ran out of microwave dinners, and I'm not much of a chef."

"It's perfect, Marilyn. My ... wife wasn't much of a cook, herself. I usually made most of our meals." Fred bites into the turkey, cheese, and lettuce sandwich with a muted smile. "I ought to make you two the best dinner when I'm up and moving again as a thank you for saving me. I can't believe I ... Well, I wouldn't be here now if you didn't intervene. I'd be a pile of ash."

"I appreciate that, Fred. I'm looking forward to eating a homemade dinner for once."

"How does chicken parmigiana sound?"

Marilyn forces a plastic smile. "Sounds delicious. My favorite."

The truth is, she's survived off of canned food, boxed macaroni, and things of that nature for years, having lost the desire for any sort of gourmet delicacies along the way. Dan's the same, living off of TV dinners and takeout food like a college student. They might as well be a couple soldiers stranded in the desert eating MREs for sustenance, too singularly focused on the end goal to worry about such simple pleasures as how food tastes.

"Well, I owe you both big time. More than a dinner, for sure." He laughs. "Maybe more like a lifetime of dinners to pay for the life I shouldn't even have. I tell ya, I really thought my number was about to be called. I really did." Fred takes another bite of his simple sandwich with an expression of glee that suggests it's the best sandwich he ever had.

Marilyn remembers this phase—irrational optimism after escaping desolation, like the opposite of a hangover with the rushing of elation following a level of stress that's indescribable to anyone who hasn't experienced it. A new, albeit short-lived, lease on life before the darkness shrouds him. The calm before the storm. He's floating in a momentary solitude of silence like a lucid interval.

"That's not necessary, Fred," she says, "but I won't turn down a great dinner for as long as you want to make them." There's a scratch at the back of her throat, a question itching and burning to expel itself. "So, you really don't want your revenge? You're going to just walk away?"

Fred holds the sandwich in front of his open mouth, ready for another bite. He places it back on the plate. "I don't think I have it in me right now. Walking back into that place—smelling the residue of metal shavings and burning bodies ... Reliving however many days we all spent locked in that tiny closet, praying for death in whatever form it would take us, getting stuck back in that headspace. I don't think I can do it. I'm sorry."

Don't worry, Fred. Those nightmares are coming, regardless. "Don't be sorry. You don't owe us anything aside from a few dinners." She tries out a wink like

Dan would do but immediately feels awkward.

"But I do. I owe you guys *everything*, although it's more than I can handle right now. I would only be a burden beside you, and I really believe that the work you're doing is too important to let some jackass like me disrupt it. I'll be cheering you on from home." Fred finally takes another bite of the sandwich, seeming satisfied with the conclusion of the conversation.

"That's okay, Fred. You're always welcome with us, but hunting serial killers isn't for everyone. I wasn't even sure that I could do it at first, myself."

He nods as he finishes chewing and swallows the bite. "So. How does it feel?"

"You mean killing a monster?"

"Yes."

"I'm not sure that I've found the right words yet." Marilyn pauses and briefly bites her bottom lip. "It felt like a soul-crushing weight had been lifted, a weight that had been holding me back for years. Not only did it help me release my repressed trauma, but I learned how to help others with theirs, as well."

"Sounds fantastic. I have to admit, there's a small part of me that can envision cutting them all down. Hacking all their masked heads off and throwing them into the furnace. Maybe I'd use a gun to kill them all. I don't know, I haven't thought that far ahead."

"It's incredibly different to fantasize about it and to actually kill them. I know—I was stuck in fantasy mode until Dan found me. Without him, I would've probably died alone in my apartment, assassinated in the middle of the night by some serial killer who finally worked up the balls to do it. And I was ready for death, or at least the concept of it. Dying seemed like a solution to all my problems."

Fred sighs, his previously jubilant face now sullen with intrusive thoughts. "A part of me thinks that, too. I know it's wrong, and I'll be better off fighting those demons for the rest of my life, but that thought has still been lodged in the back of my mind since I've been here. The sooner I die, the sooner I'll be reunited with my wife."

"But we know it isn't true, no matter how loud that voice gets. We have the rest of eternity to be dead, but only a short window of time spent alive—it's always better to fight than roll over."

"I believe you, Marilyn, especially after all that you've been through. I *want* to fight. I want to live. I'll remember your words even through my darkest moments, because I'd be a fool to think that the road to recovery won't be rough."

"Yes, it will be tough, but let's get you healthy again before you have to worry about that part. Your skin is looking better. I think the infection has mostly cleared up." Marilyn pulls a purple nitrile glove over her right hand and gently runs a finger over the burnt skin.

"Thank you so much for helping me. I'm going to say it a thousand times." Fred grins, and a rush of tears flood his eyes. "You know, my wife ... Sorry, I shouldn't."

"You can say whatever you want here, Fred. We're past the point of holding secrets with one another."

"It's not really a secret, but you just remind me of her. When they took her ... She didn't scream or anything. We were the last two left in the room, having already watched everyone else die, so we knew what was coming. We accepted it as the only way out. But they pulled us from the closet, and she walked right out on her own with her head held high, and she didn't even cry out when they ... when they stabbed her. Not me, though. Her death felt like they stabbed me a thousand times, let the wounds heal, then stabbed me again. She died with her pride intact."

"I'm glad to hear that, Fred—not that either of you suffered, but that she went out with grace. You should be proud. There's no bigger *fuck you* than refusing those savages the satisfaction they crave." Marilyn affirms the statement with a nod as she peels off the glove and tosses it in the trashcan atop a pile of used gauze coated with gunk and ointment.

"That's why you make me think of her. She thought the same as you, that it was better to die on our feet than beg on our knees. Yet, she still died, while you survived over and over again."

Marilyn chuckles awkwardly. "Just lucky, I guess."

No, Helen was *afraid*. She might've hidden it well behind a mask of apathy, a suit of armor that would shield her emotions from the perceptions of a normal person like Fred, but predators have a highly-tuned sense for sniffing it out. They smelled Helen's fear like sharks circling a pool of blood. Marilyn only survived so long because her particular predator sensed something entirely different from her—something reptilian, something primal and inedible. Is Dan more of a Helen or a Marilyn behind his thick masks?

"Do you need anything else aside from your medications?" she asks.

"Not right now. The morphine makes me sleepy, so I'll probably be out before too long. I'm not complaining."

"You need plenty of sleep to heal anyway. You're lucky we didn't have to take you to a hospital."

"Sounds almost as bad as having my body thrown into the furnace. I'm glad I could stay here."

Marilyn agrees and hangs a new bag on the IV pole that Dan mixed for her before going on hiatus. Electrolytes, antibiotics, steroids, and morphine. Plenty of morphine to keep the demons at bay.

28

———

EMANCIPATION

Nightfall overtakes the house, another quiet evening at home alone sans chaos. Although something tells Marilyn that the level of solitude has more to do with a coming torrential downpour than the sudden development of paradise.

She walks from room to room, ensuring that the lights are all turned off and the windows are locked like some kind of maid, though she enjoys the responsibility. She slept soundly every night in her apartment without a second thought of who might be preparing to pounce, but the thought of them sneaking into the house and finishing Fred off feels uncomfortable, a failure of her newfound duties as a quasi-mentor and caregiver. The instincts almost feel maternal, although Fred is at least a few years older than her.

Marilyn passes through the dark kitchen and notices light seeping through the windows from the back porch. A silhouette of a figure sits in a chair without moving, seemingly without noticing her presence. She reaches for the silverware drawer to her right and slowly draws it out to grab a serrated steak knife, having left her own blade in the office. The goal is to take as many of them down as possible before they eventually outnumber her.

She opens the slider door silently with the knife held in front of her chest like a mercenary. "Dan?"

180

"Hi, Marilyn. Have a seat." He sits in one of his wooden patio chairs next to a circular table that holds a fresh bottle of the eighteen-year-old single malt from his office. "I figured you'd be here eventually, so I grabbed you a glass." He tips his own back and takes a drag from a cigar, the smoke of which floats lazily away into the darkness.

"I didn't know you were home. I almost stabbed you."

"Did you? I suppose I deserve it for dragging you into this mess. Have a drink. I'm inviting you this time."

She pulls out another wooden chair across from Dan and pours herself a glass, looking periodically into his eyes all the while. There's a darkness to his face, even in the dim light, and it seems to be deeper than skin-level and from something stronger than the whisky. "Long time, no see."

"I've been busy with patients. Had a few personal things to attend to in the city." He takes another drag of the cigar and downs his drink. "I figured you'd call if you needed anything."

"I didn't. We've been perfectly fine."

"That's good. I'll be home for the next few days now to help." Dan's mannerisms aren't typical of his usually sharp self, his movements too sloppy and his voice lacking wit. He's obviously had a bit much to drink.

"Glad to have you back, but we've been fine. Fred's doing much better."

"Good, very good." He leans forward and fills his glass to the rim and tops off Marilyn's, too. "Do you ever dream about them?"

"Who?"

"The people you've seen die. Do you ever dream about them? Your family and friends."

Marilyn exhales a cloud of condensation that resembles Dan's cigar smoke. A shiver traverses her body, though she prevents herself from showing it. Screams echo in her mind of deeply-buried memories and bottled pain and whispers muted by six feet of soil. "Yes. I see them often."

"And? Do they seem happy?"

"No. Never."

"Hm." Dan puffs the cigar and takes a long sip, staring into some void in the nightscape as if it were speaking back to him instead of Marilyn. "I dream about Vivian almost every night. She never seems happy, either. What do you think that's about?"

"I don't know for sure. Maybe that's just the last impression they left on us, and so it's how we picture them now. Pain, sorrow, agony."

"Yeah. Maybe." His eyes remain pinned on the same spot somewhere among the backyard trees. "It's usually the same dream. A nightmare, really. Vivian comes to me half-skeleton and half her normal self, yet there's something not human about her. She's always crying desperately, pleading for my help, but I can never hear her voice. It's always silent. We can't communicate even though she's *right ... fucking ... there*. You know? And then she starts digging, her bones rattling in the midnight cold, the good half of her body decaying and eroding rapidly in front of me and turning to the very dirt she digs. And there isn't a goddamn thing I can do to help her."

Marilyn sips the whisky without speaking. Dan's words still float among the moisture in the humid air, trapped in stasis, the story alone being cold enough to leave her frostbit.

"Vivian digs her own grave, and I only stand there watching. She weeps and begs for help, for mercy, I know that's what she's saying, but I can only stand on the grass and watch. She's always sad, always distressed, always asking me questions that I can't even hear to answer. And I only stand there, feeling some sort of vacuous anti-pressure in my chest as if my heart is being sucked out through a straw. Yet Vivian continues to dig and dig until the rusted shovel strikes the coffin lid, at which point it's immediately clear of debris and as clean as the day we lowered her into that hole. Then a voice that sounds like my own, though I would never say this to her myself, but it tells her that I can't continue with her, and she must go alone. I find myself trapped in that same nightmare all the time, just the same fucking thing every time." Dan's eye twitches as he empties the glass down his throat, then pours another. The cigar smoke hangs thick and obscures his face behind it into something other than human.

"That sounds awful, Dan."

"It is." He nods. "It is. Had the same dream last night, in fact. The demons in those dreams … they linger all day … It weighs heavily in the morning and remains lodged in there all day like a parasitic black mass feeding off my happiness. My will to continue. Life itself. Before long, that mass becomes a cancer, attacking its own body, and there's nothing anyone can do to help, because there's nothing wrong with you clinically." He continues nodding aimlessly even after he stops speaking. "What about you? What happens in your dreams?"

"They're all faceless, but they just seem really tired, like the type of tired where the light is completely gone from them. I can't tell who each individual person is, but I know their names from memory. Mostly, it's in the same situations where they were killed. The college graduation party when I first met the Butcher. My friends run in slow motion with their screams rebounding inside the room we were in, but they're only shadows of memories at this point. That probably sounds horrible—my murdered friends are nothing more to me now than the stories they created by dying. The stories people tell of them are probably more vivid than how much I actually remember." Marilyn chooses not to disclose the nightmare she had the day Victor was killed.

"That's only normal after all you've been through. We can't cling to every bit of trauma we've ever experienced. Our brains aren't built to withstand that amount of input. We'd explode." He chuckles drunkenly. "Although mine seems dead set on reminding me of my trauma constantly. The more I try to run from those demons, they only seem to get faster and smarter. I feel like I'm playing a game of hide-and-seek against myself."

A gust of wind knocks two barren branches against each other with a whistle and scratching sound, and Marilyn's first thought is that they're being invaded, her internal alarm system already on high alert after thinking Dan was one of them. "How do you feel now? After killing Victor?"

"Better and worse in different ways. The kill was a release, as sick as it may be for me to say, but I fear now that the relief will only be temporary. The sickness of grief felt better until the medicine began wearing off. Years of agonizing and drinking and hoping and praying and renouncing those prayers and rotting in the great creator's forsaken wasteland like red-headed stepchildren have taken their toll. That's the real pain of it all, Marilyn. And all pain must eventually be accompanied by some sort of release. It's inevitable. We can't live that way, in perpetual pain. Believe me. There *has* to be some sort of light at the end of the tunnel, some sort of respite, or existence suddenly becomes a living hell, a never-ending nightmare, the worst sort of drug trip that you could imagine.

"I first felt that release watching Wayne die, absorbing his agonized screams as you sliced his fucking face off. What was it you said in his trailer? Ah, yes. *Cut off his face to see through his eyes.* I realized then, in that moment, that the release we crave must be equal to the magnitude of pain suffered. All the drinking and drugging in the world can't numb this sort of fucked up. It takes the murder of a wicked one to nullify the murder of an innocent. That's why you're so special, Marilyn, far better than me, the fact that you were even able to *appear* unbothered after your world was repeatedly shattered. All it took for me to spiral into chaos was the death of my one true love, the most perfect being to ever grace this desolate world." Dan's eyes glisten for half a second before he blinks them dry and takes a long drink.

Marilyn realizes that no matter how many patients he treats, no matter how many serial killers they dispatch, how many potential victims they save with their work, Dr. Dan the heralded psychologist will always just be a man with a broken heart. He may kill Odessa and all the goats and all the skulls with the wrath of God, but will it really remove the thorn that pains him?

"We're doing the right thing, Dan. You said it yourself. Neither of us have anything to lose except more innocent lives around us. Maybe that light at the end of the tunnel is actually a new horizon."

"There is no horizon. The horizon is hollow. Tomorrow is nothing but a theoretical question, until one day it simply isn't. We never know when our time will come, but the older I get, the more I realize that every day should be considered our last." He lowers his head and rubs his eyes and temples. "I'm sorry. Now I'm just being crotchety and speaking my thoughts out loud. You know, it's wild to think that you're the only person alive I can have this sort of conversation with. Same goes for you. Funny how life works."

Marilyn looks down and stares into the waves in her whisky glass from her slightly shivering hand, then she nods. "So, what's next for us? You're not quitting on me, are you?"

"Quite the opposite. It's more that I fear our work is the only thing keeping me alive." Dan pauses with the frigid breeze and takes the last sip in his glass. He eyes the bottle. "It seems the only logical step forward is to kill them all. Won't be easy, taking on the thirteen of them with only two of us, but we're in knee deep now. You aren't suddenly afraid of dying, are you?"

"No. It's a neutral thought that seems as hypothetical as being alive."

Dan chuckles sloppily. "It's definitely coming one day, but it doesn't have to happen now if we're smart. I just want to know that you're ready to walk that line if need be."

She nods.

"Of course, you are. You're Marilyn fucking Soroka—I shouldn't even have to ask. Give me until tomorrow to think of something. You know I won't put you at unnecessary risk."

A momentary silence shrouds their conversation, mentor and mentee lost in thought until Marilyn leans forward and refills her own glass.

"Your patients that took their own lives—do you think that wears on you the same as all the people I've lost? Maybe you're carrying more baggage than just Vivian."

"You're probably right. The face I show the world is that of an unflappable doctor, and none of us have ever not lost a patient before. But for me to fail so many of them, to let them slip through my fingers, no matter how difficult they were to grasp … Yeah, I'm sure it's done some damage. And my logical sense understands that cleansing the world of killers won't bring back those they've killed, but I have to do *something* about it. I have a lot to atone for."

"I wasn't implying that it's your fault," Marilyn says.

"But it is. My job is to heal broken patients, not healthy ones, yet my desire to continuously move forward never let me look back on them with remorse. It certainly wasn't a lack of caring for them, as much as survival instinct for myself."

"Yes, I understand. Just as it wasn't my responsibility to save my loved ones from the Butcher, though I still wish I could've done something about it. It always felt like more of an inevitability, not something I could control."

"Exactly." Dan nods with eyes half-closed. "If only hindsight could be foresight, but those experiences shaped who we are today. We're going to take down Odessa and the *Famuli Morte* because of it. I always knew she would cause me trouble one day."

Marilyn sits upright at full attention. "What's that supposed to mean?"

Dan sighs. "Nothing. It's not important right now."

"Sounds awfully important. You know her?"

"She was a patient of mine, and an especially troubled one. That was shortly after Vivian died, maybe a year or so. She often tried to turn the situation around on me, what we call deflecting, suggesting that I was projecting my own grief onto her, questioning my motives, implying that I was purposefully making her worse. Then she faked her own death and disappeared."

Marilyn takes a big sip of whisky and drops a small pour into Dan's glass. "You're certain it's the same woman? And how do you know she didn't actually die?"

"Never met another Odessa, and she fits the profile," he shrugs. "A few colleagues also treated her, some at the same time I was, and they reported to me later that they had seen her in the city. They thought maybe we could finally get through to her, but she changed her phone number, address, everything. I never talked to her again. A part of me wondered if maybe she'd truly died and been reborn a new person, hopefully as something better, but now that doesn't seem to be the case. I guess evil won out once again."

"Hm. How did she come to be in your care? Who did she know that was murdered?"

"Her mother. She killed her at twelve-years-old."

Marilyn scoffs. "Jesus. A serial killer in the making from the start. No wonder she couldn't be helped."

"Yeah." He flicks the ash from the end of the cigar over his chair's armrest. "We damn sure tried. All of us. From foster homes and institutions, to her team of doctors that stuck by her side even when she repeatedly pushed us away. Odessa simply didn't want to heal. She didn't think she needed it. You simply can't fix what isn't perceived as broken, no matter how flawed the logic may be."

"Why did she kill her mom?"

"She claimed self-defense. The mom apparently had a series of abusive boyfriends, and she blamed Odessa whenever the relationships fizzled out, starved her, purposefully ruined her clothes and belongings as punishment. That sort of thing. Textbook case of a bad childhood that we deal with fairly often. Very few children kill their parents, however, even when they technically deserve to."

"And now she's a cult leader," Marilyn says. "We can't leave her out there much longer. We have to strike before they do."

"I agree. The iron is definitely hot, and I can't wait to watch them all burn in their furnace."

29

SURMOUNT

"Wake up, Fred." Dan stands at the edge of the bed, looking a bit more haggard than usual after a night of over-indulgence. Otherwise, he appears as a typical shrink in his typical cardigan.

Fred mutters something as his eyes roll behind their fluttering lids. "Huh?"

"Marilyn and I are going into the city for a couple hours. How are you feeling?"

"Better than yesterday, at least."

"That's encouraging," Dan says as he pinches the empty IV bag. "Will you be fine on your own until we get back? I need her with me, if possible."

"No problem. I'll hold down the fort." Fred chuckles as he props himself up on a pillow.

"Great. I'll pump you full of meds before we go. That should easily last until we get home. Call if you need anything else."

"I'd like one of those world-famous Marilyn Soroka sandwiches before you go, if you have the time."

"I didn't know you cooked," Dan says as he swerves around a car going ten miles under the speed limit in the fast lane.

"About as much as you do."

"Nice. So, I have Odessa's patient file stored in the office. That's where I keep the paperwork for the so-called *normal* patients, as in those who needed less intensive treatment, those suffering from less severe psychiatric ailments. The files I keep at home are typically all from serial killer survivors. Not that Odessa didn't need intensive care."

"Right." Marilyn grips the overhead handle above the window, feeling uncharacteristically uneasy being out of control in the passenger seat. "Why do we need the file?"

"I want to double-check it for information that we can use against her. I haven't had any reason to dust it off for nearly ten years, and because of that, I never had a reason to enter it into my database. An old colleague of mine is going to meet us at the office, Dr. Madsen. She also attempted to treat Odessa at the same time I did, and I need you there in case I forget to ask any important questions."

The cityscape enters view as they circle around the last turn of mountains. The tops of the buildings reach high enough to crack the sky if either side were to move closer to the other. A petri dish of predators and victims, innocent bystanders and know-nothings and those who hide their heads in the sand alike. Marilyn swallows hard, feeling like she's returning once again to an old life left behind, an epoch erased, a totally different Marilyn. Like an addict in recovery returning to the root of her addiction, the drug in question being death. The city reeks of it, even through the open air vents, a stench of perpetual degradation and self-inflicted entropy.

"Is Odessa her real name?" Marilyn asks at last as Dan deftly crosses over three lanes toward their exit. He seems abnormally perturbed.

"No, but she legally changed it, so her old name was never of much interest to me. It's in the file." Dan takes the freeway exit and brings the car to a stop behind several other cars waiting at a red light. "Honestly, Odessa's old life was of little concern to me at the time. Sordid past, sure, but that's not uncommon in the mental health field. I was more interested in the person before me, the adult she had become. As far as I was concerned, the real version of her had died with the name change, and Odessa was only another mask to conceal her true face. You know?" He glances at her as the light turns green.

"Yes. I know all too well."

"And now she's orchestrating mass death upon innocent people. I'm starting to consider that maybe her early life was the mask, and Odessa is the true face, the monster that had been chained beneath all along. I should've known there was no cure for a pre-teen murderer, no matter how justified it may have been. Killing another human has to open some kind of door within a person that can't be closed." The car begins to roll, and Dan cackles. "No offense to us."

Marilyn cracks a rare smile. "On the bright side, it couldn't have fucked us up any more than trying to hide how fucked up we were."

"Poetic. And probably true. From a psychological perspective, Odessa's situation is much more akin to those found in severely psychopathic patients. She always fit the mold for a serial killer in the making, meeting the dark triad model to a tee, but we didn't have any hard evidence to suggest violent tendencies to have her committed. As I mentioned before, she blamed me for her problems, suggested there was some sort of coup against her, and believed we only had the worst intentions for her. Narcissism and Machiavellianism, check. As for psychopathy, well ... she murdered her own mother and laughed about it in the courtroom."

Dan drives them through the city streets toward his office where Marilyn first met Deb. Feels like a lifetime ago instead of a week. They pull into the parking lot located on the bottom floor of the office building and exit the car with both of them turning their heads on swivels.

"You got your weapon on you?" Dan asks.

Marilyn pats the lower back portion of her coat. "Always."

"Good." He pats the left side of his chest. "Got mine, too. Don't be afraid to use it. Any one we see could be one of *them*, the Famuli Morte, hiding in sheep's clothing. Everyone is a target, and we still don't know how broad their reach is."

She nods.

Dan leads her across the parking lot, through rows of cars hiding potential assailants waiting to strike, though the pathway is clear. They reach a metal door, opting for the stairwell instead of going through the lobby. He ascends on the right side of the stairs with her directly behind him.

Another metal door opens a few stories above causing them to freeze. Slow steps descend softly toward them from what sounds like two floors above, each one echoing in the concrete silo like a foreboding warning of danger. *Step.*

Dan turns to face Marilyn with his index finger over his mouth. He removes the revolver from his jacket, its stainless sheen shining under the dim overhead light. She does the same with her chef's knife, unsheathing it all the way to the tip beneath the cover of her coat.

Step.

Dan uses both hands to pull back the revolver's hammer silently, the right thumb on the hammer itself with the left beneath it to mute the noise. Then he holds it under the left coat flap to be withdrawn easily in case of danger.

Step.

He motions for them to move forward as if they're back in the woods surrounding Wayne's trailer, on the hunt for a singular killer, harkening back to what might be considered the good old days when not every simple citizen on the street should be treated like their own encroaching grim reaper.

Step.

Dan leads Marilyn up the stairs to the platform between flights where they'll be able to see this person taking the stairs just as they round the corner.

Step.

An elderly woman wearing a shawl rounds the top of the steps on the second floor. She appears startled when she sees them.

Dan keeps his hand on the concealed revolver. "Ma'am."

"Oh, you scared me!" Her voice ricochets off the walls all the way up to the top story. "I don't often run into folks in the stairwell. Nobody takes them anymore," she chuckles.

"That's exactly why we take them. Good for clearing the head."

The woman nods at them with a smile and continues down the steps. Dan eyes her until she walks through the door into the parking lot, then he removes the revolver from his coat and aims it down the stairs.

"Are you going to start shooting old women now?" Marilyn says.

"How do we know she isn't a messenger? They could be coming through to ambush us right now, and then we're definitely dead. I can at least take out six of them."

"Dan ... I think we're fine. How would she have known when to find us taking the stairs? We're fine."

He turns and looks back at her, then scans the stairwell for more sights or noises. "Alright, but I'm keeping the gun out. The idea of rolling the dice with my life is still new to me, and Odessa already knows where my office is."

They continue upward with each footstep echoing, walking toward whatever fate awaits on the other side of the door leading from the fourth floor of the stairs. Marilyn concedes that they could also just as easily be killed in their sleep at Dan's house, ambushed when they get back to the car, or, if her imagination were to get the best of her, they could be set up by one of his patients. Maybe even Fred. But she doesn't tell this to Dan—he might go nuclear with safety measures stricter than a maximum-security prison inside the house. Whatever happens to them will simply happen at some point. The path they've chosen is like playing Russian roulette on a daily basis, and luck can only go so far.

Dan stows the revolver just inside his coat, and he cracks the door open to inspect the hallway. "Looks clear. Keep close." He steps through and keeps his back against the wall, appearing to be in pursuit of a killer rather than walking into his place of employment. The hallway is long and plain, the apotheosis of corporate in one elongated rectangular shape.

They hustle toward Dan's office, the fifth door on the right, as if someone might leap from any of the other office doors and abduct them. There's a golden plate on the door. *Daniel Hudson, Doctor of Psychology.*

Dan fishes the keys from his pocket carefully to not make them jingle, then he slowly inserts one into the door lock. He looks back at Marilyn one last time and raises his eyebrows. The door was locked, which seems to be a good sign.

He enters his office and waits for Marilyn to follow before locking the door behind them. The reception area is quiet. "Where's your receptionist?" she asks.

"I don't have any appointments today, so Carissa is working from home. My office phone routes to a cellphone that I gave her."

"What about your colleague? Aren't we supposed to be meeting someone here?"

"She has a key. We go way back and have collaborated to cross-treat patients for years. Kat? We're here!" Dan walks past the reception desk down the hallway toward the bathroom and knocks on the door. No answer. "Kat? She must be in my office waiting. Kat? Are you here?"

Dan moves quickly past Marilyn, yet she already knows the result. She's seen this movie too many times. He pushes through the office door then his face sours. She follows closely behind to find a beheaded woman in a pantsuit sitting cross-legged on the leather couch, her stiletto on the top foot pointed at them as if she was positioned to do so. The cut is jagged, the skin swollen, and blood coats the couch and wall behind her. It seems to still be damp.

"Jesus Christ," Dan says, his stoic voice warbling beneath the surface. "This is unfortunate."

Marilyn steps closer and notices Kat's hands are folded on her lap like a typical shrink, but there's also a note pinned to her chest by a ballpoint pen stuck through the flesh with *Hudson, Doctor of Psychology* still exposed on its barrel. She leans in further to read the note. "2-2. Love, O. I guess she took offense to your message."

Dan rubs his fingers across his forehead, appearing stressed beneath the surface. "Yeah, well, that was sort of the point. I'm only sorry that my actions got Kat killed. This was a massive mistake on my part, meeting her here, but I didn't think Odessa would expose herself like this."

"I doubt she was even here. She probably sent the minions to do her dirty work."

Dan agrees. "I'm sorry, Kat, for what it's worth, even if you can't hear me. I feel foolish, if it makes you feel any better. Now I'm being out-maneuvered by a *patient*."

Marilyn scans the office, his desk, and the bloodstained carpet for signs of anything at all to jump out to her. There's a partial shoe print in the wet carpet, but they can't get any information from it. There's nothing else to suggest any signs of struggle from Kat, but there might've been enough bodies here to hold her down for the decapitation. Then Marilyn glances at the filing cabinet.

"Dan."

"What is it?" He's still staring at Kat's headless corpse as if it will start talking back.

"I'm assuming your filing cabinets aren't usually missing their drawers."

Dan jumps and turns in one motion with his eyes wide and shocked. "Oh, shit ... Shit, shit, shit, shit, shit!" He lunges toward the cabinets and drops to his hands and knees, searching for any scraps or loose papers left behind.

"What's wrong? So, they came to take her file back—what's the big deal? It's her information, and we already know where to find her."

"It's not *her* file I'm worried about, Marilyn," Dan admonishes from the floor. "They took *all* the files of *all* my patients! They took my tax documents with my home address!" He bolts upright stiff and sweating. "Don't you see? They weren't planning to kill me here, they wanted to find out where I live so they could kill me—"

Dan is interrupted by an alert on his phone that sounds like an alarm. He removes it from his pocket to reveal a notification of a break-in from his home security system. The front door camera shows three goats and three skulls forcing their way in with a fire axe, and then his phone screen transitions to movement in the hallways.

"Dan ... What about Fred? They're going to kill him!"

He shakes his head gravely. "There's nothing we can do from here. Unfortunately, he's a sitting duck."

The skulls kick open every door leading to the spare bedroom hiding Fred, then they kick his down, too. Dan's screen shows Fred lying in bed, passed out and floating amongst the morphine clouds as the Famuli Morte assailants approach. One of the skulls passes the red fireman's axe to a goat, who raises it high and chops through Fred's neck and into the mattress as if he were nothing more than a piece of firewood for their furnace. Blood spouts from Fred's open neck wound in the horizontal position, and it sprays like crimson confetti over the white bedsheets, the headboard, the wall, and spills onto the hardwood floor. The red liquid runs down the wall and headboard like corn syrup, while the droplets puddle and begin to sink into the bedspread.

The same skull grabs Fred's head by the side of it that still has hair and tosses it into a black leather bag that clasps at the top, like something an old doctor would use when making house calls. They exit the room quickly as Fred's headless body, a carbon copy of Kat's sans suit, twitches with one last spurt from the hole in his snipped neck.

Dan turns his phone off and sets it face down on the walnut desk, then he plops down restlessly on the leather sofa without saying another word.

30

DEFENESTRATION

"What are we going to do?" Marilyn asks, her voice crackling with the barely audible wavelength of excitement. "Dan ... Fred is dead. We can't just sit here!"

"I'm thinking."

"They could be coming back here, knowing we're trapped. We have to go."

"I said I'm thinking." Dan presses his palms together and rests the index fingers on his nose. He takes a deep breath and exhales loudly into his hands. "They won't come back here, not right away, at least. They have Fred's head, something they probably already prepared a ritual for, and that should buy us some time for today. It seems to me that the ceremony of the kill is more important to them than some sort of blood lust, meaning they won't immediately come after us like hounds. They also might try to split up and blanket a larger area. It's me they want—you should be safe, for now."

"I didn't get into this with you to be fucking safe, Dan." She sighs, exasperated. "I would rather take them all out and die in the process than live in fear anymore. All those years ... I *was* afraid, but I'd so completely resigned myself to death that the thought of dying couldn't scare me. That's all it was. I've learned that there's much more to life than simply surviving."

"I know you have, and I'm proud of you for that. Truly, I'm amazed at how far you've come. I say we hit them hard where they live. Guns blazing, storm the factory."

Marilyn flashes a full smile for the first time in nearly a decade. "Let's do it. Let's crash the party during their ritual."

Dan returns the grin. He rises from the sofa with a renewed sense of color in his previously pale face, and he scours the office, grabbing personal trinkets and items that seem as if they might be of some importance.

"Not to be callous, but what are we going to do with Kat's body? If we call the cops, they'll obviously suspect you at first. At best, you'll be tied up in the investigation for days, and your face will be plastered all over the news. Not the kind of attention we need."

"Shit, you're right. Well, I can't just leave her in here, either. Carissa will be back in the office tomorrow, and by that point, the place will stink something awful."

"And we can't take her through the lobby. The stairwell obviously can't be trusted."

"No." Dan puts his thinking face back on, the quick calculations dancing behind his eyes. "But the back window by the restroom opens pretty wide."

Marilyn pushes the back-alley dumpster against the rear wall of the office building, already feeling somewhat regretful for agreeing to the plan. *By the time anyone finds her, we'll be long gone,* Dan said. *We don't have time to give her a proper burial.*

She lines the dumpster beneath Dan's fourth story office window, the drop seeming much further from street level. Once they're aligned, Marilyn pulls the steel bin outward by a few feet to account for outward travel, as were Dan's instructions, her slight frame struggling against the weight of the several-hundred-pound container. Whatever the day seemed to have in store when she woke up, defenestration of a decapitated doctor wasn't on the list.

Dan opens the window and leans out with his thumb pointed upward, the sleeve of his cardigan gently flapping in the wind.

Marilyn looks left and right, scanning the alleyway for peering eyes and passersby. She raises her thumb in return.

Dan disappears into the building for a moment, leaving Marilyn destitute in the cold and vulnerable to witnesses, attackers, and nosy-types. Thankfully, none of them come. Kat's body is suddenly expelled from the window without warning, her figure spinning in the wind like something between a starfish and a ragdoll. Marilyn watches helplessly as the corpse drifts outward further and further, yet it's too late to push the dumpster in any more.

Kat's upper half strikes the outer rim of the metal dumpster first, expelling a sprinkler spray of blood into the garbage as if she'd been juiced, and then her body lands on the asphalt with a sickening splat and cracks from bones breaking and joints bending backwards. Marilyn stares at the woman she never had the pleasure of meeting in life, the accomplished and headless woman who's now reduced to extremely pulpy cranberry sauce in a stain-laden back alley.

"Shit," Dan says from the window. "I'll be right down."

Marilyn eyes the roads on both sides of the alley, just waiting for some errant jackass to stumble behind the building, looking to get high, and ruin the entire disposal act. "Any time now, Dan," she mutters.

Another minute passes before he bursts through the back door, red in the face and panting. His arms are full, carrying a bottle of bleach, two white bed sheets, and a box of nitrile gloves. "Ran as fast as I could. We need to move fast."

"You had all that in your office?"

"The bleach and gloves were for cleaning the bathroom, and the sheets were for the many nights I fell asleep on that couch in there. More than I'd care to admit. Come on." He pulls a pair of purple gloves from the box and tosses them to Marilyn, then they both pull them on with several snaps of the nitrile. "This won't be pleasant, but we need to get out of here before the situation turns FUBAR. For now, it's only simply fucked up."

She takes one of the folded bedsheets and carefully tucks the ends of it beneath Kat's mangled carcass as if making a meat bed. Dan helps her with the second sheet, and they lift the corpse to heave it into the garbage. He saturates the blood spatter in the street with bleach directly from the bottle, then he dumps the rest over the front rim of the dumpster and tosses the bottle in with the body.

Marilyn scoffs. "Won't the garbage men put two and two together and assume the blood belongs to the person in the trash?"

"All we need is enough time to get out of here. Besides, the bleach is already working."

She looks down at the asphalt to see an off-brown colored puddle instead of vivid red. The hue continues to fade into something less definable, something amorphous and amoebic.

"And, no offense to the many great sanitation workers out there, but I doubt they're going to do a deep dive into some brownish stain in the road. The city sidewalks are full of mysterious markings. The last thing we need to do is pull a few broken-down boxes from the recycle bin and cover her up, just to be sure." Dan hurries to the dumpster and leans over the edge, coming back with three flattened pieces of cardboard. He covers the majority of Kat's oversized metallic coffin with the boxes and snaps the gloves off, tossing them in behind the refuse.

"Are we good to go now?" Marilyn asks.

"Not quite. I need to go back upstairs and give my office a quick cleaning to be on the safe side. I'll call Carissa and have her cancel all my appointments tomorrow. I need you to wait in the car while I do this. You hear me? Don't leave the car. I'm okay with those ghouls coming back and killing me in my office, but there's no hope left in this world if you're gone. Alright?"

Marilyn agrees solemnly.

"Good. Take the car keys. I won't be long."

Dan approaches the driver's side of his car, his cardigan and hair both disheveled, and he climbs into the seat. "Told you I'd be fast. Anything eventful happen out here?"

"Nothing at all. Just normal city shenanigans. The key's in the ignition."

"Normal is good." He turns the key to fire up the engine, the dramatic rumbling of his old Charger a sign of safety. "I know we're in a mess at the moment, but I promise I'll fix it all. We'll be fine soon."

Marilyn sits quietly in the passenger seat, again uncomfortable with being out of control as they exit the parking lot and pull into the crowded street. "What about Fred?"

"What about him? He's gone."

"His body. What are we going to do with it? We can't just throw it in the garbage at your house like Kat's."

"No, we can't." Dan keeps his sunglassed eyes on the road like a hawk, not once turning to look at her. "He's a low priority at the moment, being isolated inside the house where nobody will find him. We can't even go back there ourselves until the Famuli Morte have been dealt with. I say we hit them tonight before they catch us off-guard."

"Tonight? Without a plan?"

"I'd rather be too soon than too late. I also figure they won't wait long to finish the ritual with Fred's head. They'll all be inside the factory tonight, ready to be killed like prisoners in the gallows line."

Marilyn thinks through the alternatives, maybe picking them off one by one to avoid suspicion, but it would take too long to do so while ensuring their survival. "Let's do it. This might be the best chance we ever have."

Dan nods, still laser focused on the road. "We aren't safe here anymore,

Marilyn. Not while they live. We can't go back to my house, and we can't stay in my office. Although, the city might be the best place to hide in plain sight until we kill them tonight."

"Where do you want to go? We should probably find some place quiet to prepare."

"I was thinking maybe your apartment." He turns and looks at her now, his eyes persuasive even through the sunglasses. "Odessa probably doesn't even know you're involved, unless Victor told her your name specifically. My gut says he didn't—she would've had him killed for letting us walk free."

Her apartment. The notion seems as foreign as returning to her childhood home where only the fading echoes of ghosts linger. Memories of a different time, a different life, as if she herself had been killed and reborn since then. But it makes the most sense. "Sure. There's a spare bedroom, if you need it. As long as you don't mind it being Tara's room."

"Won't be necessary. Either the Famuli Morte die tonight, or something went horribly wrong for us. No quarter."

"No quarter," Marilyn repeats, sounding decidedly unlike herself.

"The further execution of our work depends on it. Either they all die, or we do."

"I want to live free or not at all."

Marilyn notices a smirk creep up Dan's cheek. "That's right. We're at a fork in the road, and I intend to lead us down the right path."

31

CULMINATION

Dan walked Marilyn up the stairs to her sixth-floor apartment with his revolver drawn, just like at his office. He poked around corners carefully like an infantry soldier after each flight, and he pushed her door open and made them wait a full five minutes before entering.

The apartment was exactly as she'd left it however many weeks ago, although it felt more like walking into a well-preserved relic than her old home. Now she sits in the same seat where she watched the Butcher shoot herself, and she inspects the postmodern architecture and interior design that pass as normal to city dwellers. The walls are plain and cold, the view from the windows made up of concrete and other glass panels and steel.

Dan left her there (the safest place he could think of, he said) with the revolver and made one final supply run to prepare them for an evening raid, assuring her he would be back well before dusk. Just a few small things to do, he said. She's learned that he'll never be forthcoming with information until he has something to actually share, so she stopped asking. For as brooding and stoic as Dan can be, he's also the most cunning and clever man she's ever met.

Marilyn thinks of what they could call themselves as a duo, something to rival Famuli Morte as an intimidating team name for all the predators out there to fear. The Bloodhounds, Grim Pursuit, and Vigilante Vigil all made her cringe, so she stopped trying. Dan and Marilyn will do, nondescript enough to leave killers guessing, and anyone who doesn't know will find out soon enough.

The front door handle turns, and Marilyn leaps off the couch with the gun aimed at the entryway. Her hand is steady, at ease, ready to fire at will.

"You didn't lock it?" Dan asks with his back toward her as he closes and locks the door. He's carrying an overstuffed plastic bag tied at the top, with a paper bag secured under his arm.

She shrugs. "Old habits. Did you get everything you wanted?"

"I did. Chinese food with a few containers of egg drop soup."

Marilyn scoffs. "You put your life at risk for some orange chicken and soup?"

"Plus a few other things in the car. And this is the *best* Chinese food in the city. You don't want to die hungry, do you?"

Her stomach feels like it's being eviscerated from the inside out. "No, I'm starving from hiding bodies all day. What else do you have there?"

Dan grabs the bottle by the neck and allows the bag to drop like a pair of too-big pants without a belt. He smiles, the sense of boyish glee he displayed when they first met coating his face, and, for just a moment, that sharp-edged predatorial glint in his eyes is gone. "The *really* good stuff. I splurged a bit. Figured now's the time."

Marilyn squints, trying to read the label from across the living room. "What is it?"

"Twenty-five-year Islay single malt. You can fix yourself a plate while I pour the glasses." Dan sets the bulging plastic bag on the coffee table and turns to rifle through Marilyn's cabinets, same as the Butcher did moments before her death.

"You mean I won't die hungry *or* sober?"

"Not on my watch." He continues searching aimlessly without turning around, without asking for help.

Marilyn scoffs quietly to leave his ego unbruised. "Here, let me do it. It's my place, after all, I'll be the host." She stacks two glasses, forks, and spoons on a pair of plates and places them next to the bag of Chinese food. "There you go.

Dig in."

Dan breaks the foil seal on the single malt first before touching the food, then he pours a couple fingers in each of their glasses with a genuinely joyful smile. "A toast to us before we eat. You know, Vivian would've thought I was crazy for spending over five hundred bucks on one bottle of whisky, but the importance lies in the circumstances, not the details. I've never been one to make decisions based on monetary value, or lack thereof, but rather the significance of said circumstances surrounding an event. Weddings, birthdays, holidays, graduations. Each of these signifies a certain passing of time or effort in order to properly celebrate them, and some require both. Marriages and graduations—a culmination of years' worth of singular dedication toward a goal with lifelong rewards. Birthdays and holidays to celebrate another full year with our loved ones—sorry, no offense. Our goal is similar to all four of these things wrapped in one, a lifetime of circumstances and situations we didn't ask for that led us to this moment, an impossibly complicated butterfly effect and spider web interwoven to present us with this unique opportunity—an opportunity to save innocent lives with righteous justice. I'll drink to that."

Dan tips his glass back slowly and takes a sip with a sigh of satisfaction.

Marilyn points the rim toward him in a cheers motion, then she does the same. "Tastes like a campfire and Band-Aids. Almost like someone threw those Band-Aids into the campfire, and now we're drinking the juice of it."

"Sure is good, though, isn't it?"

"Surprisingly. Thanks for the last supper, Dan." Marilyn grabs her plate and silverware, and rips the top of the bag open without untying it. "Thanks for everything, really."

"It's me that needs to thank *you* for making my dream a reality. A void opened within me when Vivian died, the type of emptiness that seemed incurable, but where there's life there's hope. And I'll stake my own life to ensure a safer future for others. That's directly because of you, Marilyn. You planted your flag publicly on the side of righteousness and others followed."

She scoops a forkful of orange chicken on her plate and raises an eyebrow. "Yeah. Although, sometimes I wonder how many people took that notion as a challenge to be *worse* than the Butcher. Did I really help or hurt people?"

"Not for us to decide. Their actions were their own, just as yours belong to you. An alcoholic is still an alcoholic even if they relapse because they saw a beer commercial on TV, you know? It doesn't absolve responsibility." Dan piles his plate high with orange chicken, chow mein, and broccoli beef, staring at the meal as if it's the best thing he's ever seen. "Anyway, it's a dirty process, but the end justifies the means. Someone on our side has to get their hands dirty to see any sort of progress. The police would cuff the entire Famuli Morte and walk them into the station like a group of angsty kids who got into an argument at recess. People would celebrate those savages like anti-heroes but not after we get done with them. Nobody will even know their names."

"Root and stem, like you said. The city might finally find some peace until the next batch of savages pops up." Marilyn takes her first bite of orange chicken and her eyes widen. "I hate to admit it when you're right, but this *is* pretty damn good."

Dan bows his head slightly as he chews. "Best in the city. Almost makes the thought of potentially dying tonight seem regretful, yet the food may not be as good without walking that tightrope between life and death. Try the chow mein."

She scoops a serving of noodles from the box with her fork and swirls them around the utensil to have a bite. "Mm. Sorry, I might have to cancel on you tonight. Can't risk never eating this again." She smiles as her lower jaw moves up and down.

"Was that a *joke*? From *Marilyn Soroka*? Now I know we're in the end times." Dan leans back and cackles, the type of warm laugh only shared between true friends. The type of laugh he might've shared with his wife, back before the brutal ways of this wicked world chewed him up and spit him out. Maybe Marilyn might've made an even funnier joke before the same happened to her, but she doesn't remember anymore. Doesn't matter now.

"I can be funny, when I want to. There just hasn't been much to laugh about these days."

"That's where you and I disagree, my friend. Once we lose laughter, it's all over. There's a joke to be had for every situation, every circumstance, even the darkest of them. The darker, the better, the more healing, that's what I think. What happened to the Butcher, after all she put you through—fucking hilarious."

"It was pretty funny, I guess," Marilyn says as she takes another sip of campfire-tinged whisky. "It felt more like I was watching a movie than anything."

"Yeah, a comedy. I could only imagine seeing her so incredibly distressed, so distraught, that she shot herself in front of you just to prove a point. I'll never feel an ounce of sympathy for any of them, and I invite you to howl mockery at their every misfortune alongside me. It's healing. It's growth."

"I guess I just felt relief. I wasn't really happy or sad, just glad that it was all finally over. Or so I thought at the time."

Dan holds a finger up while he chews, pausing the conversation at that thought until he swallows. "It's never over. We're only shuttling from one tragedy to the next like wayward tumbleweeds with brief lapses of happiness in between. Relief—tension and release like we talked about before. Those are the moments to revel in, the moments that remind us why we're wired to endure the many storms that come our way. Like this Chinese food. It's a small remembrance of why life is worth living."

"This whisky ain't half bad, either, once you get used to the Band-Aid taste." Marilyn closes her eyes as she takes a sip and allows the fiery liquid to roll down her throat. "I get that, reveling in the beautiful moments. I mean, I wouldn't have understood before, only recently, but it makes sense to me now. Just a few months ago, even the most beautiful moments felt like a façade. A Trojan horse concealing a cavalcade of horror."

"You've been reborn. I can see the change, and it's stunning. Life is about balance in all aspects, though it's unfortunately also prone to asymmetry from time to time. And with that asymmetry the occasional stunning imbalance sometimes follows, and, every so often, it can shatter us into tiny bits of who we used to be. We then either remain a collection of fragments, missing too many pieces to properly reform, or we climb from the ashes as an evolution of our former selves. Then comes genesis."

Marilyn stares intently, unsure if Dan is talking about himself or her or any number of clients he's treated as a professional. Must be easily in the hundreds. *Genesis*. "And? What's the distinction? What determines whether someone remains broken or reincarnates into their new self?"

"I've had that same conversation with myself for years. What causes some to frantically seek a way out, be it via drugs or other vices or worse, while others willingly walk through the fire just to see what's on the other side? I'm not sure there's an easy answer or at least nothing I've come across yet."

"Give it your best shot."

Dan stabs his fork through a piece of orange chicken, beef, and broccoli, then he takes it all in one bite. His plate is empty now, and he begins to refill it with seconds. "I used to think it might be due to willpower, or lack thereof, or maybe simply dumb luck to find our way out of the flames. Now I believe that it's just how we're wired. Distress versus eustress, remember?"

Marilyn nods. "Yes, I remember. I apparently don't experience distress when normal people would."

"Exactly. That's not to say that one is better than the other, but some people are willing to endure the pain for the prospect of growth, and others would prefer relief by any means necessary. I used to think I was lucky for being one of the former, but eustress is still *stress*. It's essentially a compulsion to keep moving forward, no matter the cost, and it still takes a toll."

A door slams upstairs, causing Dan to leap up, revolver drawn, and aim it at the entryway.

Marilyn chuckles. "You really aren't used to the apartment life, are you? That was just another nameless person coming or going. Happens all the time."

"That loud?"

"All hours of the day. People work weird hours, come home late from get-to-gethers, and who knows what else. Maybe affairs."

"Jesus." Dan scratches his beard stubble with an eyebrow raised. "And you never think the noises might be something bad? Someone coming for you?"

"I don't think about them at all. I barely even hear the noise anymore, even in the dead of night. A few hundred people live in this building alone."

"You're a different breed, Marilyn, truly special. I don't know how you do it."

She looks down at her plate, mostly empty now, with a silent longing for the days when she *wasn't* special. She was simply Marilyn Soroka, an unknown, the idealistic college student and psychology major who still held reverence for the field before the professionals inadvertently made her loathe everything about her life. Maybe it was the Butcher's fault for killing everyone in her circle or maybe it was her own for shutting down in the name of self-preservation to guard against outside influences. That's when life started to head south for years to come.

"Do you want any more food before I eat it all?" Dan asks.

"No, thanks. I'm stuffed. Here's to hoping we get to eat the same meal again tomorrow night."

He nods and smirks. "You're ready to go, then? It's nearly dark."

She downs the rest of her glass and slams it down on the table. "I'll take a refill first and then we can go. I don't want to die never tasting good whisky again. Seems like the worst sort of tragedy."

32

BACKLASH

"You're sure of the plan?" Dan asks. They stand at the trunk of his car parked just off the main road. A steady flow of traffic streams by on the other side of the bushes.

"I'm sure. Ready as I'll ever be."

"If we don't make it back here ... Well, it's been an absolute pleasure." He leans in and hugs Marilyn tightly, which would normally cause her to recoil as if she were in the jaws of Death itself. Instead, she embraces him back, her arms wrapped tightly around Dan's ribs.

"Likewise. But we'll be fine. You haven't steered me wrong yet."

He releases his grip and nods with a smile. "Here's what else I picked up today." Dan pops the trunk and shines a flashlight into the hole, revealing two large guns, one with a scope, a pair of vests, an ammo can, and a tactical backpack.

"Machine guns? How the hell did you find those in the city?"

"It's an assault rifle, an M4 to be precise, and it was at my house. My dad was an Army Ranger. He left his collection to me when he passed." Dan reaches into the trunk and grabs the gun without the scope and hands it to Marilyn. "Here, this one's for you."

"I get an M4, too?"

"It's a shotgun, twelve gauge, and be careful with it. She kicks like a mule."

Marilyn holds the dark gray shotgun in her hands, staring at its many parts and components as if they were some foreign, advanced technology. "How do I use it?"

"The simple answer: point it at the bad people and fire." Dan takes the twelve gauge from her, pressing the butt of it into his inner shoulder. "Make sure you have it in the meat of your arm so it doesn't dislocate your shoulder. Then you pull the forend here back and forward again to cock it, the sound of which should be enough to scare any self-respecting wrong-doer into acting right, then you point it at your target and squeeze the trigger. Six pounds of pressure is all it takes to end a life. Make sure it's the right life to take." He hands the shotgun back to Marilyn proudly and watches her practice the exact motions he just showed her. "Careful, it's already loaded."

She nods, her left hand on the forend, the right resting on the grip and trigger, and she points the gun at a bush with her left eye closed like she's seen in action movies.

Dan chuckles. "That won't be necessary. Anything even close to where you shoot won't be walking again. The shotgun is the perfect defense weapon—versatile, powerful, resilient. Ready to go out of the box, just point and shoot, and that's why I brought it for you. Anyone moves out of turn, you light 'em up." He grabs the M4 from the trunk and stares at it with admiration. "This here's a weapon built for war. My dad made me shoot it a million times, or so it seemed, until my aim was impeccable. Then he moved me back further until I hit the target over and over. This rifle in my hands will be the end of the Famuli Morte ... and, right now, that makes me their god."

Marilyn feels a sense of excitement overtake her as her heart knocks twice in her chest. She and Dan are cowboy and cowgirl, riding toward danger with their guns drawn, ready to die gracefully in the name of righteousness if the moment calls for it. Though the world's benevolence seems to be on their side, the united will of all its people who would rather not live in fear of being murdered for sport. "I'm ready. Are you?"

Dan scoffs. "I've been ready for ten years. This is the moment I've dreamed of since, and now it's here." He empties the trunk of its contents, tucking several spare magazines into his belt, then he tosses Marilyn a vest. "Put that on. I don't anticipate them having guns, but worst case, it will protect your vitals from stab wounds, too."

"Thank you." She inspects the vest carefully to understand how the Velcro should fit around her chest, then she unfastens it and fits it around her torso as Dan does the same. "I'm ready to blow these fuckers away."

"Good. All we have to do is make it inside the factory without incident, and the rest should go smoothly."

They wade their way through dry bushes and gullies on their way toward the dark shadow of a factory that looms maybe a mile away from their position. The building lacks light, just as they suspected, as the Famuli Morte prepare to perform their business in the cover of darkness.

Dan and Marilyn move quietly, careful not to step on dry brush that makes a crunch to carry over the open plain, although she assumes the killers couldn't hear anything this far out from inside the mausoleum-like building. They keep low, their guns and heads pointed at the ground for maximum concealability amongst the cover of dead foliage.

Left, right, left, right, they continue in lockstep toward the foreboding factory as armed assailants, in their own right, prepared to kill the killers that haunt the somber nights of so many citizens who don't even know exactly what they're afraid of. Marilyn remembers the feeling, secretly fearing the darkness that could be festering inside anyone beyond their cozy apartment, and her childhood home before that. Small circles of safety that likely weren't actually all that safe in retrospect.

The factory grows larger on the field's horizon, its rustic steel construction seemingly a shade of navy blue in the distance. Marilyn shoulders the shotgun over her left arm to feel for the birchwood handle holstered on the back of her belt, a safety statement as they traverse the darkness into the maw of death. Her outlook on their survival feels just a bit better, enough so that she can hold her head that much higher as they march. *Everything will be just fine*, she continues to remind herself, the subtle knock behind her ribs a foreign reaction when staring into the eyes of oblivion.

Dan stops walking and drops to one knee, so she does the same. He pivots in the hard-packed dirt to face her with his head and the rifle held down low and shoulders hunched, then he raises his right thumb. Marilyn raises hers back.

"*Stick to the plan,*" he whispers almost inaudibly. "*This is the end zone.*" Then he smiles. It's a genuine smile, wide and joyful despite that vicious glint in his eyes that's magnified in the moonlight. The duality of Dan's two inner faces encapsulated in one expression. The smile melts into something made of steel, something barbaric. Then he spins around, facing the factory again, and rises.

Marilyn follows suit and stands tall, keeping a close distance of three feet behind Dan as he walks. They're within a hundred yards of the building now, where its shadows would've extended only a few hours ago, yet he maintains a slow and controlled pace toward the sprawling effigy.

He points them toward the rear of the factory with his index and middle fingers extended, although Marilyn studied the plan obsessively, and she already knows the moves he'll make before they're executed. The front door is typically locked like a bank vault, but there's a standard metal door in the back with nothing but a latch and a circular, keyed lock that can be easily picked. He took photos of the door the last time they were here with Deb, and he brought a lock picking kit that should grant them entry into the factory just outside the ritual room.

A flickering of orange flashes through the high windows of the back third of the metallic factory, signaling that the ritual has already begun or at least is in its early stages. Dan lowers his head again and rushes forward in a low combat glide, gripping the rifle in both hands and moving swiftly toward the towering walls to round the rear corner.

He slings the M4 on his shoulder by its strap, then pulls the kit from his belt and fiddles with a tension wrench, hook, and rake pick for several moments before the lock pops free. "Keep your eyes peeled for assailants in the dark," he said back in her apartment. "I'm not an expert locksmith. It won't exactly be a simple task."

Dan pulls the door open and ushers Marilyn inside with the butt of his rifle pressed into his hip, aimed toward the inside of the building. She shuffles through the doorway, which they leave open to not risk any more noise. None of them will leave alive anyway, he had said.

They walk through an abandoned conference room, the chairs and elongated desktops coated in dust, and follow the beckoning call of chanting voices. The ritual room that contains the furnace is the last main room in the factory, and the echoes of the Famuli Morte ring louder throughout the catacombs as they draw closer.

"Grant me that your infinite power and strength may be the shield and sword of my inner will ..."

Dan raises the M4 to his shoulder and holds it steady with his left hand as the right reaches under his jacket, and he pulls two black cylindrical canisters into view. Then he smirks sharply and pulls out a third, passing it to Marilyn. "Concussion grenades to disorient them. Just pull the pin and throw when I do," he whispers, his voice drowned out by the thirteen voices chanting loudly.

"Transcend me so that my spirit never fails in the true purpose of my life and that my actions and feelings may be equitable as your sword of justice."

Dan nods, holding both grenades in one hand with his fingers looped through the metal pins. "Pull."

He yanks the pins free as Marilyn does the same, and they bounce the grenades across the concrete floor and take cover behind the partition wall with their ears covered. The chanting ceases abruptly as the metallic cylinders clink over the grimy cement.

The high windows rattle and blow out of their frames from the blast. The sonic explosion leaves a ringing in Marilyn's ears, even through the cover of her hands pressed against them. There's moaning and groaning from the other side of the wall, and she and Dan raise their guns to their shoulders, ready to rock. They round the partition wall into the clouded great room, where the fire of the furnace glows with a soft, orange light bouncing off the concrete.

Dan fires three rounds into the first goat head he sees, the body already lying on the ground from the concussion blast. It's a warning shot to the other twelve to signify dominance that serial murder will no longer be tolerated in their town as long as he's still standing. "Howdy, motherfuckers."

33

INEVITABILITY

"On your knees, all of you!" Dan shouts, his M4 rifle aimed into the crowd of cloaked murderers stuck in fetal positions. "I said right fucking now!" He fires another shot into the hip of a skull laying on its side and rocking back and forth grasping its head.

Another skull on the far side of the room, near the furnace, leaps to its feet and charges them with a blade drawn. Marilyn steps forward and fires the shotgun into the skull's chest, lifting it off its feet and causing it to land flat on the concrete floor in a splayed star pattern. A spattering of blood showers the floor next. She approaches the fallen savage, stepping her boot into the speckled chest wounds, then she fires another shell through the skull mask as the other eleven cower with their heads bowed. She stares into the red and white mess of eviscerated flesh and skull matter with a now familiar feeling rising in her chest. Two down.

A tall, slender figure wearing a velvety black cloak and gold Venetian-styled mask rises and saunters from the shadows beyond the furnace. "Do as he says. On your knees before you all find yourselves murdered."

"Odessa. So good to see you again," Dan says as he trains the rifle on her. "Looks like you haven't changed one damn bit."

"Dr. Hudson. Seems like you still use your patients as disposable commodities to fit your needs. How *Machiavellian* of you."

He chuckles with a sinister snarl that doesn't sound quite like him. "I should say the same. This is the end, Odessa. You're all going to die mercilessly."

"Oh. Is that so? By my count, we outnumber you eleven to two."

"Hm. Do any of you have guns hidden behind those cloaks?"

Odessa scoffs behind her gold mask, the echo of which lingers in the hollow room. "I'm afraid we don't."

"Then I'd say we outnumber you with sheer strength alone. We're going to execute you one by one until this city is safe again. And I'm going to enjoy the hell out of it."

"No sudden movements, do you all hear me? I'll blow your skulls out across the concrete!" Marilyn shouts, her voice carrying as she pumps the shotgun and the spent shell bounces on the floor.

"Oh, my dear. It's so good to finally meet you." Odessa steps forward, her voice both soothing and oppressive. "You would be *great* with us, Marilyn. We don't look down upon your predisposition towards death here."

Marilyn swings the shotgun toward Odessa's chest region. "Don't move. I'm itching to blow a hole in you."

Odessa's body language softens. "I'm assuming Dr. Hudson didn't tell you—I was the one who suggested vigilantism to him, that there were people in this world who deserved to die. He disagreed at the time, but it seems he's since had a change of heart."

"Always the manipulator, this one," he chuckles. "If only it were that simple."

"Then why don't you explain it to me in simpler terms? Or are you not the pompous, self-righteous psychiatrist I remember? Go on, talk down to me."

"Yes, Odessa," Dan sighs, "we talked about all the people *you* believed deserved to die. Your father for abandoning you, your sister for hiding during your beatings instead of defending you, your mother's many despicable boyfriends for driving her to hurt you." He squints his eyes in a showing of repressed rage that appears to be boiling to the surface.

"And what gives you, a simple psychiatrist, the right to choose who lives and dies? Why is your judgement more valid than mine?"

"We murder killers to save lives. Nothing more, nothing less. You kill people who piss you off for whatever odd reason. We aren't the same." Dan inhales deeply, then releases the breath in a sudden whoosh of air. "I truly felt sympathy for you when we met, Odessa. I did. I didn't necessarily agree with you killing your mother from a principled standpoint, but I understood. Where else is an emaciated and neglected child to turn except outward? I respected your willingness to fight back, to take control when most adolescents don't know any better but to accept inevitability and cower. But *this*? Odessa, there's no defending what you're doing here."

She laughs behind the gold mask, her voice muffled like one of their strangulated victims. "The very nature of the inner self prevents any other living being from understanding it in full. Isn't that what you said to me? My mother deserved her death more than any of the miscreants that you've been wasting your time pursuing. Her demise saved my life from certain self-extinction, which freed me to pursue my eventual destiny here, with my new family. The Famuli Morte."

A shotgun blast rings through the massive room, reverberating sharply off the metal walls. Another skull slumps forward with the back of its black mask blown out in a viscous red jelly concoction. The savage lies still on its chest, head cocked to one side, blood seeping through the small holes produced by escaped pellets in the white skeleton face like rolling tears of crimson. The forend slides back with a distinctive click, followed by the sound of a plastic shell ricocheting across concrete.

"That's enough pontificating bullshit for one night," Marilyn decrees as a thin trail of smoke rises from her gun's barrel. "I came here to exterminate killers, and I don't give a fuck about the trauma that drove you to become who you are." She stomps the factory floor with each forceful step forward, and she drives the heel of her black boot into the side of a goat's head then blows a twelve-gauge slug through the boot print. The forend cocks, the shell hits the ground, then another slides into position.

"I yield! That's enough bloodshed for one day." Odessa raises her arms upward at right angles awkwardly like a trident, her hands covered in black leather gloves. "I'm going to assume that you'll kill every one of us in this room."

Dan nods. "Sure as the sun rising each morning. Count on it."

Odessa steps backward subtly, but Marilyn notices. "There are more of us out there—the Famuli Morte doesn't end within these walls. Execute everyone in this room, but spare me so I can lead you to the others. You can kill them, too, kill them all, but you'll need me to root them out." She shuffles backward another couple inches.

"Ha! I almost forgot how ruthlessly manipulative you can be." Dan's cackles echo long after they leave his mouth seemingly in conjunction with the furnace fires roaring behind its metal grate. He aims the M4 at her. "I would've been a dead man long ago if I trusted every psychopath in my company."

"And what about Marilyn? You trust her?"

"With my life, obviously. You'd be surprised how well-adjusted she is given the amount of death she's seen. Unlike you."

Odessa lowers her hands slowly. "You *like* death. Don't you, Marilyn? That's why you can't seem to stay away from it. You find comfort in its cold finality, don't you? Shoot this lunatic doctor in the head and live a life of freedom for the first time. Release yourself!"

"Shut your mouth, bitch," Marilyn seethes. "Not another word."

"All you have to do is point your gun. Shoot him dead. Finally release that demon you've been trying desperately to keep chained because I know it's in there. I see it."

Marilyn turns her head toward Dan, who looks at her with his rifle still trained on Odessa. His brows are furrowed with the same predatorial intensity, but he cracks a small smile. Then he nods.

Marilyn kicks a goat in the back of its head, propelling it forward flat on the concrete, then she stomps its skull with primal screams that carry throughout the factory until the goat's skull audibly cracks. She flips the body over and crushes the nose of the mask in with her heel. Another squelchy crunch, followed by another, and another. The beastly wails cease.

"You'll have to forgive my partner. She can be a bit brash when unchained, but I'm rather fond of her." Dan smirks in the fire light, his cheek pressed against the butt of the M4.

Odessa holds her gaze, hidden behind the golden mask like something less than human, a graven image in the dark of something below a human god. "Go on, then. Do what you must. But be warned, for our every action holds equitable consequence. This is not the end."

"I'm well aware. The heavy weight of my great many sins hides my benevolence in their shadows. This is my cross to bear as he who straddles the line between both light and dark, though I'm prepared to pay my penance in full. Are any of you?" Dan says.

Several goats and skulls shudder on their knees like cattle for the slaughter. Odessa remains still. "Nunc!" she screams. They rise to their feet hastily and converge in a lengthy line to block Odessa, charging toward Dan and Marilyn. Odessa takes a bullet through her arm and jerks as if shot again as she drops down low and rolls out of sight while the firing commences into the crowd.

Dan sends military-style rounds through the backs and heads of goats and skulls, while Marilyn fires slugs that tear through flesh like buzzsaws and create exit wounds that burst like M-80s. The killers fall flat in lifeless heaps two by two, their corpses piling rapidly on a hill of carrion until nothing left in the room remains moving. "Find her!"

Marilyn dashes around the mound of bodies toward a metal plate in the floor. She throws the door open and slides down a short, wall-mounted ladder into a crawl space that she has to hunch to fit inside. Dan follows closely behind. The tunnel resembles an access point for machine maintenance, with valves lining the walls and thick, dusty power lines overhead. "There."

A black-cloaked body wearing a golden Venetian mask lies in the tunnel beside a man slumped against the opposite wall. Marilyn shuffles forward with her shotgun drawn and pointed at the prone carcass, and she flips the mask off to reveal a woman's face coated in spatter. Her throat is slit, with the wound pumping the last bits of blood over her chest and onto the concrete floor. Just like Deb. She still holds the knife in her left hand, the blade and leather glove both coated in crimson.

The man's face is pale, his open eyes dim and listless, and at least a half-dozen leaking stab wounds garnish his chest. Ligature marks adorn his wrists, though they lay free at his sides with no other evidence of the rope that was used.

"What do you think?" Marilyn asks. "That her?"

"Hard to say beneath the blood." He scoots forward and drops to one knee to inspect closer. "Looks like her, yet she always was quite the chameleon. Odessa always seemed to look different every time I saw her."

"What about him? Did they kill each other, or is this a murder-suicide?"

Dan presses his thumb to the upper edge of her throat and pulls the wound open. "The upward angle of the slice would suggest a suicide, but again, there's no telling with Odessa. She was the definition of chaos, with every move seemingly more surprising than the last." He wipes his thumb on the cloak then pulls the mask back down over her dead face. "Let's get her upstairs with the others. Leave him."

Marilyn grabs Odessa's right shoulder while Dan takes the left. She's shockingly light as they pull her across the slick cement coated with grime and old machine oil. Marilyn freezes in position while they approach the few stairs leading toward the great room. "Fred."

Fred's head rests on a stack of square stone plates with a dim candle burning beside both of his ears. His eyes are closed with dark parabolas descending beneath them down to his sagging cheeks, and the cut where his head was severed has begun to rot with shades of green and purple reaching up to his scorched jaw.

"We interrupted the ritual—they never sacrificed his head. This poor schlub behind us was probably next in line to be murdered, so Odessa left him with a parting gift."

Marilyn stops at the stairs with her hand resting on the upper rung. "Do you believe what she said about the Famuli Morte continuing on? Do you think there are more of them out there? Maybe she killed this guy to leave behind for whoever comes next."

"No, I don't believe it. She was always full of delusions about being some sort of demigod. Like I said before, she's the apotheosis of the dark triad—narcissism, psychopathy, and Machiavellianism. Those traits tend to lead one to believe things we would refer to as batshit. Sacrificing dead bodies to Death? Esoteric religious rituals, infernal icons, occult ideologies. Definitely batshit. Let's get her out on the floor with the rest."

Marilyn nods and ascends the short ladder to climb back to the main floor. Dan squats to a knee and hoists Odessa's torso over his shoulder and lifts her left arm upward for Marilyn to help pull, then he forces her corpse through the open metal plate.

Marilyn yanks the lifeless body free and drops it like a sack of cement mix, causing a cloud of dust on the floor to expel from both sides of Odessa. Dan follows through then pats the front of his duster, his face simultaneously distracted and focused on something behind Marilyn.

"What is it?" she asks.

"We've got a straggler." He walks past her, his boots echoing ominously as he raises his M4 atop his shoulder with the barrel pointed upward and his finger on the trigger.

A goat crawls forward inch by inch, digging its nails into the grease-stained cement floor to will itself to freedom. Dan steps on the back of the goat's ankle, and a shiver of panic shakes its body. He flips the goat over by the gun-shot shoulder and slams it on its back, then yanks the rubber mask from its head.

Marilyn approaches and joins Dan by his side, standing over the fear-stricken killer with her shadow obscuring his features in darkness. She can see that his chin is soaked in blood running from his quivering mouth.

"Not so fun being on the victim's side, is it? What's your name?" Dan asks.

"Please …"

"Please? Your name is Please?"

The unmasked goat swallows hard with a visible convulsion. "Please, just let me go. You proved your point. I'll … I'll never kill again."

"You have one opportunity to speak your last words, to repent for your countless sins, and your only response is to grovel like a sniveling little asshole?" Dan lowers the rifle and pushes the bore of the barrel into his cheek hard enough to create ripples in the sweat-glistened skin.

"Please … Please!"

"You're pathetic. Be honest with me—what did you do when your victims begged for their lives?"

The nameless killer sniffles as if he's going to cry. "I would get excited and kill them anyway."

"Thank you." Dan pulls the trigger, sending an explosion of sound and flesh and bone bits and concrete pebbles propelling from the exit wound. The echo of the blast lingers in Marilyn's ears. "No quarter. Shoot the rest again."

"Gladly," Marilyn says. She quickly walks through the aisle and deposits five more shotgun slugs into the backs of skulls of killers and sympathizers alike before her gun goes click. Empty.

Dan takes the rest, stepping on their necks to be sure they won't move again as he blows the backs of their heads out with military rounds until all twelve goats and skulls have been permanently immobilized in puddles of their own inner filth. Odessa lies to their left, her face and head still intact. "Here comes the fun part." His face contorts into an expression of demonic glee, obscured in the fire's flickering shadows, his smile pulling upward into sharp corners that make him look like a new person. "Toss them all in the furnace."

Marilyn returns the grin. "Divine justice."

She grabs the shoes of the first skull, and Dan grabs its shoulders. They carry the cadaver to the roaring furnace and drop it on the floor so Dan can open the oven's door. He wraps his hand in the lower portion of his duster and grabs the scorching handle to swing it upward. Then the skull is rocked back and forth by its appendages and tossed in the furnace like a heavy trash bag into a dumpster.

They grab a nearly-headless goat, what's left of its skull jagged and dripping and dangling from the extension of flesh protruding from its neck like gelatin—the result of the twelve gauge, to be certain—and they heave it, too, into the furnace. The fire burns brightly with fresh fuel loaded in the flames, human logs that ignite as if they were soaked in gasoline. Physically human, at least.

Dan and Marilyn toss in another goat, then another skull, and so on and so forth until the air in the factory is rank with the stench of death, the pungent scent of boiling flesh and singed hair and enkindled teeth. The purification of organic matter into an ashen substance that ceases to be human yet no longer classifies as anything else but the residual dust of past lives left behind. The echoes of their grisly actions reflect into eternity.

"That only leaves Odessa, the full-headed bitch responsible for this mess." Dan spits on the floor to his side.

"What do you want to do with her?"

"I have an idea … but we have to be careful not to burn her entire body just yet. You take her head, and I'll grab her feet." Dan leads Odessa by her bottom half to the furnace, placing her legs in the fires that lap at the fabric of her cloak like ravenous piranhas. "Help me slide her forward, just a bit more."

Marilyn does so, pushing Odessa by the shoulders until her neck rests on the door's landing plate, and her head dangles beyond the opening.

"Right there," Dan says as he extends his duster's sleeves past his hands. He grasps the handle of the furnace door and swings it downward like a sledgehammer onto Odessa's breathless throat. Then he raises it high and brings it down again with the squelch of smashed fruit. And he does so again. And again. And again, until her head pops free and rolls across the squalid floor toward them, the gold Venetian mask and hood still in place. "She doesn't deserve the ending she craved, at the feet of some demon to serve in death."

Dan kicks the head in the direction of the steel plate then he picks it up by the handful of spinal column exposed from her disguise. He flips opens the door and tosses it into the maintenance crawlspace with the unnamed man and Fred. Marilyn hears the dilapidated rolling of a misshapen severed head traversing the hallway before Dan slams the steel door shut in an emphatic act of finality. Closure.

34

REVOLUTIONARY

"Do you feel it? The tranquility in the air, the peace. It's almost like there's a renewed sense of balance that was immediately restored the second we rid this world of the Famuli Morte." Dan bites off the head of a cigar and spits it into the bushes, then he pulls a metal lighter from his duster and ignites it. The M4 is slung over his shoulder as he leans against the hood of his old muscle car and takes a long draw.

Almost. "Yeah, I feel it. Feels like a cold breeze on a winter night."

He laughs, the smoke pouring from his mouth in differing bursts of volume. "Always the smartass. But that's why we all love you." He takes two more puffs on the cigar.

There *is* something different about the chilled air, a certain stillness in the breeze that she hasn't felt in years. A feeling she attributes to change. "That sense of peace can be ascribed to both of us. You led the charge."

"Yeah." Dan leans against his old muscle car with his head tilted backward as he watches the clouds of smoke billow from his mouth. "Ten years I waited for this feeling. Ten. I lurked from the shadows, a sleeping giant ready to awaken as soon as the opportune moment arose. I battled through my own doubts, moral quandaries, and my true sense of purpose to get here."

He doesn't move, and Marilyn doesn't speak. She listens intently to the words unspoken in silence, years of scheming on Dan's part to get them both to this moment, years' worth of internalized suffering that forced evolution into the man standing before her now, the absolute belief in an idea to devise a system revolving around the end result at any cost. Years when Marilyn floated aimlessly in entropy, when she perpetually rode the undulating waves of chaos until it was the inevitable lack of motion that made her feel seasick.

"I guess what I'm feeling now can only be compared to Christmas morning as a kid," he says at last. "You waited all year to get to that moment, which felt like a decade through a child's eyes, then the anticipation got out of control as the moment neared. You barely slept a wink on Christmas Eve, then the excitement was over in a flash. All that waiting, building up the moment in your head for months, then you realized there would be another excruciating waiting period ahead. That's where we are now—a decade of waiting for a moment that's come and gone. It's bittersweet to the fullest."

"We'll just have to get back to work sooner than later. There will always be cretins out there that deserve to die. We'll stay busy for a long time to come."

"Yeah," he says again, taking another draw from the cigar, followed by a peaceful exhalation of smoke that soothes the both of them. "This was the *big one*, you know? This will be that *one* Christmas morning we'll always remember, where we got everything on the list, everything we could possibly want and more, and that's a great feeling."

Marilyn walks toward Dan and grabs the cigar from him and takes a deep drag. "I know you're a deep thinker and all, but this is the time to stop thinking for once and breathe it all in. We won—that's all that matters. We took on thirteen of those savages, yet here we are. Don't think about it. Just be happy that we're still alive and they're dead."

Dan takes the cigar back and laughs. "That's the Marilyn secret, eh? You know, after all the time we've spent together, and all of my schooling and experience with the most fucked up minds imaginable, I'm still not sure that I fully understand what makes yours tick. And I like that."

She shrugs. "I can't say for certain that I'm doing much better than you in that aspect. Just live, be alive, and try not to think about anything else." She takes the cigar again and releases a large puff and passes it back. "It's hard to care too much about the little problems in life when you've been through hell. The things that the average person out there stresses themselves into an early grave over, the appearances and social interactions and status symbols. I couldn't care less. Fuck it."

Dan chuckles again as he shakes his head. "Fuck it, indeed. You're a unique sort, Marilyn Soroka. Too rare for this world, I fear, but you're worth protecting at all costs. One of one, for sure."

"Thank you. It's been a long time since I've actually meant those words, but thanks for saving me. I guess it's difficult to understand how broken you are until the pieces start to fit back together."

"You were perfect when I found you. The only difference is now you understand the purpose that was waiting to be discovered your whole life. Unfortunately, the path was drenched in plenty of bloodshed, but we can't change that now. From the pressure forged a diamond."

The swelling of emotion in her chest is overwhelming, causing her throat to tighten and her head to feel full. There are so many things she'd like to say about the relief that came with taking control of her life, the fulfillment of caring for others, the empowerment of putting down killers like rabid dogs. But she only nods. "What are we going to do about your house? Do you think it's safe now?"

"I would imagine so, but I want to be cautious for a couple more days to be sure. I'll keep an eye on the cameras to check for any movement in the meantime. I'm going to get you a hotel room until we're out of the woods."

"What about you?"

"I have a hell of a mess to clean up between the office and my house." He laughs weakly, shifting from the car into an upright position. "I'll be fine. Neither place will take me long."

"Then shouldn't I go with you? We can finish twice as fast."

"No. I can move more secretly alone and thus be more evasive." Dan steps toward Marilyn and places a hand on her shoulder. "Remember, we're not running from anyone anymore. We're just so used to feeling as if we're surrounded by enemies both real and imaginary, even in the brief lapses of time when there were none."

Dr. Dan dropped Marilyn off at a rather upscale hotel building about half a mile from her apartment. "Hiding in plain sight," he said, although Marilyn hasn't felt safer since she became a media icon following the Butcher's first massacre. She even forgot to lock the door before she fell asleep.

There's nothing to fear anymore, or pretend not to fear, especially now that the big chunk of the killers in the city have been murdered and the rest will be easy to pick off like isolated stragglers. The tides have turned—once word gets around that the Famuli Morte were murdered by the woman they were obsessed with hunting, they'll go into hiding like the pissant cowards they are.

She slept a hard five hours before the sound of a door slamming upstairs jerked her awake, although it was the best sleep she'd had in weeks. She's become accustomed to suburban solitude.

Dan told her to stay in the hotel until he called and said that it was safe to leave, but she's grown stir crazy in the twelve hours spent inside the room. The sudden involuntary solitude wasn't something she was prepared for, having been so recently readjusted into a role of socialization. She needs a change of clothes out of the militaristic outfit that she still wears the morning after a spree killing. Maybe a shower in her own bathroom, the only thing she's missed about the old apartment, then right back to the hotel until Dan calls. She still feels bloody.

Marilyn grabs the hotel keycard and leather sheath that houses her Damascus blade with the birchwood handle, the ultimate feeling of safety since it was gifted to her. She slides the sheath down the front of her waistband for easier access on the city streets, the handle hidden inside her coat to not attract attention, then she pulls her hair into a ponytail and lifts the jacket's hood over her head and blankets her eyes with sunglasses.

A woman who could be a poorly-veiled prostitute by night smiles at Marilyn as soon as they meet on the sidewalk just outside the hotel, then she carries on down the sidewalk in her short skirt and pumps none the wiser.

Another man nearly bumps shoulders with Marilyn as he hurries by, the fabric of his business suit brushing against her black denim. Everyone in the city looks their own brand of unusual, including Marilyn, and thus, none of them do. It's a colorful amalgamation of amorphous shapes coming together like an abstract painting, the many different textures blended together to conceal the blurred edges.

Marilyn lowers her head just enough to appear non-confrontational to the passersby, though the monster lies in wait for any hidden predators in sheep's clothing, the implied danger that Dan keeps warning about. *But they're all dead.*

The apartment building approaches on the sidewalk's horizon, that structure that for the longest time felt like a mausoleum in which she had already died. Now, she rushes toward it as her last living testament to freedom, an escape from the outside world as opposed to the prison cell it had been for years.

A middle-aged man holds the glass doors of the apartment building open for Marilyn as she rushes toward them. She thanks him, to which he only gives a half nod with a mustachioed, stoic smile. The smell in the lobby is surprisingly comforting, something of a mix between its vintage and oily brass architecture and the cleaning product used by the janitors to keep the marble floor glistening.

Marilyn approaches the elevator and reaches for the up button on the stainless panel, then pauses as she notices the cab is on its way down, already on the second floor. She steps back to allow the passenger or passengers to exit unobstructed, as is only polite, when the door opens to reveal a woman who appears slightly shocked to see someone on the other side. She seems to be only a few years older than Marilyn.

They continue staring at one another, each of them waiting for the other to make a move. Marilyn takes the initiative and steps through the doors, wanting to get upstairs to her apartment instead of playing a game of elevator politics. The doors close slowly and seal in position.

"Oh my God … I've seen you on TV!" The woman speaks giddily as her eyes widen and illuminate. The cab begins to move.

Marilyn glances down at the black leather bag that the woman holds as if she's going off to work in some corporate office, although it also looks like the type of bag an old-timey doctor would use. She forces a grin and nods. "Yes, that's me. *The survivor.*"

"That's so cool! I can't believe we live in the same building!"

"I suppose I live in the same building as a lot of people who don't know that I'm here. Weren't you heading down? We're on the ground floor."

"Oh, well I don't mind a few more minutes, especially to meet a *celebrity.*" She shrugs and steps forward with her index finger outstretched toward the button panel. "What floor?"

"Six."

She presses the six, then she leans back against the brass handrail with a smile plastered across her face. "None of my friends will believe me when I tell them I met you. They'll probably just *die* of excitement."

"Unfortunately, there's not much to tell. I'm a pretty normal person, despite the media coverage." Marilyn also leans back and slowly reaches her hand up her jacket to grasp the birchwood handle. A safety blanket. The light above the door changes from one to two.

"I disagree! I've heard all the stories about you, the woman who totally *refuses* to die. Do you fear her ever catching you off-guard? That must be a ton of stress to live with all the time."

"The Butcher? Actually, she's dead. But I wasn't worried before, and I'm not worried now." Marilyn squints her eyes slightly and stares at the overly-enthusiastic woman—her neighbor, apparently. The light moves to three. "Are you sure we haven't run into each other before? Maybe in the hallways or the lobby? You seem familiar."

She shakes her head. "Nope. I definitely would've remembered. You're like ... a *really* big deal for us."

"Us? Whose *us*?"

"All of us out there. You're an inspiration! The whole city talks about you, like only all the time." Three to four. "Would you ... mind?"

"Mind what?"

"Would you show me the fingers for a picture? That would be the most amazing thing ever. Only if you don't mind, of course."

Marilyn sighs, feeling slightly cornered in the elevator, and she's always hated being recorded or photographed, even before the rise to fame. This woman already knows where she lives, or at least the building and floor. "Sure, why not? Just one finger, though."

She turns and raises her left hand with the middle finger standing tall, truly meaning this particular *fuck you* towards the spectacle that her life has become and the killers that built her legacy, but different people are impacted positively by different things. If flipping this woman the bird makes her day, then so be it. It's easier than hunting killers for her. They reach the fifth floor.

The woman raises her phone and snaps a picture with the flash on, blinding Marilyn momentarily in the confined space. She blinks the spots away and unsheathes the blade halfway inside her jacket in case it's an attempt at an ambush. The woman only grins from ear to ear.

"Oh my God, this is the coolest! Thank you so much, Marilyn. You don't know how much this means to me."

"You're welcome. Glad to do it," Marilyn lies. The light turns to six, and the elevator dings before the doors open. She steps into the hallway and turns back to face the woman. "Nice meeting you."

"The pleasure was all mine." The woman reaches out for a handshake, caus-ing her shirt sleeve to rise a few inches, exposing a fresh, white bandage around her bicep.

"What happened to your arm?" Marilyn asks without reciprocating the ges-ture.

"How nice it was to finally meet you *face to face*!" The elevator door seals as the woman smirks sharply. The numbers atop the door shift from six to five, sending the woman back down to the lobby where she was supposed to exit a few minutes ago.

Marilyn shakes her head, and she turns back toward her apartment at the far end of the hallway, where the string of wall-mounted lights beside the doors offer a dizzying display. Her eyes still feel a bit fuzzy from the phone's camera flash. She removes the Damascus blade fully but keeps it tucked inside her jacket like a service pistol.

The rows of doors on either side of her are identical to one another, each one seemingly more plain than the last. Each of them houses another individual or individuals hiding in plain sight, just like her, another drop of water in a collection of them that makes up an ocean, each of them hiding behind masks of anonymity to blend in for safety.

But what happened to her arm?

Marilyn reaches her door, the brass room number gleaming from the collec-tion of lights. 624. She extends her hand to reach for the handle, and it turns freely. Dan specifically made her lock it when they left the night before, stating that any number of people might be hunting them now, and none of them would be for charitable reasons. It's simply a good habit, he said.

The wise decision would be to turn back and take the stairs and run all the way until she reaches the anonymity of her hotel room, just another drop of water in the sea. But something inside her bares its teeth to defend its territory.

Maybe this is all just a game ... Come and get me, killers.

She eases the door open slowly to avoid attention from anyone inside, if possible, although the inevitable is already in motion. Nothing, no sound or movement. She steps inside and locks the door behind her in case they try to ambush. She'll at least hear the key turning, and she has home field advantage.

Marilyn glides silently through the entryway and stops suddenly as if she ran into a wall, like a gunshot went off and she's waiting for the impact, for the blood, for the pain. But there was no gunshot.

Dan sits on her sofa where the Butcher committed suicide, staring in her direction with glazed eyes that still display his typical expression of something between fiery and stoic.

Marilyn clears her throat as she stares into his eviscerated chest, the individual rib bones bent and broken outward from the sternum like the gaping maw of some cornered beast, the assortment of organs from his torso spilling out onto his lap and the hardwood floor in a potpourri of disembowelment. Yet his heart is gone. *The black bag.*

His blood spills still fresh and not yet congealed from the open wound, a cavity the size of a beach ball extending from throat to pelvic bone, intestines dangling down his legs into flesh coils on the floor, bits of broken bone snapped free from his ribcage and tossed haphazardly onto the cushions beside him like discards at a cookout, his sternum sawed open jaggedly from the solar plexus upward, his duster jacket coated in blood and gore and the shattered dreams of future patients associated with such.

But the real kicker is what catches her eye next.

Dan's right arm is affixed at a crooked angle with his middle finger erected. Pointed straight at Marilyn.

It's a howling mockery of their attempts to create a better world, a bastardization of justice, of righteousness, of morality. It's a reminder that true evil will never quit because it has nothing of value to lose, and thus, it can't be beaten.

Another killer will always fill the power vacuum voided by the death of another, the universe seemingly willing it to happen by force for gain.

Marilyn's phone vibrates in her pants pocket, a shocking sensation when the only person she'd expect to be texting her sits in front of her looking like he spent the night in an abattoir. She pulls out her phone and opens the overly saturated and washed-out picture of her standing in the elevator with her middle finger pointed upward and now aiming at her present self, too. It's sent from Dan's phone with a message beneath.

Talk soon!

Odessa, the chameleon. The seemingly unkillable spectre who defies the same god she claims to worship—Death itself.

Marilyn looks like a runaway fugitive in the photo, wearing her military-style outfit with the hood pulled over her head and sunglasses shading her eyes, and she essentially is. The apartment isn't safe, Dan's house is compromised, and his city office is a warzone.

This display was meant to break her, to destroy her will to live again like it was before Dan entered her life. He, too, became a victim of the Marilyn Soroka travelling shitshow, yet his teachings live on. She would rather die than break again, but neither will happen today. Life is worth fighting for, even against insurmountable odds. Where there's life there's hope.

Maybe this is all just a game ... Come and get me, killers.

Marilyn closes the photo and dials 911.

"911, what's your emergency?"

"This is Marilyn Soroka. I'm calling to report a murder in my apartment." She ends the call abruptly then digs the point of her blade into the phone's SIM card slot and pops it free before exiting the apartment with the door wide open.

Catch me if you can.